The whole situation was crazy,

Tate told himself. There could never be anything between him and lush, leggy reporter Natalie Grant.

She was a threat to his family. He felt nothing but disdain for her job. And he… Sweet hell, he was lying to her with every conversation, every look, every damned breath he took.

All excellent reasons to keep his distance and ignore his rampant attraction to the sweet Southern redhead.

But that might be easier said than done.

For one thing, in a ranch house normally filled with male voices and Okie twangs, Natalie sounded like a songbird among crows. Undeniably Southern, achingly feminine, her voice was made for whispering sweet, seductive invitations.

But not to Tate.

After all, he wasn't even the man she thought he was. He was an impostor, telling her sweet, loving lies…

Available in May 2003 from Silhouette Special Edition

The Truth About Tate

MARILYN PAPPANO

SILHOUETTE®
SPECIAL EDITION™

*First published in Great Britain 2003
Silhouette Books, Eton House, 18-24 Paradise Road,
Richmond, Surrey TW9 1SR*

© Marilyn Pappano 2001

ISBN 0 373 24425 8

23-0503

*Printed and bound in Spain
by Litografia Rosés S.A., Barcelona*

MARILYN PAPPANO

brings impeccable credentials to her writing career—a lifelong habit of gazing out windows, not paying attention in class, daydreaming and spinning tales for her own entertainment. The sale of her first book brought great relief to her family, proving that she wasn't crazy but was, instead, creative. Since then she's sold more than forty books to various publishers and even a film production company.

She writes in an office nestled among the oaks that surround her country home. In winter she stays inside with her husband and their four dogs, and in summer she spends her free time mowing the garden that never stops growing and daydreams about grass that never gets taller than two inches.

You can write to her at PO Box 643, Sapulpa, OK, 74067-0643, USA.

Chapter One

The letter came in Tuesday morning's mail—a pale-green envelope postmarked Alabama, addressed to J. T. Rawlins in a delicate script and lacking a return address. Alabama, the Heart of Dixie, home to a decent college football team, the venerable and newly retired U.S. senator, Boyd Chaney, and an incredibly determined, tenacious reporter by the name of Natalie Grant, who was writing said senator's biography.

The single sheet of stationery inside the envelope was also pale green, textured. The tone was polite, professional, but the letter was a warning all the same. It was enough to justify a gathering of all four members of the Rawlins family at a time when each of them needed to be someplace else.

Tate Rawlins sat in his usual seat, to the left of his mother, Lucinda, who claimed the head of the dining table. His sixteen-year-old son, Jordan, sat on her right, and Tate's half brother, Josh, was beside him. Tate's and Josh's fathers had never been part of the family. Ditto for Jordan's mother. As families went, they were small, and not exactly traditional, but they were close.

Everyone wore the same somber expression, except Lucinda, who also looked guilty, worried and ashamed. So far she hadn't said a word, hadn't even hinted at what she wanted, except for this whole mess to go away.

But Natalie Grant wasn't going to go away. In fact, according to the letter lying in the middle of the table, she would be appearing on their doorstep first thing in the morning, and she wasn't leaving until, one way or another, she'd gotten the information she wanted. That was a fact, she'd written in the last line of the letter.

A threat, to Tate's way of thinking.

"Well?" Josh prodded.

Tate felt three pairs of brown eyes, identical to his own, turn his way. While they'd waited for him to come in from the pasture, they'd hatched a plan for dealing with the reporter. No, correct that—a plan for Tate to deal with the reporter. Josh and their mother had already made arrangements, before the letter's arrival, to spend the next few weeks at her parents' ranch down in southern Oklahoma, and they wanted—needed—to go ahead. Grandpop had broken his leg two days before, and while Gran was convinced she could look after the place just fine by herself, the rest of the family wasn't about to let her prove it.

Let me help Grandpop, Tate had suggested, and Josh could handle Ms. Alabama. After all, though they shared the same initials, Josh was the J. T. Rawlins she wanted.

Even Jordan had winced at the idea. Josh wasn't the most cautious or even-tempered person around. Lucinda excused his behavior as impulsive. Grandpop said he let his mouth run without engaging his brain first. In his twenty-nine years, he'd sometimes talked his way into more trouble than Tate could get him out of. He'd gotten the two of them suspended from school, thrown out of bars and, on a few occasions, thrown into jail. There was no telling what kind of trouble he could stir up with a nosy reporter—especially one who was bound and determined to uncover every last detail in all the Rawlinses' lives.

All because of a stupid affair Lucinda had had thirty years ago.

Tate shifted to face his mother. "What do you want me to do?"

Her gaze dropped to the tabletop, but not before he caught another glimpse of the guilt in her eyes. "This has to be your decision."

His decision, when he was the one least affected by Alabama's snooping. Josh was the reporter's prime target, and Lucinda came next. Tate and Jordan were of interest only in that they were family.

"Why don't you go on down to Grandpop's? When she shows up, I'll tell her you're out of town and won't be back for several weeks."

"Read the letter again, Tate," Josh said angrily. "The part about staying 'as long as it takes.' Besides, how hard would it be for her to find out where we've gone from someone in town? You want her showing up unannounced at Gran's?"

No, Tate admitted silently. To this day, the mere mention of Boyd Chaney's name could make AnnaMae Rawlins spittin' mad or sorrowful and weepy. With Grandpop in the hospital, the last thing she needed was Natalie Grant's questions about the bastard child.

Josh's chair scraped the floor as he stood up. "Can I talk to you outside?"

Tate followed him onto the porch. It was a miserable day. The heat index had climbed past 110 for eighteen days in a row, they hadn't had rain in more than a month, and things were likely to get worse before they got better. Hell had nothing on Oklahoma in August.

Josh rested his hands on the rail cap and stared at the horses in the pasture across the yard. "Look, I know you don't want to do this. I know it's sneaky and underhanded. But she's not exactly playing fair, either. I told her I wanted no part of her project. I told her politely, and I told her rudely, and she's coming here, anyway. I don't owe her anything else. Mom for damn sure doesn't owe her anything. Now it's time to look out for our best interests.''

For an instant the tightness in Tate's chest made it difficult to breathe. Lying to a stranger, impersonating his brother—it was wrong, and he wouldn't consider it for an instant if his brother's privacy and his mother's reputation weren't at stake. If his son weren't at risk of getting tarnished by the same brush.

But Natalie Grant was nothing if not persistent. She'd been harassing Josh for months, wanting his cooperation for her book. She'd called. He'd turned her down, hung up on her and ignored her messages. She'd written, and he'd written back once—''No, thanks, not interested''—then returned her following letters unopened. But none of that had stopped her from making the trip from Montgomery to Hickory Bluff.

And why shouldn't she be persistent? Given Chaney's political power, his wealth, his family's penchant for scandal and the American people's penchant for gossip, her book was bound for the bestseller lists. She stood to make a nice chunk of money by exposing Tate's family to ridicule.

But maybe he could minimize the damage.

As if he sensed Tate was wavering, Josh asked, ''How much effort do you think Ms. Alabama will make to be fair? *He* handpicked her to write the book. You can be damned sure everything will be skewed to make him out to be the good guy. She'll say Mom—'' With a glance toward the house, as if Lucinda could hear through the solid walls, he broke off. But he didn't need to go on.

Tate had only one memory of the illustrious senator. He'd been about five years old when Chaney had come to their apartment in Montgomery. The election was coming up, and he'd brought money to persuade a very pregnant Lucinda to leave the state and keep the identity of her baby's father secret. Tate hadn't understood most of the conversation, or why the man was giving his mother so much money. But he'd never forgotten the ugliness in Chaney's voice when he'd made one last remark before walking out the door. "Gold-digging whore." The insult had made her cry, leaving Tate afraid to ask what it meant. Eventually, of course, he'd learned on his own, and he'd hated Chaney ever since.

Josh's quiet voice pulled him back from the memory. "You think this reporter won't make it look like Mom made a habit of having affairs with married men, getting pregnant and blackmailing a little cash out of them? And let's toss in the fact that her older illegitimate son is raising his own illegitimate son. You think she won't twist that so it reflects badly on you? On Mom? Hell, even on Jordan?"

Though he'd already made his decision, Tate continued to raise objections. "What if she finds out the truth?"

"You put the word out around town that you don't want anyone talking to her." The answer came from Jordan, standing in the doorway. Sixteen years old, and already showing his uncle Josh's talent for deception. "Then make it one of the terms of your agreement, that she can only ask questions of you and me. Not Grandma, not the neighbors, not anyone who knows us."

"And if she agrees to that, I'm supposed to trust her to keep her word?" A writer snooping around in people's private lives didn't strike him as the best candidate to trust. Anyone working in any capacity for that bastard Chaney couldn't be too upright in the morals department.

"We won't let her go into town alone."

Tate shook his head as Jordan came closer. "There's no 'we' in this. I don't want you involved. You stay away from her, don't talk to her and—"

"Dad, I live here, and unlike Josh and Grandma, I can't leave. I've got football practice. Besides, I'm old enough to watch what I say."

"You can't go to Grandpop's, but you *can* stay with Steve while she's in town."

"Aw, Dad…" Suddenly he grinned. "You need me here as a chaperon. Grandma and I think it would be a good idea if she stays here. That way we can watch her and you won't have to trust her to keep her word.''

Josh slapped Jordan on the back. ''Good thinking. Keep her on a short leash and control everything she does.''

''I don't want her staying here,'' Tate protested. Inviting a strange woman into his house? Sharing a bathroom with her? Letting her sleep in the empty room between his and Jordan's rooms? Worse, giving her free run of the house while they were working?

''Not *here*,'' Jordan replied, gesturing toward the house. ''At Grandma's. She'll lock away all her personal stuff so there won't be anything for her to snoop through. Besides, the nearest motel is twenty miles away. If you make her stay there, she'll spend half her time driving back and forth.''

Tate turned to look at his mother's quarters. The two houses shared a roof, but were separated by a broad deck with flower beds all around. It was a great place for cooking out, watching storms or just kicking back, and gave them at least the illusion of privacy.

''What do we care if she spends half her time commuting?'' he asked as he turned back to Jordan and Josh.

The two of them exchanged a damn-he's-slow sort of look, then Jordan explained. ''The more time she's out without one of us, the more chances she has of meeting other people, and the more people she gets to know, the more likely it is that she'll start asking questions and they'll start answering them. A stranger asking questions is one thing. A friend is different.''

The floorboards creaked as Tate moved to lean against the rail. Sweat was trickling down his back, his stomach was queasy, his head was starting to ache, and it was so damn hot. Better get used to it, though, because he was going to hell.

He was an honest man. He'd never cheated on a test, his taxes or a woman. He'd accepted every responsibility that ever came his way, whether he was ready for it or not. For thirty-four years, he'd lived right, loved well—if not always wisely—and earned a reputation a man could be proud of. But if he agreed to this fool-minded scheme, he was surely going to burn in hell.

He took a deep breath of dry air that seared his lungs, then faced Jordan and Josh. "All right." The words were stiff and reluctant. There was nothing he wouldn't do for his family. They'd never had a lot, but they had each other, and that was all that mattered. When one was in trouble, they all were. When one needed help, they all gave it. It was how they'd lived their lives, how they always would.

But that didn't mean he had to be happy about the help he was giving this time. "I'm sure I'll live to regret it, but…all right. Let's get our stories straight and see if I can pull this off."

And if he did, or even if he didn't, he would surely burn in hell.

But maybe he could take Natalie Grant and Boyd Chaney with him.

Natalie Grant scanned her laptop screen:

Luther Boyd Chaney was born in the heart of Alabama, not far from the Coosa River, in a sharecropper's shack that let in the rain and the heat and the cold. He watched his father work himself to death, and a few years later saw his mother do the same, and he swore his own life would be different. Seventy-some years later, he's made good on that vow. He put himself through school, got elected to the Alabama state senate, went on to Congress. He became the confidant of presidents and the unofficial advisor to prime ministers and kings the world over. He was unarguably the most influential man in the last century of American politics.

Muttering to herself, Natalie paged down to a blank screen and started typing again.

It would be difficult, if not impossible, to find an American citizen whose life hasn't been greatly improved by Boyd Chaney. Every major piece of legislation in the past forty years dealing with education, families and social programs bears the stamp of the senator from Alabama. If he didn't author it himself, he ensured that it passed into law. From his first Congressional term to his last, he was, first and foremost, an advocate for the American family.

One might expect such an advocate to be a family man himself, but Boyd Chaney doesn't always do what one might expect. Oh, he married six times and divorced six times, and he had children—nine of them. He knows his children's names, and their mothers', but birthdays, ages, occupations, marital status? Not with any degree of accuracy.

With a sigh Natalie pushed the computer away and stood up. She'd slept in until eight, then gone straight to the computer and had written a dozen pages, none of it keeper stuff. Like many reporters, she'd always planned to write a book whenever she found the time. Now she had the time, and the contract, and the full cooperation of the subject and a hundred or so of his nearest and dearest. She had reams of research and thousands of hours of taped interviews. She'd gathered enough material to write a dozen volumes on the senator who'd virtually run the country for all of her life and beyond.

She had everything…except the cooperation of one of the Chaney offspring. That one man's stubbornness could cost her the project.

It had been a deal-breaker in the negotiations. Upon his retirement from political life, Chaney had chosen her to write his biography, but he'd insisted that she personally gain the cooperation of each and every one of his six ex-wives, nine children and seven grandchildren. She'd known it was a red flag, because he'd already secured agreements from half of them. The other half had signed on readily enough, except for one. The fourth son, the fifth child, the only illegitimate one in the bunch. J. T. Rawlins.

She turned on the water in the shower, then stripped out of her pajamas. She'd tried for months to set up an interview with the elusive son no one had ever heard of. She'd tracked him down in an end-of-the-line Oklahoma town called Hickory Bluff and sent him a letter politely requesting an interview. He'd returned it with a terse note scrawled across the bottom: No, thanks, not interested. She'd called repeatedly. He'd hung up on her. She'd written time and again. The letters had come back unopened.

So here she was, in a cheap motel nineteen miles from Hickory Bluff. She intended to show up at J.T.'s house, to talk to him reasonably, persuasively, to let him see for himself that she wasn't a threat. She wasn't looking to disrupt his life any more than was necessary.

Yeah, right, she thought scornfully as she rinsed magnolia-scented suds from her body. She just wanted all the personal details of his life so she could put them in a book for everyone to read. She wanted to announce to the world that his mother had had an affair with a tremendously rich and powerful married man and that he was the best-kept secret of one of the most flamboyant, tabloid-fodder families in the country. What would that do to his reputation, and to his mother's? How would it affect their relationships with the people currently in their lives?

She was sorry, but she had no choice. She *needed* this project. She'd already screwed up once, and it had cost her career, her relationship with her family and her own self-respect. This was her chance to recover those things. Failing wasn't an option.

After rubbing herself dry with a threadbare towel, Natalie quickly dressed. She applied the few cosmetics that were her major effort at looking good, tied her curls back with a strip of ribbon, then gathered everything she needed for a day's work—steno notebook, ink pens, microcassette recorder, tapes and batteries, 35-mm camera and film, as well as digital camera. It all fit handily in the oversize tote she used for a purse. With sunglasses on and keys in hand, she left her motel room, deposited the laptop in the trunk for safekeeping, then slid behind the wheel of her classic Ford Mustang convertible and headed for Hickory Bluff.

With The Doors blasting on the stereo, she cruised along the two-lane highway at ten miles over the limit and thought about the events of the past fifteen months that, together, had brought her to this place. The award-winning articles she'd written, the accolades and recognition, the jealousy, the scandal and the truth that only she and one other person knew. No one had stood beside her—not her editor, not her best friend of five years, certainly not her father. An entire career of outstanding work had been forgotten, destroyed in one careless moment by the simple act of trusting someone she'd loved. I hope you learned a lesson, her father had unsympathetically told her, and she had. Don't trust, don't love, don't care about anyone or anything except the story. Natalie Grant's New Rules to Live By.

Dealing with Senator Chaney and his self-absorbed family made them easy to stick to. She hadn't yet met any Chaney kin that she would give a plug nickel for. For a man who had accomplished so much good in his career, he'd married and helped give life to some of the most beautiful, charming, shallow, irresponsible and worthless human beings she'd ever met. Maybe J.T., being the exception as far as legitimacy went, would also be the exception in other ways, but she wasn't holding her breath.

At the sight of a large wooden sign up ahead, Natalie slowed and pulled onto the shoulder, stopping twenty feet back. *Welcome to Hickory Bluff,* it read. *Home of the Fighting Wildcats. Class 2A State Champions in Football, Basketball, Baseball.* Each sport was listed on a separate line, followed by the years the team had won the championships. Spray-painted in hot pink across the bottom was an afterthought— *Lady Cats Rule!*

Was J. T. Rawlins an athlete? Had he suited up every fall

Friday night in the Wildcats' green and gold? Did he relive former glories every time basketball season rolled around or each time the crack of a baseball on a bat split the air?

Making a mental note to check the yearbooks for his high school years, Natalie pulled back onto the road and rounded the curve that led into Hickory Bluff. It wasn't a prosperous town and never had been. Situated at the crossroads of two state highways, it consisted of four blocks of businesses, houses backing them up on both sides of the street and a water tower, painted green and gold and honoring the boys' teams. There was a church on every block, or so it seemed, and a redbrick schoolhouse, a football stadium and a complex of baseball fields.

She parked in front of a store that announced its services in white letters painted across the plate glass. *Hunting, fishing licenses. Ice. Bait. Video rental. Cold beer. Sandwiches. Notions. Driver's licenses and car tags.* Next door to it was her destination—the post office. The building was small, fronted with yellow brick and devoid of personality. If a tornado swept through the downtown area, it would probably take all the old stone-and-glass buildings with it and leave the amazingly unimaginative post office standing untouched.

The plate-glass door led into a room no more than eight feet deep and ten feet wide. Customer boxes filled the two end walls, and a counter took up most of the back wall. There were no customers other than her, and no employees visible other than a white-haired man sorting through a stack of mail. He glanced at her but didn't speak or stop his work. She waited patiently, assuming that when he finished, he would turn his attention to her.

"Well?" he prodded after a moment. "You plannin' on standin' there all day, missy, or is there somethin' you want?"

"Actually, there is. I'm looking for J. T. Rawlins."

"Have you looked out at his place? Call me strange, but if I was lookin' for someone, I'd start with where they're supposed to be."

"I don't know where he lives. The address I have is 2111 Rawlins Ranch Road."

"Yep, that's right."

She waited expectantly, but he didn't go on. "Can you tell me where that is?"

"Sure can. It's outside of town. West, then north. 'Bout…oh, four, five miles. You can't miss it." This time he was the one who waited expectantly. When she didn't do anything—such as leave—he laid the mail aside. "Well? Is there somethin' else you want?"

"According to the map, practically the entire state of Oklahoma is west of here. Could you be a little more specific?"

The old man rolled his eyes, then pointed out the window. "See that street? Not Main Street here in front. The one over there that runs east and west. You follow it outta town until you come to the old Mayfield barn on the left. Make a right turn and stay on that road a couple miles north until you come to the Rawlins place."

"And how will I recognize the old Mayfield barn?"

He laughed. "You'll know it. You'll know the Rawlins place when you come to it, too. Trust me."

With a tight smile Natalie thanked him and returned to the car. It was tempting to run across the street to Norma Sue's Café and ask for directions there. Instead, she decided to test the old man's "you'll know it when you see it" theory. If she didn't find J. T. Rawlins, she could always come back, ask for help and get some lunch while she was at it.

She turned right onto the street the clerk had pointed out, drove past a few businesses, an elementary school, two mobile home parks and a now-defunct plant that, according to the faded, peeling sign on one building, had once manufactured bricks. Now it was secured by a tall chain-link fence that trapped windblown leaves and trash inside, and looked empty and forlorn.

The odometer slowly rolled over—one mile, two, three. She was beginning to wonder if she'd been sent on a wild-goose chase, when a barn came into sight ahead on the left. It was octagonal in shape, painted bright red, and in huge block letters around the sides was painted The Old Mayfield Barn. Directing muttered curses toward the postal clerk, she slowed to turn right onto a dirt road.

About four or five miles, he'd said. She'd gone exactly four and a half miles when she turned into a driveway and stopped. A pipe gate formed an arch over the cattle guard that stretched across the drive, and a sign dangling from the arch announced that this was, indeed, the Rawlins Ranch. For a moment she simply sat there, engine idling. Since she'd come up with this less-than-brilliant plan to visit J. T. Rawlins on his own turf, she'd convinced herself that he would be so impressed by her professionalism, won over by her sincerity or maybe simply worn-out by her determination, and would agree to cooperate fully. In fact, she hadn't let herself consider any other outcome.

But what if he wasn't impressed, won over or worn-out? What if his determination to have nothing to do with her was stronger than her determination to write this book? What were the chances she could persuade Senator Chaney that twenty-one out of twenty-two wasn't bad—that no one else could do better?

Slim to none. He'd been adamant that, without even one of the brood, as he called his ex-wives and children, there would be no book. Simple enough, then. She wouldn't take no for an answer. However stubborn J. T. Rawlins was, she would be more so. He would talk to her if for no other reason than to get rid of her.

Slowly she shifted her foot to the accelerator. The driveway was dirt and gravel and ran between two fenced pastures. Several hundred yards back from the road sat a house the color of an unbaked pumpkin pie, with trim the same hue as fresh cream. The house was oddly laid out—two halves side by side, connected by a deck. The neatly maintained lawn was yellowed from lack of rain, but the flowers planted in

beds around the house and in pots all over the deck bloomed
as beautifully as if the climate was fit to sustain life.

Natalie parked in the shade of a massive tree that was
already losing its leaves, climbed out and smoothed her dress.
The place wasn't exactly quiet—a dog barked somewhere,
music was coming from the direction of the barn, and there
were birds, crickets, wind rustling in the trees—but it was a
different type of noise than she was accustomed to. At home
in Alabama, she lived in an apartment complex where something was always going on—TVs blaring, kids playing, cou-
ples fighting. There was a fire station two blocks away, so
sirens were a daily part of life, as well as traffic, construction
and aircraft flying overhead.

She tried the house first, knocking on one front door, then
the other. When she got no answer at either, she headed out
back. The dead grass crunched underfoot, and the horses in
the pasture lined up at the fence to watch her pass. As she
neared the barn, she could tell the music came not from there,
but somewhere on the other side. She followed it around the
corner, then came to a sudden stop.

The source of the music—country, she thought, wrinkling
her nose—was a portable radio sitting on a tree stump. Parked
a few feet beyond it was an old pickup truck, its green paint
sadly faded by the sun. The hood was propped open, and
bent under it was a man. In faded jeans. Dirty boots. With
lots of warm tanned skin exposed that glistened with sweat
under the blazing sun. A white T-shirt hung from the truck's
outside mirror, and an oil-stained rag was draped over the
open window.

Natalie swallowed hard. She'd always had a fine appreciation for men in snug-fitting jeans. The harder the body, the
more faded the jeans should be, because faded denim was
soft, yielding, gloving—and these jeans were pretty damned
faded.

After all but drooling for a moment or two, she cleared
her throat. "Excuse me. I'm looking for J. T. Rawlins."

The man straightened, turned and gave her a long look.

She stared back into a seriously handsome, seriously boyish face. He might be anywhere from fifteen to twenty, she guessed—way too young for her womanly appreciation. He didn't smile, come closer or offer his hand, but subjected her to a thorough appraisal before he spoke. "Who are you?"

"Natalie Grant. I believe Mr. Rawlins is expecting me."

The next response came from behind her. "Why would he be expecting you when he told you very plainly that he wasn't interested in your book?"

She turned to find a bigger, impossibly harder version of the boy standing a few yards away. He, too, wore scuffed boots and snug jeans that rode low on narrow hips, and had discarded his shirt in deference to the day's heat. He, too, showed lots of warm, tanned skin, stretched taut over muscle and bone, and wore the same unwelcoming look as the boy. "Mr. Rawlins, I presume."

"Ms. Grant."

"I take it you didn't receive my most recent letter."

"We got it. We considered barring the gate to you and having the sheriff run you out of the county."

"But you didn't."

He shifted the toolbox he carried from one hand to the other. "Some pests will go away if you ignore them long enough. Others require a different solution."

She didn't particularly appreciate being called a pest, but she could hardly blame him. She *had* been a bit persistent. "And what solution did you decide on for me? Capitulation?"

"Hardly." His expression was as dry as the air. "More like compromise."

She mimicked the dry reply. "The sooner you deal with me, the sooner you get rid of me?"

He responded with a shrug that made the muscles of his chest and belly ripple enticingly. She'd known the odds were better than even that J. T. Rawlins was a handsome man. His father was. His eight half siblings were as beautiful as genetics, pampering and virtually unlimited wealth could provide. There wasn't a crooked or unbleached tooth in the bunch. Not an inch of untanned skin or a pinch of untoned flab. Not one single hair on one head that would dare rebel enough to create a bad-hair day. They were all artificially, phonily gorgeous.

And they couldn't hold a candle to their illegitimate half brother. His tan came from hours in the sun, his muscles from hard work. His dark hair was perfectly tousled, as if he'd combed it with his fingers. His smile, she would bet, was naturally perfect, as everything else was, though she doubted she would get the chance to see it. That would be her loss.

"Compromise," she repeated. "As in you'll tell me everything I need to know, and then I'll disappear from your life?"

"As in I'll answer the questions I want. As for the rest of them…well, you'll have to live without the answers."

"Or get them someplace else."

With a glint in his dark eyes, he shook his head. "That's part of the deal. You talk only to us. We don't want you asking a lot of questions about us in town, or bothering our friends and neighbors. And my mother and my brother are off-limits. You don't ask about them, you don't get to talk to them, and you don't mention them or Jordan any more than necessary in your book."

Natalie studied him for a moment. Though his skin glistened with sweat, he didn't seem to notice the miserable heat or the dryness that sucked the moisture from her pores. He didn't seem to notice anything at all besides her, though it was a wary prey-watching-predator sort of attention. She wondered what it would be like to have that same intense focus in a man-woman way. Not that she was looking for a relationship. *No trust, no love, no concern for anything but the story.*

With that in mind, she turned her own attention back to the story. She could do without the brother—he was important only in that he *was* J.T.'s brother—but she really wanted an interview with Lucinda Rawlins. She wanted to know how the affair had started, how an unsophisticated waitress from Oklahoma had caught the eye of the powerful senator from Alabama thirty years ago. Had the woman fallen in love with Chaney? Had he given her anything besides a baby—sweet lies, affection, excitement, money? How had it felt, raising her son all alone and seeing his father on television traveling with the president, being presented to the queen of England, touring Israel with the prime minister? Had she kept her secret about J.T.'s father willingly, or had Chaney bought her silence?

So she would get those answers some other way.

"Are those your only conditions?" she asked evenly.

"There's one other. You'll stay here. My mother's out of town, so you can use her place."

She glanced at the divided house, then back at him with a wry smile. "And if I go into town, one of you will just happen to be going along, right?"

That negligible shrug again.

It was a smart idea on his part—restricting her movements, therefore restricting her access to the friends and neighbors he didn't want her talking to. "This was a rather convenient time for your mother to go out of town, wasn't it? When did she leave? Sometime after my letter arrived in the mail yesterday?"

"Actually, the trip was already planned. She and my brother went to help a…friend. But if she hadn't already made plans, she would have. You're not dragging her into this mess."

Natalie resisted the urge to point out that it was Lucinda who had dragged J.T. into this "mess." She was the one who'd chosen to have the affair, who Chaney believed got pregnant deliberately to get something from him, who chose to go through with the pregnancy, planned or not, and raise the senator's son. Instead, she turned back to the boy, who watched them silently. "You must be Jordan." Closing the small distance between them, she offered her hand. "I'm Natalie."

He raised both hands palm out to show that they were greasy, and she lowered her hand to her side. "Who exactly are you, Jordan?"

He looked at J.T., then uncomfortably replied, "I'm—I'm Tate's son."

Tate, she knew from her sketchy information, was the elder of the two Rawlins sons. They both lived and worked on the ranch with their mother, and both were single. J.T. had a habit of picking up speeding tickets, and he and his brother had landed in the county jail for a few youthful offenses involving too much booze, pretty women and hostile competition for the ladies' affection. They owned the ranch outright, though occasionally they had to take out a mortgage to get through a tough season, and they were both good credit risks, Tate more so than J.T., though they were never going to get rich from ranching. That was about the extent of what she'd learned before leaving Montgomery.

"Do I get to put any conditions on this agreement?" she asked J.T. as he finally came close enough to hand the tool box to Jordan.

"Sure. You can take it…or leave it."

"My, you're so generous." She smiled in spite of the sarcasm underlying her words. "I'll take it, of course. I've already checked into a motel in Dixon. I need to pick up my stuff."

"Any reason why Jordan can't get it?"

She gave the same sugar-atop-sarcasm smile. "You mean, did I leave anything of an intimate nature lying about? Files? Drafts of the book? Notes of the senator's comments about you?"

"You and I obviously have different definitions of 'intimate nature,'" J.T. said.

With a faint flush warming her cheeks, she tried to remember what she'd done with the clothing—including a black lace bra with matching bikini panties—she'd taken off the night before. She'd been tired when she'd checked into the motel, and she'd changed into her pajamas and fallen into bed…but not before stuffing the clothes into a mesh laundry bag.

Removing the motel key from her key ring, she offered it to the boy. "If you'd save me forty more miles on the road after yesterday's trip, Jordan, I would be ever so grateful. There are a couple of suitcases, a laundry bag, some papers on the table…oh, and the stuff on the bathroom counter."

Jordan accepted the key, then, at a nod from his uncle, he grabbed his T-shirt and headed for the house.

"So…would you prefer that I call you J.T., Joshua or Josh?"

"I'd prefer that you call me long-distance."

"A sense of humor. None of the other Chaney kids have one."

That earned her a scowl and a hostile response. "I'm *not* one of the Chaney kids. Don't call me that." He circled the truck, then came back with a chambray shirt. She watched as he thrust his arms into the shirtsleeves, then started fastening the buttons. It was a simple task, one she'd seen done a million times, but he made it look…easy. Fluid. Sexy.

And that wasn't something she should be thinking about the subject of her most important interview ever.

He finished up, not bothering to tuck the wrinkled tails into his jeans—a sight she would have paid money to see. Instead he simply stood there, waiting for her to say something, and finally she did. "J.T., Joshua or Josh?"

There was a certain reluctance to his voice when he answered. "J.T. will do."

"Then shall we get started, J.T.?"

Chapter Two

If Tate had given it any thought, he would have expected Natalie Grant to be…hell, he didn't know. Older. Stuffier. More the type to be interested in the affairs, both governmental and personal, of an old man. He would have imagined her as shorter, stockier, grayer and wearing sensible clothes.

The woman walking beside him toward the house was none of those things. She was beautiful. Leggy. Wearing a summery-looking dress that was short and sleeveless and clung from shoulder to midthigh. And she was a redhead.

When he'd come around the corner from the barn and seen that, his breath had caught in his chest, robbing his groan of any sound. Red hair came fourth on his list of weaknesses—right after Jordan, Lucinda and Josh—especially that particular shade of shiny-new-penny red. And long legs ranked right up there, too, along with sultry Southern accents.

Not only was he going to hell, but God was going to see to it that he suffered here on earth first.

"Interesting layout."

He glanced at her and saw her gesture toward the house. "Mother-in-law troubles."

"Whose?"

"The man who built the place sixty years ago. His wife insisted on her mother living with them. Unfortunately, the old lady's only purpose in life was to make him miserable, so he built this house, but instead of putting the porch across the back, he stuck it between the two halves. The mother-in-law lived in the north half, while he and his wife lived in the south half. Now Mom lives in the north half."

"And you, Tate and Jordan live in the other half?"

Tate swallowed convulsively. When he'd agreed to impersonate his brother, he'd realized he was going to have to answer to Josh's name—though he was glad she'd offered him the chance to use J.T. instead. He'd actually been called that, off and on in his life, so it didn't feel totally foreign.

But somehow he hadn't realized that he was also going to wind up talking about himself as if he were someone else. Listening to Jordan admit to being Tate's son, hearing her refer to Tate just now…it was too strange an experience.

"Actually, I have…my own place, but I'm…staying here while Tate's gone."

"He doesn't trust Jordan to be alone," she said with a knowing nod.

His anger flared. "He trusts Jordan completely. He's a good kid."

"I'm sure he is. But teenagers, no matter how good, are trouble waiting to happen."

No one knew that better than Tate. He'd been sixteen and planning on going to college and having a career, instead of a backbreaking job on a ranch, when he'd met Stefani Blake, and he was seventeen and devastated when she'd told him she was pregnant. He'd offered to marry her, but she wasn't interested. She'd had her future planned, like him, and there was no place in it for him or his kid. Two weeks after his eighteenth birthday, she'd given birth to Jordan, signed away all her rights and they'd never seen her again.

Tate had forgotten about college, a career elsewhere and everything else, and had put all his energy into being a father and making a go of the ranch. He'd changed diapers, fixed bottles and learned to bathe and dress a wriggly, squirmy kid, and he and Jordan had done a bit of growing up together.

He had no doubt Stefani had given him the better deal. Wherever she was, whatever she was doing, it couldn't be as satisfying as his life.

"This is a nice place. Have you always lived here?"

"Pretty much."

"Do you have any employees?"

"We hire on help when we need it, but usually it's just us."

"And what do you raise?"

"We're a cow-calf operation." At her blank look, he explained, "We have a dozen bulls we breed with our cows. We sell the little boy calves, keep the little girls and let them be girlfriends with the bulls when they're old enough."

She gave him a chastising look. "I don't need the explanations quite that simple."

"Sorry," he said, though he wasn't. Digging in his pocket for his keys, he led the way up the steps and across the deck to the side door of Lucinda's quarters, then inside. The door opened into a broad room that doubled as a mudroom and laundry room. Off the connecting hallway, there was a bathroom on one side, a closet on the other, then a small dining room and kitchen straight ahead. From the kitchen a doorway opened into the living room, and from there another hallway led to the three bedrooms and the bathroom they shared.

The house was about twenty degrees cooler than outside, and was dimly lit, the blinds having been tightly closed against the sun. It smelled of furniture polish and mulberry, his mother's favorite scent in the world, and it felt strangely empty.

Natalie gave a soft sigh as she closed the door behind her. "I don't care what anyone says. Dry heat is *not* more comfortable than humid heat. At least you can breathe when there's moisture in the air."

"Have you always lived in Alabama?"

"No. We moved a lot because of my father's job. I settled there about nine years ago."

"What was his job?"

She turned from her study of the rooms they were walking through to give him an uneasy look. "He's retired now, but he was a—a journalist. Maybe you've heard of him—Thaddeus Grant."

Tate shook his head, wondering why she called herself a reporter and her old man a journalist. A mild case of hero worship, maybe. After all, she had followed in his footsteps.

"He won the Pulitzer Prize so many times they considered just automatically giving it to him every year, and the college he went to renamed its journalism school after him. He's one of those people who becomes so much more than the job. Instead of merely reporting the news, oftentimes he *is* the news. These days he spends his time entertaining the rich and powerful, lecturing and giving promising young journalism students the full benefit of his years of experience."

"Sounds intimidating." Definitely hero worship, with a little something else underneath. Resentment? Jealousy? Anxiety?

He gestured toward the first bedroom they approached. "This is my mother's room." Then, down the hall, "Bathroom, guest room, guest room."

She walked into the third bedroom, went to the windows that looked out on yard and pasture out back, yard and woods on the north, and nodded once. "This is fine. Am I allowed to go shopping for groceries?"

"Sure. You can go with me when I pick up a few things."

"I'm surprised you aren't taking my car keys away from me."

"Why would I do that when you've already agreed to my conditions? Especially when breaking the agreement will mean leaving here immediately?" A few steps down the narrow back hall returned them to the kitchen. He glanced inside the refrigerator—pretty bare since Lucinda had transferred most of the perishables into his own refrigerator—then said without thinking, "You can eat with Jordan and me next door. Breakfast is at five-thirty, dinner's around noon, and supper's about six-thirty."

"Thank you." She sounded surprised, as if she hadn't expected such an invitation—which was fair, since he hadn't intended to make it. He would take it back if he possibly could. The last thing he needed was her in his house, sitting at his table three times a day.

But what did it matter whether they ate together when he was going to be spending plenty of other time with her? Lying to her. Pretending to be somebody he wasn't to her. Deliberately misleading her. Even thinking about it made his stomach queasy.

Opening the silverware drawer, he withdrew the extra key his mother kept in the corner and laid it on the counter halfway between them. "Any questions?"

"Only about a thousand. Starting with—" In the brief silence came the rumble of her stomach, making her blush. "Well, gee, starting with the fact that I haven't eaten since dinner last night so can I get some lunch?"

"Come on." She was close on his heels as he left the house, crossed the deck and unlocked the door to his own house. He'd neglected to tell her that the same key that opened Lucinda's door also opened his, but figured that was something she didn't need to know. Unlike Lucinda, he hadn't had the time to lock away anything he might not want a nosy reporter to see.

The layout of his half of the house was identical to his

mother's, but his mudroom/laundry room had been turned into an office. A battered oak desk with a computer was pushed into one corner, Jordan had built shelves into one wall, and two oak file cabinets stood side by side against another. Papers, records, magazines and stacks of mail were piled on most of the flat surfaces, including the old-fashioned desk chair made of hickory. He saw the glint of amusement in Natalie's gaze as it swept over the mess, and felt his face grow warm. "It's not as bad as it looks."

"Actually, it looks like home. This is the Thaddeus Grant Method of Record Keeping."

"And yours?"

"Uh, no. I'm a bit more…compulsive. You'll see." Without waiting for an invitation, she went ahead of him into the kitchen. He stood where he was for a moment, watching her move with a lazy grace as if she had all the time in the world, and enjoying the view, before giving himself a mental shake and starting after her.

His kitchen was just like Lucinda's, but where she had floral wallpaper and oak-stained cabinets, his walls were painted yellow and his cabinets and all the trim were white. Her appliances were harvest gold and practically antique. His were white and practically new. He wondered how it compared to Senator Chaney's kitchen, or if any of the Chaneys had ever actually set foot in their kitchen. He also wondered idly if there was any money in winning Pulitzer Prizes, having a school named after you or lecturing students. He assumed there was, since she'd said these days her old man entertained the rich and powerful.

"Sandwiches okay?" he asked as he scrubbed his hands at the double sink.

"Sure. Can I help?"

"Just have a seat."

With a nod Natalie turned toward the table. It was oval, massive and looked about a hundred years old. She could easily imagine generations of Rawlinses gathered around it, sharing meals and the events of their days. If her memory was good enough, she could probably count on both hands the number of times she and her father had sat down to a cozy dinner together. He'd traveled so much when she was growing up, and even when he was home, it seemed that work just naturally required his attention in the evening. She'd spent so much time alone, wishing for his company and vowing to grow up to be just like him.

She'd tried…and failed miserably.

Shying away from thoughts that would only depress her, she forced her attention to the walls behind the table. More than two dozen framed photos hung there, some recent, some discolored with age. Jordan's pictures were easy to pick out by their sheer newness, but J.T.'s were identifiable, even if half a lifetime had passed since the most recent. "Is this your brother?" she asked, studying the third subject.

"Yeah."

"How much older is he than you?"

"About five years."

"Jordan looks more like you than his father." In fact, she thought, if not for the obvious difference in the age of the photographs, a person could easily mistake Jordan in his football uniform for the teenaged J.T. in *his* uniform.

He set two plates on the table with more force than necessary. "Jordan and—Tate aren't part of your interview or your book, remember?"

As he slid into a chair, she claimed the seat across from him. "Sorry. I'm more than a little fascinated by families."

"So write about your own."

"I don't really have one. It was always just my father and me."

"You didn't have a mother? Guess that proves my theory that reporters aren't born. They're created in a lab somewhere."

"I had a mother," she said with a faint smile. "She died when I was six. I just have a few memories of her."

"Sorry." He said it brusquely, but she suspected he was sincere. "What about grandparents? Aunts and uncles?"

"My father was an only child who wasn't close to his parents. My mother was the youngest of four children, but her family resented my father for taking her away. After she died, we never had any contact with them." She glanced at her plate, at a ham sandwich too large by half for her appetite, a pile of potato chips and two home-baked chocolate chip cookies. J.T.'s plate held the same, plus an additional sandwich. "You know, I'm supposed to be asking the questions, not answering them."

"So ask."

She chewed a bite or two before leading into her first question. "I understand that your father—"

"Chaney was a sperm donor, not a father. Call him whatever you want, but not 'father.'"

Natalie nodded in agreement. "Senator Chaney tried to establish a relationship with you some time back, but you refused to return his calls or answer his letters. Sounds like a pattern, doesn't it?"

"Sounds like you people from Alabama are pushy."

"Some of us more than others," she replied with a smile. "At least he didn't show up on your doorstep."

J.T. wasn't the least bit amused. "If he had, I really would have called the sheriff."

"Aren't you even curious about him?"

"No."

"There's nothing you want to say to him? No answers you'd like to get from him?"

He shook his head.

"I think he's very curious about you. I think he regrets not acknowledging you all those years ago—not claiming you and giving you the same sort of privileged life the rest of his children had."

"I'm not a possession to be claimed."

"No, of course not. But you understand what I'm saying."

"If the good senator has any regrets," he said snidely, "I imagine they have to do with leaving office and losing some of that power and constant media attention. I think that's the whole reason behind this book, and the whole reason for sending you here. His illegitimate son is the only surprise the old man has left to get people's attention.''

Natalie disagreed with him, though she didn't say so. She truly believed Chaney wanted to meet J.T., to know what kind of son he and Lucinda Rawlins had produced together. He'd made his own attempts and had been rebuffed, and so he'd turned to her to get the information for him.

''You're very close to your half brother, Tate, and your nephew, Jordan.'' When she paused, a wary look turned his brown eyes a few shades darker and cranked up the intensity in his gaze a few notches. ''You have eight half brothers and sisters and seven nieces and nephews on your fa—on the Chaney side of the family. Do you have any interest in meeting them?''

''You've met them, haven't you?''

She nodded. She'd had the dubious pleasure of spending weeks with every one of them.

''Do I have anything in common with even one of them?''

As far as she could recall, not one of the Chaney offspring had ever held a job. Oh, they'd been given titles in the family business and positions in their father's campaign, but they were empty titles, responsibility-free positions. None of them had actually worked at anything beyond enjoying life to the fullest as one of the privileged elite. They partied. They indulged their every whim. They spent their father's money as if the supply was inexhaustible—as it seemed to be. They carried on scandalously and considered themselves above the dictates the rest of the world lived by.

''Other than the brown hair and eyes, no,'' she admitted. Then she smiled. ''Of course, I don't know that much about you yet.'' But she knew enough to be certain that he wasn't the typical lazy, self-centered, greedy narcissist the rest of the Chaney children were. She knew they would have no more interest in claiming him as their half brother than he had in being claimed.

"Are your mother's parents still alive?"

The abrupt subject change made her blink. "I—I don't know."

"Why haven't you found out?"

"I don't even know where they lived."

"You know their names?"

"Yes, but—"

"You found me, when I would have preferred to remain lost. Surely, if they're still living, you can find them."

"And what would I say?"

"How about starting with, 'I'm your granddaughter'? Then moving on to 'I'm fascinated by families and thought it was time to get to know my own.'"

Natalie's laugh felt choked and phony. "Remember—I ask the questions and you answer them."

His shrug was every bit as enticing as it had been earlier by the truck, with his shirt off. "Have you never even thought about tracking them down?"

"No."

"Why not? Their problem was with your father, not you. They would probably be thrilled to meet their youngest daughter's only child."

Maybe, she admitted to herself. But her father would go ballistic if he ever found out. He'd made it clear enough when she was a child that her loyalties belonged to him, no one else. His parents, her mother's parents—who needed them? They had each other.

But she had never really had him.

She cleared her mind. "Back to the Chaneys..."

"Let's stick with the Grants, or actually...what is your grandparents' name?"

"Stevenson."

"You have a whole family out there somewhere. Wouldn't you like to meet the Stevensons?"

"Wouldn't you like to meet the Chaneys?"

"Aunts, uncles, cousins…"

"Half brothers, half sisters, stepmothers—several of whom are just about your age."

"You think I'd be interested in one of the old man's ex-wives? How sick would that be?"

"Stranger things have happened."

"Not in the Rawlins family."

Natalie took a few moments to eat, polishing off half of the sandwich and the chips and both cookies, then pushed her plate back. "What kind of schedule do you keep?"

"I get up around five-fifteen and work until everything that needs doing is done, and I'm usually in bed by ten."

Some days she awakened with an excess of energy and did everything that needed doing, too. Other days she hung around her apartment, not getting dressed or combing her hair, eating junk food and taking naps between movies on TV. She considered those days the refilling-her-creative-well days. No doubt J.T. would think of them as damn-what-a-lazy-slug days.

"You don't have a regular quitting time?" she asked.

With a brow raised, he reached for her plate. When she nodded, he took it and his own plate to the counter. After putting the remaining sandwich half in a plastic bag in the refrigerator, he returned. "I usually quit around six or six-thirty, depending on what I'm doing. Sometimes I have to work later. Occasionally I can quit earlier."

"Doesn't leave much time for a social life."

He shrugged.

"You've never been married." She waited for his nod. "I assume there are women in your life. Anyone in particular?"

For a long, still moment he simply looked at her. Though her gaze remained steady on him, some part of her mind noticed that it wasn't as cool in the house as it had initially seemed, coming in from the searing oven outside. In fact, in the past few minutes she'd gotten distinctly warmer, almost uncomfortably so, and found herself wishing for a blast of chilly air, an industrial-strength fan...or maybe a cold shower.

"You don't really think I'd tell you if there were, do you? Considering who—or rather what—you are...."

Though his tone was mild, his words measured, Natalie felt the insult's sting. "This may come as a surprise to you, J.T., but not everyone regards reporters as the spawn of Satan."

"Not everyone has one sticking her pretty little nose into their personal lives."

She smiled smugly. Every Chaney male eventually got around to a compliment of some sort—though she had to admit, J.T. was the first one to select her nose. The number-one son had liked her legs, number two her breasts, number three her mouth. Number five had expressed great appreciation for the way she moved and the way she talked, and even the senator himself, old enough to be her grandfather, had made a few indecent suggestions the first time they met.

But of course she had better sense than to mention the reason for her smile to J.T.

"I've got to get to work," he said, pushing his chair back.

She popped to her feet, too. "Can I come with you?"

His gaze started at her shoulders and glided all the way down to her sandaled feet before sweeping up again. She would bet the partial payment she'd received on the book's advance that he was doing nothing more than taking note of how inappropriate her dress was to a working ranch— which didn't deter her one bit from finding the look... sensual. Heated. A threat to the professional detachment she always maintained with her interview subjects.

"You're not exactly dressed to ride one of my horses," he said at last. "Jordan should be back before long. Get settled in, and we'll talk at dinner."

She couldn't even argue the point about riding. There was no way she could make it into the saddle in this dress, and there was one other minor problem in that she didn't know how to ride. She'd lived thirty-one years without getting closer to a horse than when they'd cut across the yard on the way to her temporary quarters, and she was convinced she could happily keep her distance for the next sixty years.

After thanking him for lunch, she returned to Lucinda's place, nudged the thermostat into a cooler range, then wandered into the living room. With the sun already on its afternoon slide into the west, she opened the blinds, then turned to study the room.

It was a little on the small side and decorated in a rather fussy manner. There were hand-crocheted doilies on the arms of the sofa and chairs, dried flower arrangements, a ruffled cloth on one round end table. More pictures of the three Rawlins boys hung on the walls, along with a couple of snapshots of Lucinda. The one that appeared most recent had been taken in the spring, with that old green truck and the weathered barn for a backdrop. The photographer's shadow fell across lush green grass and stretched toward the feet of the family gathered there—Jordan, wearing crisp indigo jeans and a vertically striped rugby shirt, the heartthrob every high school should have for its own; J.T. in faded jeans and a white dress shirt and holding a cream-colored cowboy hat in his hands; the absent brother, Tate, five years older than J.T., several inches shorter, less handsome, less sexy, more forgettable; and Lucinda.

From the time the senator had told Natalie about his affair with Lucinda Rawlins and the illegitimate son it had produced, she'd wondered about the woman. Was she as pretty as Chaney remembered, as sly, deceitful and cunning as he claimed? Had she pursued him, seduced him and deliberately set out to trap him, or had it been just one more instance of the senator's lack of self-control?

In the photograph with her sons and grandson, Lucinda didn't look sly, deceitful or cunning. What she looked like, in fact, was the senator's preferred type—slim, blond, pretty, delicate. She had a lovely smile and held herself with a certain grace, though her life certainly hadn't been easy. According to the senator, her marriage to Tate's father had ended when he'd found himself one girlfriend too many. She'd been left to raise two kids alone, with no help from either father, and she had apparently been very successful. Well, except for the fact that Tate had apparently repeated her mistake and wound up raising Jordan alone.

"Hey."

She gave a start, then turned to face the subject of her last thought, standing in the kitchen doorway.

"I knocked, but I guess you didn't hear. I don't know if—if Uncle J.T. told you, but the doorbell at the side door doesn't work. We got hit by lightning in the last storm, and it fried the doorbell and Grandma's cable and the telephone. We got the telephone fixed, but if you want to watch cable, you have to come over to our place, and Dad will fix the doorbell—" he swallowed hard, and his cheeks turned pink "—or—or maybe Uncle J.T. will. When he gets the time. Maybe."

Natalie offered her warmest smile to put the boy at ease. "I appreciate your picking up my stuff for me. It was nice of your uncle to volunteer you."

"They're always doing that," he said with a shrug that was an unconscious imitation of J.T.'s. "But I don't mind. I just got my driver's license a couple months ago. Your bags are by the door. Want me to put them in the guest room?"

"That's okay. I'll get them later. Do you have to get to work, or can you sit down and talk?"

He shifted uneasily. "I've got football practice in a little bit."

"In this heat?"

"We just run some laps, and mostly work out in the weight room. It's air-conditioned. And we drink a lot of water and Gatorade and stuff. We won't spend a lot of time outside until week after next."

"I saw the sign outside town that said you were the state champions last year."

He seemed intent on dragging the toe of his boot back

and forth across the seam where vinyl flooring met carpet. "Yeah, we did okay."

"I bet you did better than okay." He was six feet tall, broad-shouldered, about 180 pounds of muscle—and acting as shy as a tongue-tied six-year-old. "Is football your only sport?"

"I play baseball, too. Pitcher, just like my dad. He was one of the best jocks Hickory Bluff ever saw. He was recruited by the OU Sooners and the Razorbacks his senior year."

"What happened?"

Jordan stared at the floor for a moment. When he looked up, his brown eyes were dark with regret. "Me."

"Oh." Natalie's smile felt forced. "Look at it this way—you probably saved him from a lifetime of aches and pains from too many injuries."

"Yeah, I saved him a chance at the pros and making millions and retiring when he's thirty-five."

"Do you think he'd rather have the chance at the pros and making millions than you?"

Jordan raised his head and slowly smiled at her—the naturally perfect smile that she doubted she would get to see his uncle wearing. "Nope. My grandma says I'm the light of their lives."

"I'm sure you are," she said dryly. "What's your favorite subject in school?"

They answered in unison. "Football."

"What's your favorite academic subject?"

"Algebra. I think after college I'll teach math and be a coach."

"And you'll be the most popular math teacher the school has ever seen—with the girls, at least." She hesitated, debated the wisdom of her next question, then asked anyway. "Your father's not married, is he?"

"No."

"And J.T. isn't married, either, is he?"

"Nope. Are you?"

She shook her head.

"Why not?"

He looked like J.T., his mannerisms were like J.T.'s, and he was quick to ask questions like J.T. Kind of made her wonder just how much effort his father had put into raising him, and how much of the responsibility J.T. had shouldered.

With a sigh, she sat down in the nearest chair. Jordan took a seat on the sofa arm. "Why am I not married.... Nobody ever asked. I didn't particularly want to get married. I haven't had much time in the past year or so for dating." Or much desire. In fact, the thing she'd wanted to do most in that time was hibernate. Disappear off the face of the earth. Find some way to turn back time and make right everything she'd done wrong.

"Take your pick, or make your own excuse." She smiled tautly. "Do you have a girlfriend?"

A faint blush stained Jordan's cheeks. "Sort of. We go out, but she sees other guys, too."

"Are you free to see other girls?"

"Yeah, but who's got the time?"

Or the desire, Natalie suspected. A faithful man—a rarity in her experience. She wondered—purely for the sake of the book—if his uncle shared that trait or took after the fidelity-challenged Chaneys.

"Her name is Shelley. Here's a picture of her." He passed over a brass frame from the end table. It held an eight-by-ten-inch photograph of a dozen or more teenagers. Jordan and a tiny blonde were front and center, looking like Ken and Barbie, Jr.

"She's pretty," Natalie said of Shelley, then pointed to another girl. "Who is she?"

"That's Mike. She lives down the road a ways. Her real name is Michaela." With a glance at his watch, he jumped to his feet. "I gotta go. See you later."

While listening to his footsteps, then the slam of the door, Natalie continued to study the photo. The kids all looked so young, so fresh-faced and innocent, starting lives that were brimming with potential. It seemed *she* had always been the new kid in school, there and gone before she'd had the chance to make any lasting friendships. She envied the kids and hoped they enjoyed the camaraderie while they could.

Poor Mike didn't look as if she was enjoying anything in the moment captured on film. She was taller than every girl and most of the boys in the shot, a brunette in a sea of blondes, her glasses unflattering and her clothes ill-fitting, and she was looking at Jordan as if he'd hung the moon. Unfortunately, Jordan was looking at Cheerleader Barbie's Best Friend, Shelley, in exactly the same way.

Young love. Young heartache.

Natalie's only experience with heartache had been of a nonromantic nature. She'd been betrayed by her only best friend ever, and she couldn't imagine a lover's betrayal could hurt any worse. She didn't intend to find out, though. In the foreseeable future, her life was going to revolve around work—the book on Senator Chaney, undoing the mistakes of the past, righting the wrongs, winning back her father's respect.

Like Jordan, she had no time or desire for anything more.

Chapter Three

It was after six when Tate returned to the house with only two things on his mind—a long, cool shower and a quiet, peaceful evening sacked out on the couch in front of the TV. The instant he saw the Mustang parked under the tree, though, the hope for a quiet evening went right out of his mind. He had to spend the evening with the woman of a thousand questions. He'd have no peace tonight.

As he reined in his horse, then swung from the saddle, he smiled without humor. He *had* to spend the evening with Natalie Grant. When was the last time he'd spent three whole hours with a beautiful woman and complained about it? Hell, he couldn't remember his last date. Sometime last winter, he thought, with one of Jordan's teachers. The kid had been mortified and had done all but beg him not to make a second date.

Tate hadn't. Ms. Blythe, the English teacher, had been about as interesting as the subject she taught, and she'd spoken to him as if he were one of her students...at least until she'd sucked the oxygen right out of his lungs.

He didn't think he had to worry about anything like that with Natalie—though given a choice, he'd rather kiss her than lie to her.

Damn, given the choice, he'd rather kiss Ms. Blythe than lie to Natalie. He just wasn't cut out for deception and dishonesty.

He'd just finished tending his horse and tack and was heading for the house when he saw Natalie come out next door and start toward her car. When she saw him, she angled toward him, strolling across the yard as if she belonged there. The rays from the evening sun made her burnished hair glow and gave her creamy skin a golden gleam. She'd removed the ribbon that contained her hair in a ponytail, and now it hung wild and unrestrained down her back, so thick and electric that touching it, he thought, might send out sparks.

Burying his hands in it might generate more heat than he could bear.

"Hey," she said, turning and falling into step beside him. "Long day."

"The usual." He removed his hat and drew his arm across his forehead. His sleeve came away wet and grimy. He was dripping with sweat, coated with dust and stank to high heaven...but he would swear he could smell the subtle fragrance of her perfume. Sweet. Clean. Light. "Did Jordan get back okay with your stuff?"

"Yes."

"Did he take it inside for you?"

"Yes, he did. Then he left for football practice. Isn't it way too hot for that?"

"If life stopped around here for the heat and the drought, we'd be shut down part of July, all of August and most of September every year. The kids are used to it, and the coaches keep an eye on them."

"I know you played football in high school because I saw the picture. Any other sports?"

"Baseball. I was a pitcher."

"You, too?" At his questioning glance, she shrugged. "Jordan said he's a pitcher, and so was his dad. So all three Rawlins boys have a good arm."

Through sheer will, Tate kept his grimace inside. This damned charade offered a million chances to screw up, and he'd just taken one. Truth was, Josh couldn't hit the barn with a rock unless he was standing within spittin' distance. He'd rodeoed and chased girls, and that was it.

He climbed the steps to the back door, then turned to find her following. Deliberately he blocked her way. "Yeah... well..." Brilliant observations, but all he could think of at the moment. Then he turned the conversation back on her. "I know Jordan didn't say, 'Here's your luggage and, by the way, did you know my dad and I both pitched for the Wildcats?'"

"No, of course not. We were talking, and I asked—" She broke off and backed down a step, then another. Because she realized she'd already broken their agreement? Or because he was scowling at her? "I wasn't *questioning* him. We were talking. He asked me if I was married. I asked him if he played anything besides football. It was just idle conversation."

Like father, like son. Under better circumstances, whether she was married would be one of his first questions, too. It was too late for that now, but... "Are you? Married, I mean?"

Confusion shadowed her blue eyes momentarily, then cleared. "No. I'm not."

It was an unimportant detail. She might as well be, for all it mattered. She was still a reporter snooping into his family's lives. He was still lying to her with every breath he took. He couldn't summon any respect for her or her job, and at the moment he was fresh out of it for himself, too.

Even so, it seemed harder to break her gaze than it should

be. He managed by digging out his keys and turning to unlock the door. "Give me half an hour to clean up, then we'll eat supper."

"I can fix something—"

"It's taken care of." Leaving her at the foot of the steps, he went inside, closed and locked the door, then drew a deep breath. He needed a date. Soon.

He left his boots by the door, put a pan of Lucinda's lasagna in the oven, tossed his clothes into the hamper, then stepped into the shower under a stream of cool water. Once his body temperature dropped below steaming, he warmed the water, then scrubbed away layers of grime. He also, for reasons he didn't look at too closely, shaved before he got out.

With a towel wrapped around his middle, he went into his bedroom...and stopped a fair distance back from the south window. There he had a clear view of the big old blackjack and the Mustang—and Natalie and Jordan. She was removing items from the trunk—Tate recognized a laptop-computer carrying case slung over one shoulder—while Jordan walked in an admiring circle around the car. When she closed the trunk, he picked up a box of the type used to store files, and they started toward the house, talking easily. Of course, she *was* a reporter, paid for getting people to open up, and Jordan had never met a stranger in his life.

As they disappeared from sight, the phone beside the bed rang. Tate got it on the third ring, bracing it between his ear and shoulder while he started dressing. "Hello."

It was Josh. "How's it going?"

"So far, so good. How's Grandpop?"

"Not feeling too hot. So far, he's found fault with everything I've done—and he's not even out of the hospital yet."

Tate chuckled at the aggrieved tone of his brother's voice. "I'd trade places with you in a heartbeat. I'd rather have Grandpop griping at me than Ms. Alabama following me around with all her questions."

"I think for once I got the lesser of two evils. What's the lady reporter like?"

"About what we expected," Tate replied with a twinge of guilt. She *was* persistent and stubborn, as they'd known she would be. But she was also so much more.

"What's the plan?"

His plan was to avoid any slipups, to be as truthful with Natalie as possible while pretending to be someone else, to not tell her too much and to not notice any more than necessary how pretty she was...how good she smelled...how he was a sucker for leggy redheads and Southern drawls.

"I'm not sure," he hedged. "She's coming over for dinner in a few minutes. I guess I'll find out then. Tell Mom I love her, and Gran and Grandpop, too."

"Sure. Tate...? Thanks."

"Hey, Rawlinses stick together, right? See you." Tate hung up, pulled on a T-shirt and combed his fingers through his hair, then headed for the kitchen. He was buttering a loaf of French bread when Jordan came in from the office. Natalie was two steps behind him.

"How was practice?"

"Okay." Jordan took a carton of milk from the refrigerator, gave it a shake, then drained it straight from the carton.

It was a habit Lucinda had tried to break, but since it was one Tate shared, he let it slide, except for a comment for Natalie's benefit. "We don't drink out of the carton unless we know we're going to finish it, do we, son?"

Too late—when Jordan's gaze jerked to him—Tate remembered. A glance at Natalie, though, showed no reason to worry. Men called boys son. She obviously thought nothing of it.

"Hey, uh, Uncle J.T., can I get online until supper's ready?" Jordan asked.

"Yeah, go ahead."

Once he was gone from the room, Natalie came closer,

leaning against the counter a few feet away. "Does he have any chores besides tinkering with old engines?"

"Are you kidding? He could run this place if he had to. There's not a job here he can't handle. After all, it'll belong to him someday."

"Along with any children *you* might have. But what if he doesn't want to be a rancher?"

"He can be whatever he wants...but the land will be here for him."

"It's the Rawlins Ranch, right?" She waited for his nod. "Does the elder Rawlins—Tate's father—mind that you're a partner in his family's spread?"

Tate opened a bottle of pop and started filling three glasses. This wasn't the time to tell her that the only elder Rawlins around was his grandfather, that Rawlins was Lucinda's family name and not that of her elder son's father. As long as he could keep things straight in his head, she didn't need to know all the details of his family's lives. "T-Tate's father can't complain about me being a partner for several reasons. First, he hasn't been around for a long time." Truth—his old man had disappeared five months before *he* had appeared. He hadn't offered to shoulder any responsibilities or pay any support. He'd kissed Lucinda goodbye and walked out the door. "Second, this place was never in his family. The Rawlinses of Rawlins Ranch are us—my mother, my brother, Jordan and me."

"He calls you 'uncle.'"

"Yeah? So?"

She shrugged. "No older than you are, I'd expect him to simply use your name."

"I'm old enough to be his father."

"Not quite. Not unless you discovered sex *very* young. Did you?"

Tate slowly looked at her. No one would guess, just by looking, that she'd asked such a provocative question, or raised his body temperature about twenty degrees, or made his throat clamp down so tightly that he wasn't sure he could speak. No, she simply stood there, a bright splash of color and texture, cool, calm, unaffected.

"You tell me about your first time, and I'll tell you about mine," he said in a low, thick voice.

She moved, revealing an edge of restlessness that hadn't been present earlier. "I'm not the subject of this book. No one's interested in my first time."

"I am."

"You'd be bored."

"Try me."

She shuffled her feet, slid her hands behind her back, then clasped them in front of her. "I was nineteen. He was in too big a hurry. It was painful, messy and thoroughly unpleasant. End of story."

"And I wasn't bored at all."

Her cheeks pink, she gestured. "Your turn."

When the oven timer went off, he removed the lasagna and slid the bread under the broiler. He took plates from the cabinet, utensils from the drawer and serving utensils from another drawer. Out of diversions, finally he faced her. "I was seventeen, and I wasn't in a hurry at all. It was better than I expected, not as good as it could be, and I enjoyed it thoroughly."

She picked up one of the glasses and took a long drink of pop before continuing. "Jordan is only a year younger than you were then. Do you worry about him?"

"We've talked." His smile was sardonic. "It's one of the benefits of being no older than I am. We can easily discuss things that might be more difficult if I were ten or fifteen years older."

"*You've* talked. Not Jordan and his father, but him and you. Why? Isn't his father interested?"

Tate scowled as he used hot pads to carry the lasagna to the table. She followed with the dishes. "Of course his father is interested. They're very close."

"But...?"

"But nothing. They get along just fine. Why don't you take notes?"

The abrupt change of subject threw her, as he'd intended. She blinked, then gave a shake of her head. "I will when it's necessary. Right now we're just getting acquainted."

"So that's what you call it," he said dryly, then raised his voice. "Jordan, come on and eat."

"I'll be right there."

Their voices sounded alike, Natalie thought as she slid into the same seat where she'd had lunch. They also looked a lot alike. She wondered about Tate, and if his son resembled *him* half as much as his uncle.

Carrying the bread and his own pop, J.T. sat across from her, leaving the chair at the head of the table for Jordan.

"Is there any work around here that doesn't require a horse?" she asked while they waited for the boy to join them.

"Plenty. Why?"

"I'd like to follow you around for a few days, to get a feel for what you do."

He didn't miss a beat. "But I'll be using Rusty all week. And you probably don't know how to ride, do you? Too bad."

"You're not funny, Mr. Rawlins," she said primly as she tried to suppress a smile.

"I wasn't trying to be. How did you manage to reach the age of— How old are you?"

"Thirty-one."

"—without learning to ride?"

"Gee, I don't know. I guess horses were just too cumbersome for the high-rise apartments where we mostly lived."

"Around here kids learn to ride as soon as they can sit up by themselves."

Natalie studied him skeptically. "You're exaggerating."

"Not by much. Hold your ears for a minute." Pursing

his lips, he let out a shrill whistle that could vibrate loose the fillings in her back teeth.

From down the hall came a grumbled, "All right, I'm coming." A moment later, Jordan joined them. "I was just talking to some girls in California."

"Here's a novel idea—why don't you pick up the phone and have a *real* conversation?" J.T. countered. "Better yet, after you do the dishes, why don't you saddle up Cougar and ride over to see Mike in person?"

"Nah." Then the boy's eyes lit up. "But if you want to give me the keys, I can go into town and see a bunch of people. Then you two can talk all evening."

"If you're back by ten. Why don't you invite Mike?"

"Aw, Da—Uncle J.T. If I show up with Mike, Shelley's gonna spend the whole evening ignoring me. She doesn't like Mike."

"Why not?"

"I don't know," Jordan mumbled.

I do, Natalie thought to herself. The Barbie clone wanted everyone's attention all for herself, especially Jordan's. She wanted to be the only girl he cared about, even if she was stringing him along while going out with other guys. As for Mike's dislike…she was tall, flat-chested, lacking in curves, bespectacled and plain. How could she *not* dislike the gorgeous little cheerleader doll?

Then, of course, there was Jordan. Mike wanted him. Shelley had him.

After a moment J.T. gave in. Jordan scarfed down two large helpings of lasagna and half a loaf of bread, then left. Both the door and the screen door slammed behind him.

In the silence that followed, Natalie finished her first and only helping of the dish while J.T. worked on his second. "You're not really going to hide behind your horses to avoid me, are you?"

"It's a thought."

"You know, the more you restrict my access to you, the longer my visit will have to last."

"You'll have to go home eventually."

She grinned. "I have plenty of clothes, my notes on the senator, my cell phone and my computer. I could survive indefinitely with nothing else."

"What about your life back in Alabama? Your friends, your boyfriend, your other work?"

"I don't have a life in Alabama." No friends. Just people who'd once pretended to be. No boyfriend. No other work. This book had become her life.

And she wouldn't have it any other way. Even if she was a little lonely. Really, she wouldn't.

"No life?" J.T. repeated skeptically. "No boyfriend?"

She was flattered that he found it so difficult to believe that there wasn't at least one man in the state of Alabama who wanted her, and was amused by her own feeling of flattery. "Do you have a girlfriend?"

"Not at the moment."

"Well, at the moment I've got much more important things in my life. Men come pretty low on my list."

"Why?"

With a shake of her head, she gave a low laugh. "You really have trouble grasping this question-and-answer process, don't you? It's really very simple. I ask. You answer. I can write it down for you to look at from time to time if you'd like."

Between bites he said, "You said we were getting acquainted. That implies an exchange of information. You can't get acquainted with me and remain a stranger to me. So why don't you like men?"

"I like men. They have their uses." Under different circumstances, she could like him *a lot*. She could find plenty of uses for him. "I just don't want one in my life."

"Why not?"

For a time Natalie considered various answers and lies, as well as simply refusing any answer at all. She thought about pointing out to him that his getting to know her wasn't part of the deal, that he should be grateful she was trying to learn everything about him, that she could write the book as easily without his cooperation as with. The only difference was in the degree of accuracy—getting the chance to put his spin on things.

In the end, though, she answered. Maybe not completely, but truthfully, as far as it went. "My father is one of the greatest journalists who ever lived. I've known since I was a little kid that I wanted to be just like him. I know I'll never be as good, but I'm trying." She thought of the headlines fifteen months ago and inwardly cringed. She really was trying. Too bad she was failing. "One of the things he taught me was that this job requires dedication. Commitment. Doing it right—doing it Thaddeus Grant's way—isn't conducive to maintaining relationships or raising a family. I see no point in getting involved with a man who can't compete with the job for my attention, and I certainly see no sense in bringing kids into the picture."

"So your father didn't love you, and you're following in his footsteps by refusing to love anyone, in the same way."

"My father loved me!" she protested.

"Not as much as he loved the job. Hey, my old man never gave a damn about me, either. But shutting yourself off from everyone else isn't the way to deal with it."

"I'm not shut off from anyone. I have plenty of contact with people. In fact, I spend so much time with people that most evenings it's a pleasure to go home to an empty apartment. By the end of most days, I crave peace and quiet and solitude." Usually that was true. Some days, though, she wanted what J.T. had—a close-knit family whose members cared about each other, who were there for each other. All she had was her father, and far from being there for her when she'd needed him, he'd withdrawn. He'd spoken to her only once, to tell her what a disappointment she'd become. He'd helped break her heart.

Shutting out the memory of the chill in his voice and his eyes, she toyed with her fork for a moment before meeting

J.T.'s gaze again. "You ask awfully personal questions, considering that we're strangers."

He gave that sexy little shrug. "Have I asked you anything you didn't ask me first?"

"But I'm being paid to ask questions."

"So this is my payment. You want answers from me? You have to provide your own answers."

When he pushed his plate back, she stood up, gathered the dishes and carried them to the sink, where she began rinsing them.

"After-supper cleanup is Jordan's job." J.T.'s voice came from somewhere behind her.

She resisted the urge to look over her shoulder and instead concentrated on scrubbing away every particle of pasta, cheese and sauce before loading the dishes in the dishwasher. "I don't mind."

"It's not a matter of minding. It's *his* responsibility."

"But I'm already finished." She dried her hands, then faced him. "Can I go out with you tomorrow?"

"We start early."

"I know. You get up at five-fifteen and have breakfast at five-thirty. When I interviewed Boyd, Jr., the oldest of your half brothers, I usually got back to the hotel around five-thirty. I doubt he's been out of bed before noon since he graduated from high school."

"And what did you and Boyd, Jr., do until five-thirty in the morning?"

"He partied, gambled, drank, ate, flirted. I watched. When I interviewed Kathleen, the second child, I was lucky to get four hours of sleep a night. She indulges in all of Junior's pastimes, and is a world-class shopper, as well."

"So they party, they play, they spend money. And your publisher actually thinks people want to read about this?"

"People are fascinated by the idle rich, especially when they attract scandal like…like Jordan's Barbie doll attracts admirers."

"Jordan's—" Breaking off, J.T. grinned. It was a sight

to see—white teeth, crinkled brown skin, a light in his dark eyes. "You saw Shelley's picture at Mom's."

She nodded. "The most popular girl in Hickory Bluff. The cheerleader, the class president, the princess in the homecoming queen's court, the star of the school play, the sweetest voice in the school choir. The golden girl whose life so far has been perfect, who makes other girls' lives miserable."

He gestured, and she preceded him into the living room. "You learned all that from a photograph? Or were you describing yourself back in high school?"

With a chuckle Natalie chose to sit on the sofa. It was one of those really comfortable overstuffed models, the perfect place to snuggle in among puffy pillows and cushions and drift off to sleep. "I was nobody's golden girl. For me, high school was an ordeal to be endured. Graduation was one of the happiest days of my life." Except that her father hadn't been there. What had kept him away that time? Another terrorist attack in the Middle East? Some new crisis in Moscow or Baghdad or Belfast?

"Where did you go to high school?"

"New York. And Connecticut, Virginia and D.C."

"I went from kindergarten through twelfth grade here in Hickory Bluff."

"You were lucky."

"Yeah, I was."

When silence settled between them, she gazed around the room. There were family photographs on every wall, but none of Jordan's mother or Tate's father. A rusty horseshoe hung above the front door, and a sandstone fireplace filled one wall, with bookcases on either side crammed with—surprise—books. Neither the room nor its furnishings could hold a candle to the lavish residences the other Chaney siblings called home. They surrounded themselves with antiques, designer names and opulent furnishings, spending fortunes on the most exquisite items money could buy…but not one of them had a sofa that invited you to nap cozily cradled in its softness. Not one that she could recall displayed personal items with pride and affection, like the photos, the child's sculpture of a horse or the handmade Best Dad Award that stood on the fireplace mantel.

Of course, she reminded herself, this was *Tate* Rawlins's house—his pride and affection and comfort. J.T. was a temporary guest here, as she was at his mother's house.

"So…" She brought her gaze back to J.T. He was sitting in an easy chair that looked as if it lived up to its name. His left knee was bent, with his foot propped on the coffee table. His other leg was stretched out half the length of the table. His jeans were soft and faded nearly white, his T-shirt was snug and worn thin, and his feet were bare.

Natalie liked the intimacy of bare feet. His were long and slender, not as dark as his face and arms, but shades darker than her own barely tanned skin. They were purely functional…and somehow appealing.

Oh, man, she needed a date. Badly.

Clearing her throat, she returned to a subject she suspected he wanted her to forget. "Can I go with you tomorrow?"

"You don't give up, do you?"

She smiled. "That was another of my father's lessons."

"All right. But dress appropriately."

"And what's appropriate?"

"Jeans. A shirt—for you, with long sleeves. A hat. Sturdy shoes. Do you have any sunscreen?"

Her expression turned admonishing. "Look at me," she said, and he did, his gaze sliding slowly over her face, down her throat and lower before lifting again. It made her voice sound funny and her heart beat faster, and she swore it raised her temperature by a degree or two. "Do I look as if I go *anywhere* without sunscreen?"

"No," he agreed. "In fact, add a few more yards to that dress, and you'd look like the stereotypical Southern belle—fragile, pampered, delicate skin untouched by the sun…"

"I'm not sure whether I've just been complimented or insulted."

"Frankly, neither am I."

She glanced at her watch. It was after eight o'clock. She was tired, and no doubt J.T. would like a little time to himself before turning in. "I'd better get to bed if I'm getting up early. I'll see you at five-thirty."

He walked to the side door with her, leaning against the frame while she crossed the deck to her own door. There she looked back. "So you don't like the dress."

"As a matter of fact, I like it just fine."

She smiled faintly, then sobered. "Don't underestimate me, J.T. I'm neither fragile nor pampered nor delicate. I'm a survivor." Or, at least, trying to be. "Good night."

She went inside, closed and locked the door, then peeked through the curtains. For a long moment he remained where he was, motionless. Then, with a shake of his head, he went inside his own house and closed the door.

By the time Tate made it into the kitchen the next morning, the coffee was ready and breakfast was almost done. Jordan handed him a mug, already filled and sweetened, then turned back to the mass of eggs he was scrambling.

Tate wasn't an easy riser. It didn't matter whether he was getting up at five or noon, after two hours' sleep or eight. He needed coffee, food and time before he was capable of any behavior remotely close to human.

He'd bet Ms. Alabama was perky and bright-eyed, he thought with a scowl as the doorbell rang. Leaving Jordan to his cooking, he went down the short hall, opened the side door, then silently swung around and headed back to the kitchen.

"And a good morning to you, too," Natalie said cheerily as she followed. "Hey, Jordan. How was Shelley last night?"

Tate sat down with his back to the wall as Jordan grinned. "She was fine," he said in a way that gave a whole new meaning to the word. "You have to excuse…Uncle J.T. He's kinda cranky in the morning."

"He's kinda cranky in the afternoon and evening, too, isn't he?"

He ignored the teasing and concentrated on his coffee. Usually it wasn't hard to do, but usually Natalie Grant wasn't standing a few feet away, a bright light in his dusky morning.

Dress appropriately, he'd told her, and she had. Her shirt was chambray, well-worn and tucked into faded jeans that fitted snugly and held a sharp crease all the way down each leg to a pair of running shoes. Her incredible hair was pulled back and caught with a glittery band, and she wore a Crimson Tide ball cap. The outfit made her look closer to Jordan's age than his own.

He wished she *was* ten or twelve years younger. Of all the women he'd ever known, she was the most dangerous. He very much needed to keep his distance from her, but that was easier said than done.

"So, Jordan," she was saying. "You're handsome, a star athlete, you cook and do dishes, too. You're going to make some lucky woman a *very* good husband someday."

"I'm not planning on getting married," he replied, his manner offhand. "Nobody else does. Go ahead and have a seat. You want coffee, milk or orange juice?"

"Juice, please."

Natalie joined Tate at the table, bringing with her a faint hint of fragrance—something light and flowery that he didn't recognize—but he hardly noticed. He was thinking instead about Jordan's comment. *I'm not planning on getting married. No one else does.*

The last thing Tate wanted was for Jordan to get any ideas of what marriage, relationships and family were supposed to be from his own family. Lucinda hadn't set out to have two sons with different fathers and no husbands. She'd expected to get married when she'd finished school—had certainly expected to be a wife before she became a mother.

Just as *he* had always expected to be married before he became a father. Sometimes things just didn't work out the way people expected.

But he still believed the ideal family included a mother *and* a father, married and committed before the kids came. That was what he wanted for Jordan when he was old enough. He didn't want his grandchildren to carry on the family tradition of illegitimacy—didn't want Jordan to give up one single dream to take on the hardships of single fatherhood. He wanted his son's future to be every bit as normal and routine as his past wasn't.

Jordan brought platters of food to the table, refilled both Tate's and his own coffee and poured Natalie's juice before sliding into his chair. They passed the food around, then ate in silence until Natalie, obviously not as comfortable with it as they were, spoke up. "When does school start?"

"In a couple weeks," Jordan replied.

"Are you looking forward to it?"

He shrugged. "It's not like I've had much time to be bored. But it's okay. I don't mind going back."

"I loved summer vacations," she said with a faint smile. "My father and I usually did some traveling—always related to his job, of course. Depending on what was happening in the world, we'd spend a few weeks in London, Paris or Rome. Of course, they *were* working trips—" her smile slowly slipped "—so I spent a lot of time alone in hotel rooms."

"Jordan doesn't *get* summer vacations," Tate said sharply. "His time off from school is spent working on the ranch."

"But at least I don't have homework." Under the table Jordan nudged Tate with his foot, then frowned.

Just what he needed—to be reprimanded by his sixteen-year-old son. The fact that the reprimand was deserved brought a rush of warmth to Tate's cheeks.

Still wearing that warning look, Jordan asked, "What's on the schedule for today, Uncle J.T.?"

"Ms. Grant wants to follow me around, so I'm putting her to work. We're going to check fence and replace that section out by the creek."

"I thought I'd try again to get the truck running, then go out and spray for weeds." After sandwiching two strips of bacon between halves of a biscuit, Jordan stood up, drained his coffee, then headed for the door. "I've got practice at three. If you need anything from town, leave a list on the table. I should be home around the usual time, unless the coach is in a bad mood."

After he left, Tate finished his own coffee while studying Natalie. She hadn't eaten a fraction as much breakfast as he and Jordan had, and seemed preoccupied at that moment with separating the half biscuit remaining on her plate layer by layer. She *didn't* seem to want to talk to him or even acknowledge him in any way.

So, naturally, he left her no choice. "Ready to go?"

Abruptly she dusted her hands, slid to her feet and began clearing the table. Instead of offering his help, he got a large cooler and filled it with ice and water. By the time he finished, she was ready, too, with a large bag slung over one shoulder.

"What's all that?" he asked after he'd locked up and they'd started across the yard.

"Tools of the trade. Tape recorder, notebook, camera." She gestured toward the materials Jordan was loading into the bed of the pickup truck parked in front of the bar. "What's all that?"

"Tools of *my* trade." He put the cooler in back, then slid into the driver's seat. "Thanks, Jordan. See you later."

Natalie settled in on the passenger side, putting her bag on the seat between them. After taking out a camera, she opened the lens cap, then looked through the viewfinder. "Looks like you've got company," she remarked as she wiped the lens with a soft cloth.

He looked in the same direction she had and saw a lone rider on horseback coming up the driveway. "That's Mike, our neighbor's kid. If Jordan can't fix the truck, she probably can.''

"Tall, plain and mechanically inclined to boot. Poor Mike.''

Tate gave her a sharp look before he drove around the bar and onto a well-used, if primitive, road that crisscrossed the ranch. "Mike is one of Jordan's best friends. She's a good kid, smart and sweet. She doesn't deserve your insults.''

"I'm not insulting her. I'm commiserating with her. You were a teenage boy yourself at one time. You were handsome, a jock and, I presume, fairly popular with the girls. Was there *one* girl in school who wanted to be best friends with you?''

He'd gotten his share of attention from girls from the time he was about thirteen years old. He'd had girlfriends and friends who were girls. But he'd always known he could have more from his girl friends. All he'd needed to do was let them know.

"Mike may be one of Jordan's best friends," Natalie went on. "But that's not all she *wants* to be. She's settled for what she can have, not what she wants.''

"And you know all this about a girl you've never met.... How?''

"I saw the way she was looking at him in the photograph.''

"What photograph?''

"The one in your mother's living room.'' When he didn't respond, she scowled. "The one with Jordan gazing adoringly at the Barbie doll. Sheesh, you didn't even realize Mike was in that picture, did you? *Men.*''

He wasn't sure how to respond to that. Okay, so he should have known Mike was in the picture. And, yeah, maybe he hadn't noticed her because Barb—Shelley had grabbed his attention, or maybe just because he was so accustomed to seeing Mike. She'd practically grown up here on the ranch.

But he wasn't any more attracted—or distracted—by a pretty face than anyone else, man or woman.

But red hair and long legs... That combination could make him a goner *real* quick.

After a moment she withdrew the tape recorder from her bag and pressed the record button. "It's Wednesday, August eighth. This interview with J. T. Rawlins is taking place at the Rawlins Ranch. Do you have a preference where we start?"

"How about next week?" At her prim, pursed-lips look, he shrugged. "No. Wherever you want."

"Did you always know who your father was, or did your mother keep it from you until you were older?"

Tate flexed his fingers on the steering wheel. This was a question he could answer for both Josh and himself. His grandparents may have been ashamed, the esteemed senator in denial and his own father uncaring, but Lucinda had always been honest and straightforward. "It was never a big secret. When I started asking questions, she gave me answers."

"What was your first question?"

"If I had a father like the other kids." He'd seen other kids with men in their lives who played catch with them, took them fishing and taught them things mothers knew nothing about, or so it seemed, and he'd wondered why he just had Lucinda. She'd chuckled and said, "Of course you have a father. Did you think the angels just delivered you out of the blue?"

He'd been older—seven, maybe eight—before he'd started asking for details. She'd told him his father's name was Hank Daniels and he'd been a rodeo cowboy. A *married* rodeo cowboy, she'd admitted when he was ten or so. It wasn't until he'd found himself in high school and trying to convince Stephani to marry him that he'd learned the rest of the story. How Lucinda had met Hank at a rodeo in Tulsa. How he'd swept her off her feet and taken her for the ride of her life. How she'd gone on the road with him, traveling from rodeo to rodeo, falling in love, living only for the moment. How she'd told him she was pregnant, and he'd told her he was already supporting a wife back in Dallas and the last thing he'd wanted was a pregnant girlfriend to add to his troubles.

"When you understood who your father was," Natalie went on, "what did you think?"

"You mean, was I impressed?" Tate made a scornful noise. Hank Daniels hadn't been as impressive as Boyd Chaney, but he'd made a name for himself. He'd won championships, had made and squandered a few small fortunes. "He was an arrogant jerk who seduced my mother, had his fun, then left her to deal with the consequences alone. The fact that he wasn't just an average jerk didn't make him any less of a jerk."

"Your mother was...twenty-five or so?" She waited for his confirming nod. "She wasn't exactly...inexperienced."

"She was twenty-five, from a dusty little podunk town, working as a waitress in a restaurant that wouldn't have let her through the door if she weren't part of the help. She was living in a strange place, she had no friends, no money, no self-esteem and no hope. She didn't stand a chance against him."

"The senator tells a different story."

"I'm sure he does." He spared a glance at her before steering the truck off the road. Ordinarily he checked the fence on horseback. Of course, ordinarily he didn't do it in hundred-degree-plus heat, or with a companion intent on probing into every corner of his life. By himself, it was a quiet way to pass the time. With Natalie's questions, it was going to be a long day.

"The senator says Lucinda was the seducer. That she targeted him from the start, that—" she looked away, obviously uncomfortable "—that she deliberately got pregnant in order to blackmail him."

Tate's temper flared, forcing him to grind his back teeth together. For the first time since agreeing to this idiotic charade, he was glad he had. Josh had never done anything to deserve this conversation. Did she even realize the full impact of what she was suggesting? That Josh had been nothing more to Lucinda than a calculated part of a blackmail scheme?

"My mother did not get pregnant on purpose," he said, his jaw taut, "and she didn't blackmail anyone."

"He says—"

"He's lying. He offered her money to go away, to leave Alabama and to never tell anyone about him."

"She says he offered. He says she demanded. Who's to say how it really happened?"

He knew, Tate thought angrily. He'd been there. He'd seen Chaney's anger, heard his mother's tears and the jerk's obscene insults. *He* knew...but he couldn't say, because he was pretending to be someone who hadn't even been born at the time.

"Maybe we should change the subject," she offered gingerly.

"Maybe I should change my mind and call the sheriff, after all."

"Please don't. I know this isn't pleasant, but—"

"Then why are you doing it?"

She stared at him a moment, an evasive look in her eyes, before directing her gaze out the side window. "Isn't it every reporter's dream to someday write a bestselling book?"

Maybe...but that wasn't the reason. Oh, maybe it appealed to her on that level, too, but if all she wanted was a bestselling book, why that look seconds ago? Why that hint of guilt underneath the wariness?

"I wouldn't know," he said at last. "I've never met any other reporters, except Mack Black. He covers Wildcat sports for the newspaper over in Dixon. His only dream was to play pro ball, but when he couldn't make the cut, he settled for selling insurance and covering the local games instead."

Her smile was tinged with relief, as if she welcomed the change of topic. "Jordan says his father could have gone pro."

"Jordan and his father are off-limits, remember?" He looked pointedly at the tape recorder she held in an attempt to cushion it from the rough ride.

She stopped the tape, then slid the recorder into her bag. "Truth is, Jordan and Tate hold little interest for my audience, beyond the impact they've had on *your* life. I was just making conversation."

Tate had never thought he'd be grateful to hear that he wasn't interesting enough to hold someone's attention, but he was. He was also a little...insulted. Okay, so being a single-father ex-jock rancher in Oklahoma wasn't exactly exciting. It wasn't the dullest life in the world, either, and at least he could be proud of what he did. He didn't destroy lives, refuse to acknowledge his own son or manipulate everyone like puppets the way Chaney did, and he didn't force his way into other people's homes or coerce them into doing things they didn't want to do, like Ms. Alabama. He certainly had no interest in broadcasting the private details of other people's lives to anyone with the price of a book in his pocket.

"That's one of the problems I have with you," he said laconically. "I can't tell when you're making conversation and when you're interviewing. Though it's real easy to tell when you're evading." A glance at her showed a flush creeping into her cheeks. She blushed easily for someone who'd chosen to earn her living intruding in other people's private business. But maybe she was fine with snooping into other people's lives. Maybe it was only when the questions were turned back on her that she got uncomfortable. And he had one more question he really wanted to ask.

"Tell me something, Natalie. Why are you mixed up with this book?"

Chapter Four

A particularly rough spot jarred Natalie's teeth and made her grab hold to keep her seat. It also gave her the chance to consider her answer. As usual, there were degrees of truth she could offer. She wanted a shot at the bestseller lists. She wanted to prove she could write two hundred thousand words as opposed to fifteen hundred. She wanted the legitimacy an acclaimed book would bring her. To rebuild her reputation. To regain her self-respect. To replace those awful memories of her disastrous journalism career with critical acceptance.

She wanted so much she didn't know where to start.

"I love to write," she said at last, "and I loved being a reporter. But news stories have a short life. Most people never even look at bylines. The articles that fill the papers every day might as well be anonymous for all the attention people pay. But a book—especially one on someone as important as Senator Chaney—will be around forever. People will remember it, and they'll remember my name. It'll make a difference.''

Her father would be impressed, and she would be vindicated. That was what she wanted most.

J.T. wore a look of distaste that suggested the difference wasn't worth making, in his opinion. ''And it'll make you rich and famous, won't it? And don't all writers want to be rich and famous?''

That argument, at least, she could take lightly. Having money was always better than not having money, and name recognition was great, but they were merely added bonuses to the success she wanted. ''You say that as if it's a dirty goal. Isn't everyone in business looking to make money? To be successful? Do you raise cattle for the pure pleasure of it? Is money not a consideration in your dealings?''

''At least my business doesn't hurt anyone.''

''The cows you've raised that have wound up as the main course at the local burger joint might argue that point with you.''

He scowled at her before bringing the truck to a stop near a barbed-wire fence. She climbed out more slowly than he did, stepping a few feet away from the truck, then turning in a slow circle. The sky had lightened to a pale blue, with only the thinnest streaks of clouds on the horizon. There was no dew on the grass, no breeze rustling through the trees. Lack of rain had turned the grass yellow and much of the foliage brown. The air literally shimmered with heat, sapping her energy, making her long for air-conditioning, a comfortable chair under a ceiling fan and a tall glass of iced tea, and the day hadn't even begun.

He didn't give her much of a reprieve. Resting his arms on the side wall of the truck bed, he faced her. ''So you want to be rich and famous. You want to make a difference, and you think writing a tasteless book on a classless, egomaniacal jerk will accomplish that for you.''

She mimicked his position, arms resting on faded blue paint. Though only the width of the truck separated them physically, ideologically they were miles apart. He didn't like what she was doing. Period. No ifs, ands or buts about it. Well, sometimes she didn't like what she was doing, either, but there was no denying that the Chaney offspring—especially the illegitimate son whom no one had known existed—would give the book the extra oomph it needed to go from successful to wildly successful. There was an audience for a serious biography of a powerful politician. There was a mega-audience for a serious biography that dished all the dirt on said politician and his family in the past half century.

"Thank you, J.T., for displaying such willingness to trash my work when you've never read anything I've written besides a letter or two," she said politely.

He wanted to ignore her sarcasm. She could see it in the shifting of his gaze and the twitch of a muscle in his jaw. After a couple of deep breaths, he asked, "You ever repaired a barbed-wire fence?"

Prepared for the subject change, she shook her head.

"I didn't think so. We're gonna have to replace the posts in this stretch. These wooden ones have lasted longer than they should have, but it's time for some new ones. Grab those gloves there—" he nodded toward a pair of leather gloves tucked next to the water cooler "—and let's get started."

As he pulled on his own gloves, she leaned inside to pick up the second pair. They were sized for a woman's smaller hands—Lucinda's, she guessed—and tried to imagine any woman of Boyd Chaney's wearing work gloves and…well, working. The image wouldn't form. His six ex-wives were all pampered little socialites, born not only with silver spoons but also nannies and nursemaids to care for their every need. The most strenuous job any of them faced was choosing which priceless gems went best with which designer gown.

"Your mother must have been a breath of fresh air to

Senator Chaney,'' she remarked as she circled the truck to stand beside J.T.

''How so?''

''She was intelligent. Independent. Capable. She didn't require someone to take care of her.'' Though she hadn't turned down Chaney's money. Whether she'd blackmailed or he'd bribed, she'd taken a sizable sum of his money with her when she'd left Alabama. Not that Natalie faulted her for it. Whether the pregnancy was accidental, as she claimed, or planned, as Chaney insisted, the simple fact remained that she *had* been pregnant, and if her son couldn't have a father, he at least deserved a father's support.

''Are you suggesting that none of the former Mrs. Chaneys are intelligent or capable?''

''Every one of them can plan a party for five hundred with a day's notice, but they can't fix their own meals, pay their own bills or launder their own clothes. Take away their money, their servants, their advisors and their drivers, and they'd be at an utter loss. But Lucinda lives on a ranch. She raised two sons and a grandson without a man's help. She cooks, cleans and presumably—'' she held up her gloved hands ''—helps out with the chores when necessary. She's capable.''

After a moment's narrowed look, he turned to the fence. He hadn't resisted asking a couple of questions, but he was apparently determined to hold to his promise to not discuss his mother with her. That was all right. Natalie wasn't going anywhere yet. He might change his mind. And if he didn't…she'd find a way.

The wood posts he'd mentioned were rough and silvered with age. Three lay broken on the ground, barbwire still attached, and a half dozen more tilted at precarious angles. ''Looks like a herd of elephants came through here,'' she remarked.

His grin was wry. ''Close. It was our neighbor's buffalo. They're not the smartest animals in the world. Give 'em a choice between walking through an open gate or a section of fence, and they'll take the fence every time."

"Buffalo…like in *Dances with Wolves?*"

"Big shaggy creatures?" he teased. "A little on the ill-tempered side. Not much to look at, but damn good eating."

"Can we see them? I've never seen one in person before."

"Maybe. If I have time to track them down."

"Why don't you have any?"

He scowled as he began removing the remains of the nearest broken post. Her job, she figured, was going to be as helper—handing him tools for cutting the wire, holding back lengths of wire that wanted to curl around him, hauling off the old posts. Girly jobs that any idiot could handle.

"For starters," he said when she'd almost forgotten her question, "I raise cattle, not buffalo. Second, they're ugly and smelly and don't stay put. Third, they require about six times more pasture than the same number of cows. Fourth, a proper fence for buffalo is pipe—at least two inches in diameter or bigger—and costs a fortune. Fifth—"

"You've gotten used to being the most stubborn and headstrong critter on the place."

For a moment J.T. just looked at her, then he laughed— a rich, deep chuckle that sounded honest, masculine and entirely too inviting. "Cute."

"I have a way with words."

"Who's talking about words?"

His murmur raised a sheen along her skin that had nothing to do with the morning heat. It made her stomach knot, her throat go dry, and made her feel breathtakingly weak. He wasn't the first Chaney to compliment her, or to give her that look with brown eyes all dark, sleepy and sexy. He certainly wasn't the first who'd sought to manipulate her into doing what he wanted…but he was the first to stand a chance. He was the first to make her muscles taut with no more than a look—the first who could leave her at a loss for words with such a simple, innocent remark.

He was the first to entice her. Not that it mattered. He'd made it clear enough that all he wanted was her out of his life permanently.

"How'd you get this job?" he asked as he wrestled the post from the hard earth.

It wasn't the first time she'd been asked the question. Hell, she'd asked it herself when Chaney had announced his choice. Why her? There'd been plenty of other writers who wanted a shot at the book—people who'd written other well-received biographies, reporters who'd followed his career for more years than she'd been alive. Why choose a one-time, up-and-coming young reporter whose career had hit the skids, for such an important project?

The senator had given her his trademark good-ole-boy campaign smile and replied in his thickest Alabama drawl, "Honey, I haven't answered to anyone since my sweet mama died fifty-some years ago. I make decisions. I don't justify them. So do you want the job or not?"

Naturally she'd accepted it. But others had continued to ask the question—and to find some less-than-savory answers.

With a creak from the wood and a grunt from J.T., the post came loose and he pulled it out. Natalie looked from him, sweat dotting his face, to the hole in the hard ground. "How are you going to dig holes for the new posts?"

"Did I forget to tell you? That's your job. There's a post-hole digger in the back of the truck."

"Okay. Gee, that should only take me—" she glanced at the section of fence "—oh, a week or so. You must be enjoying my company to want to keep me around so long."

"You're being evasive again." He removed his hat, laying it on the pickup's seat, then stripped his T-shirt over his head and tossed it inside, too.

Natalie tried not to stare and hoped she didn't look as dazed—hungry? lustful?—as she felt. He was so nicely muscled, so tanned, so mouth-wateringly tempting. There wasn't an ounce of excess fat on his body, not one inch of skin that her fingers didn't itch to touch. Could his skin possibly be as smooth and warm and soft as it looked, his muscles as hard and sculpted as they appeared?

Swallowing hard, she looked away and fixed her narrowed gaze on the fence. It didn't help much. She could still see a blur of brown skin and faded denim in her peripheral vision. She still *knew* he was half-undressed, beautiful and within easy reach.

This was silly. It wasn't as if she were an innocent young virgin, overwhelmed by her first up-close sight of a hard male body. She'd seen him like this just yesterday, and had seen totally naked men plenty of times before. Hell, she'd been intimate with her share of them…though, admittedly, not in a long time. A *very* long time, her body reminded her.

Flustered, she searched for a distraction. A question— he'd asked her something, hadn't he? *How'd you get this job?* It wasn't her favorite question, but it was a good one for tamping down a highly inappropriate attack of lust. "If I—" Her voice was husky, making her stop and clear her throat. "If I tell you I was chosen for this job based on my past job performance, would you believe me?"

Apparently unaware of her sudden hormonal overload, J.T. went back to work. "Do I have any reason not to?"

"Would you think I was talking about my performance at the newspaper or…in bed?"

He gave her a sharp, harsh look. "You and— That's disgusting."

"Yes, it is," she agreed, but not because the senator was old enough to be her grandfather, or because his brand of old-fashioned male chauvinism offended her. Trading sex with any man for a story was disgusting, and she would never, ever consider it…but that was what plenty of people believed. The six former Mrs. Chaneys, the other eight children—and especially those she'd beaten out for the job. They'd said she was Chaney's type—female and breathing.

They'd figured it must be a trade-off. They'd remarked with winks and leers how *that* would explain so much.

Of course, her reputation had preceded her. *Good writer, talented as hell, but sloppy. Can't be trusted. Unethical. Dishonest. Dishonorable.*

Dishonorable. That had broken her father's heart, which had made it only fair that he return the favor.

"Believe it or not," she went on, before J.T. could ask her if she'd slept with his father, "I am qualified to do this book. I'm a good writer. I have a knack for putting words together in a way that's both informative and entertaining. My selection had nothing to do with the fact that I'm a woman. Your fa—the senator doesn't expect anything more from me than a thoroughly researched, well-written and accurate biography, and I have no intention of offering him anything more. I don't get involved with the subjects of my writing."

"Good." Then he gave her a long, slow look, and something she thought might be regret darkened his eyes for an instant. "Or too bad."

There it was again—the sudden heat and tingle. Anticipation, sort of queasy-quivery-exciting, that something unexpected might happen. Awareness. Attraction.

But she'd told him God's honest truth. She *didn't* get involved with her subjects. As far as that went, in the past fifteen months, she hadn't gotten involved with *anyone.* Don't trust, don't love, don't care except about the story.

Why, she wondered, did that suddenly seem a sad way to live?

Supper that evening was a quiet affair. Tate hadn't accomplished as much as he would have liked, thanks to the distraction Natalie had provided. He'd settled for a temporary fix on the fence, rigging a couple of T-posts and splicing new barbwire to old, rather than hours of back-breaking work with nothing but Natalie's questions for company. When he could get away without her, he would take Jordan out, and they'd do it up right.

After the fence had been temporarily mended, he'd loaded the truck with feed supplements and endured another few hours of her questions. He hadn't been kidding earlier when he'd told her he had a problem telling when she was being friendly and when she was prying. He would have enjoyed her boundless curiosity, and might even have found it a little flattering, if he'd been able to figure out when it was Natalie the reporter speaking versus Natalie the woman.

He was never going to be comfortable with the reporter…but he could fall all too easily for the woman.

On his left Jordan was merely picking at his second helping of beef stew. He'd mentioned that he and Mike had gotten the truck running and that football practice had gone okay, but he'd had nothing to say after that. Ordinarily Tate would question him, he'd come clean, they'd talk it over, and everything would be all right. But no way was he going to question his son in front of Natalie. She'd agreed to keep any mention of him in her book to a minimum, but who knew if she would keep her word? Any private conversation with Jordan would have to wait until she was gone.

"Did you make this stew, Jordan?" Those were the first words she'd spoken since sitting down twenty minutes ago. In spite of the hat and sunscreen, her face was sunburned, her skin turning a vivid pink that clashed with the red of her hair. She'd showered, put on another too-short, too-snug sundress and sandals and tied her hair back with a bandanna, and she smelled of aloe vera, cocoa butter and other fragrances too subtle to identify.

She smelled damn good.

"I don't know," Jordan replied listlessly. "Maybe. It was in the freezer. Once every month or so, Grandma and I cook a bunch of stuff to freeze so we always have something easy for supper."

"Good idea. I can't count the number of times I just grab a fast-food burger and fries on my way home because I'm too tired to fix anything. Was it also your grandmother's idea that you should learn to cook?''

''Yeah.''

When Jordan didn't elaborate, Tate did. ''Mom doesn't believe in gender-specific roles. Jos—my brother, Jordan and I all cook and do laundry, and Mom can brand a calf, snug up a strand of barbwire or castrate a bull as good as any of us.''

''If I were her, I imagine I'd take particular satisfaction in castrating the critters,'' Natalie said evenly.

''I imagine she does.'' Deliberately he shifted the conversation back to his son. ''You going out tonight, Jordan?''

''I don't know. I told Mike I'd try to come over and help her with her car, but Shelley called and wanted to know if I'd meet her at Dairy Delight after supper.''

Was that the reason he was so quiet? Because he really wanted to see Shelley but knew he ought to keep his word to Mike? If he and Mike really were just friends, it wouldn't be such a problem. Teenagers expected last-minute changes in their plans if something better—someone of the opposite sex—came along. But if Natalie was right and Mike had a crush on Jordan, being blown off for Shelley was going to hurt.

''Can you do both?'' Tate asked. ''Help Mike, then meet Shelley?''

A strangled sound came from across the table, where Natalie looked as if she'd choked trying to stifle her snort. Tate looked from her to Jordan, only to find his son giving him a chastising look.

''Da—mn, Uncle J.T.,'' Jordan said, barely saving himself from calling Tate Dad. ''No wonder you're not married. Is it okay if I do the dishes when I get back?''

''Sure.'' Once he'd left by the back door, Tate looked at Natalie. ''What did he mean by that remark?''

''Shelley doesn't want to share Jordan or his attention— or anyone else's attention, as far as that goes,'' she explained in a patronizing voice that was laced with amusement. "If Jordan takes the time to help Mike before meeting her, her perfect little turned-up nose is going to get so far out of joint she won't be able to breathe properly for a week. And she'll make him pay for it. She dates other guys, you know. Jordan's not the only one she's stringing along."

"So why does he put up with her?"

"Because from the beginning of time, men have been willing to sacrifice anything for a pretty face, big eyes and a great body. It's a guy thing."

"What do they sacrifice for you?"

In the process of stacking their dishes, she burst into laughter.

"You're pretty and you have big eyes," he protested.

"And a sedentary job and hips that show it. I have a lot more in common with the Mikes of the world. No guy's ever looked at me the way Jordan looks at Shelley or offered to give up anything unless he was getting more in return."

Tate turned in his chair to watch her carry the dishes to the counter. From this angle—and every other—her hips looked just fine. He liked women with curves, and she had them in all the right places, from her breasts to her waist to her hips to those long legs. Lush, shapely, womanly curves. Dangerous curves.

"Then the men in Alabama—" and New York, Connecticut, Virginia and D.C. "—must be blind or foolish or both," he murmured as he removed the cast iron Dutch oven and the crumpled napkins from the table.

"What?" she asked over the sound of running water as she rinsed the dishes.

"Nothing."

"Are you insulting me again?"

He stopped beside her, deliberately closer than they'd yet been, and made a production out of scraping the few remaining bites of soup from the pot into the garbage disposal. His elbow bumped hers, skin to warm skin, and as she worked, he caught a whiff of something sweet and flowery that was quickly becoming familiar.

"I said I liked your hips," he lied. It wasn't a complete lie. He'd *thought* it, even if he hadn't said it aloud.

She stilled, then slowly eased away from him, not stopping until she'd reached the dish towel lying on the counter six feet away. After drying her hands far more thoroughly than needed, she cleared her throat and said, "I...I meant what I said this morning. I don't get involved with subjects."

"And I meant what I said, too."

Good...or too bad. Good that she'd kept her distance from Chaney and his parasitic children. Too bad that she also intended to keep her distance from *him*. Too bad, even if that was his intention, too.

It was crazy. There could never be anything between them. They lived in different states. He felt nothing but disdain for the job that supported her. The past sixteen years proved that he wasn't the type for casual affairs—and neither, he suspected, was she. She was a threat to his family, and he...sweet hell, he was lying to her with every conversation, every look, every damned breath he took.

All good reasons to keep his distance and ignore this attraction.

But that might be easier said than done.

Aware that she was watching, he washed and dried the Dutch oven, turned the oven to three hundred degrees and set the pan inside to dry thoroughly. When it came to housework, Lucinda's standards for the boys, as she called them, were relatively lax. Most of the time clean was good enough for her. But there were rules for using her cast-iron cookware, every piece of it older than he was, and there would be hell to pay for anyone not following them.

"What kind of newspaper articles did you write?" he asked, leaning against the counter and gazing out the window over the sink. The sun hung low over the horizon, and the western sky was hazy with dust. When he was a kid, his great-grandparents had told him stories about Oklahoma's Dust Bowl. Back then he'd never understood how such a thing could happen. Yet now, after three weeks of hundred-degree-plus temperatures and more than a month without rain, he had a better grasp of the process than he wanted. The grass crackled and broke underfoot, the air was heavy and dirty, and a car driving down the road out front could be in town before the cloud of dust trailing behind it disappeared. They needed rain badly—a gentle, forty-eight-hour soaker. What they would probably get, sooner or later, would be a downpour, running off before doing the parched earth much good.

"I wrote a little of everything," Natalie replied softly behind him. In a house that was normally filled with male voices and Lucinda's no-nonsense Okie twang, she sounded out of place, like a songbird among crows. She sounded undeniably Southern, unbelievably delicate, achingly feminine. Hers was a voice made for talking babies to sleep, for soothing bedtime stories, for whispering sweet invitations.

But not to him.

"Politics, city and state government, education, crime. I did everything but obituaries, sports and society pages. Thaddeus Grant did not *do* obits, sports and society, and so neither did his daughter."

He heard the edge under the airiness of her last words and wondered at its source. "Did he want you to become a reporter?"

"There was no 'becoming' to it. It's what I always was. You inherited brown hair and eyes from your father. I inherited being a reporter from mine."

"What if you didn't like writing? Would you still do it just because it's what he expected?"

"I don't know. I've never had to consider the possibility."

"Is he proud of you?"

He heard her move—the faintest rustle of cotton on skin, the tiny squeak of a sandal sole on floor. "From time to time."

She was being evasive again. Was she protecting herself

or her father? Obviously, she thought the world of the man. Just as obviously, he hadn't thought so highly of her. He'd taught her to put the job first, shown her that it was more important than family, love or anything else. He'd cut her off from the rest of her family—had taken her on vacations to exotic places only to leave her alone in a hotel room, giving her his attention only when there was nothing else to claim it. Though she was apparently respected in her field, in *his* field—why else would Chaney have chosen her?—he was only proud of her "from time to time."

Some parents did such a good job at screwing up their kids. He hoped to God he never made those mistakes with Jordan. Whatever else his son took from their relationship, Tate wanted him to be certain that he'd always loved him dearly.

Smelling the hot iron, he switched off the oven, removed the heavy pot with padded mitts and set it on the back burner to cool. After filling a glass with ice and water, he led the way into the living room, where they took the same seats as the night before. "So this book is going to make you rich and famous, and, I assume, that will be one of the times Daddy will be proud. Then what?"

"Then I go back to life as usual."

"No more books airing famous people's dirty laundry? No more disrupting the lives of innocent bystanders unfortunate enough to have some connection to them?"

Her smile came slowly and curved her mouth but didn't touch her eyes. Instead, they looked guilty, at odds with the smile and the light tone of her voice. "Don't tease, J.T. I suspect it's been a good long while since you were innocent in any way."

True. His life hadn't exactly been conducive to innocence. He'd been fatherless from the git-go, had heard one too many of his grandparents' arguments with Lucinda over her behavior first with his father, then Josh's. He'd lived through the whole Chaney affair, including its ugly end. Along with his mother, he'd more or less been run out of the state of Alabama, and he'd heard the gossip and whispers at Grandpop's before Lucinda had finally moved them someplace—Hickory Bluff—where no one would ever know the truth, where there could be an imaginary long-gone Mr. Rawlins to go with the two Rawlins boys and no one knew any different.

"What is 'life as usual' for Natalie Grant?"

She settled on the couch, turned so she faced him, with her long legs stretched out along the cushions and crossed at the ankle. With her coppery hair, royal-blue dress and pale, creamy skin, she looked as bright—and as foreign— as a hothouse flower.

And right. At ease. Comfortable. As if she belonged right there in his house...or as if she could if she wanted to.

"Let's see...a day in the life of Natalie Grant, girl reporter." She grinned, then reached up to slide the bandanna from her hair. The heavy red curls tumbled over her shoulders and made a lump lodge somewhere in his chest. "I get to work by eight and get my assignments. I might spend the whole day in meetings or doing interviews or trying to catch someone who doesn't *want* to be interviewed. You didn't realize I have far more experience at finding people than you do at avoiding them, did you? I write whatever's due that day, get home around six or seven, eat fast-food or a frozen dinner alone while the news is on, then work on other stories and the occasional in-depth articles I get to do. I watch a little TV, read a little, then go to bed."

"To dream, no doubt, of winning the Thaddeus Grant Award, formerly known as the Pulitzer Prize, for your outstanding work."

Slowly the amusement in her eyes dimmed, and the smile slipped away bit by bit. Her muscles tightened until her body was as stiff as the words that came from her mouth. "I'm not interested in awards. Doing your best should be the only reward anyone needs."

Another lesson from Daddy? Was Thaddeus afraid of being outdone by his own daughter? Had he chosen her career for her only after ensuring she wouldn't be tempted to try to surpass his accomplishments?

"Of course everyone should do their best," he agreed mildly. "But a little recognition beyond a paycheck and personal satisfaction is a good thing."

"Awards are meaningless. The opinions of a few judges are no more important—cannot be more important—than the opinions of your readers."

"Okay. You don't dream of winning more Pulitzers than your father did. Did he ever write a book?"

"No."

Interesting. So in writing Chaney's biography, she could still have the career her father had chosen for her, but on a different level. She could accomplish whatever goals she'd set for herself, without eclipsing his own successes. "He must think this Chaney book is a pretty big deal for his little girl."

She picked up the *TV Guide* from the coffee table and nonchalantly flipped through the pages. "Actually, I don't know what he thinks. The truth is…we haven't spoken in more than a year."

He shouldn't have been surprised. God knows, he understood parent-child estrangement. He wouldn't know his own father if they passed on the street, and Josh was determined to have zero contact with his father. Jordan's mother was a long-ago-and-nearly-forgotten part of their lives. Even Lucinda had had a three-year falling-out with Gran and Grandpop between Tate's and Josh's births.

But he *was* surprised. "What happened?"

"That's none of your business."

"We're compromising, remember? Getting acquainted? You want to know all my secrets, so I get to know yours."

"Not this one."

He could have argued with her, just for the hell of it, but she looked so…brittle. Fragile. If he kept pushing, he was liable to get any number of responses—anger, tears, defensiveness, striking back. All were emotional, all with the potential to be more than he knew how to handle. So instead he accepted her answer as if it were no big deal, then directed the conversation into safer territory. "Want to learn to ride while you're here?"

"Ride…a horse?"

"That's the idea."

"Uh…no."

"Why not?"

"Horses are big animals."

He chuckled. "Yes, they are. An adult doesn't do well riding on the back of a large dog, you know."

"They bite and kick and stink."

"They only bite and kick when they have reason, and they *don't* stink. They just smell…horsey."

"Yeah, like fish smell fishy."

He studied her for a moment, then shook his head with feigned regret. "And I always said I would never allow any chickens on my place."

"Bock-bock," she said dryly.

"What if I decided all future interviews would take place on horseback or not at all?"

"Then I would learn."

"So you'd do it for a stupid book, but not for pleasure. I don't understand you, Ms. Alabama."

"As long as *I* understand *you,* that's all that matters." Covering her mouth with one hand, she yawned so widely that her entire face crinkled. It wasn't even nine o'clock, but she looked as if she could doze off where she sat. She would have to stay there, too, at least until Jordan came home. There was no way Tate was getting near her when she was asleep and vulnerable—not to wake her and send her next door, not to move her to the guest room, not for *nothin'.*

"You'd better get to bed."

She yawned again, then stretched. "I think so."

Once again he walked to the side door with her, then leaned against the frame as she crossed the dimly lit deck to her own door. Her movements were quiet in the still night, as if the air molecules were too heavy with heat to stir at her passing. He doubted the temperature had dropped more than ten degrees since high noon, but that didn't deter the tree frogs croaking nearby, or the whippoorwills and bobwhites trading calls in the woods that edged the yard to the north.

The sound of metal against metal—key in lock—reached him across the width of the deck, then she faced him one more time. "Do you think Jordan went to help Mike...or to meet Shelley?"

"I hope he went to Mike's." He'd raised a good kid who understood obligation and responsibility better than most. Jordan knew a man's word was his honor. If he'd told Mike he would come over, then going over was the *only* honorable thing to do.

"I hope he did, too," Natalie murmured. "Good night, J.T."

Long after she went inside, he stood where he was. He was a fine one to talk about honor because, apparently, he had none. Every word he said to her was part of a big lie. Every question he answered as Chaney's son dug the hole around him a little deeper. Already he was in way over his head. The teetering piles of lies and deceptions could grow only so high before they toppled over and buried him underneath their weight.

He only hoped he could survive.

Chapter Five

Sunday marked the beginning of Natalie's fifth day at the ranch. For the first time, she woke up at five-thirty as if it were a completely natural thing—on the one day of the week when it was completely unnecessary. Sundays were the closest to days off around the ranch, J.T. had told her over supper the night before. They slept in an extra hour or two, had a late breakfast and pretty much took it easy once the necessary chores were completed. She intended to claim five or six hours of his time for some serious conversation…or damn near anything else he might want to indulge in.

She sleepily stretched, then rolled onto her side to gaze out the window at the dark sky. If only he weren't an integral part of her project…. It was part of the Natalie Grant School of Bad Luck that the first man she'd met in months who tempted her was automatically off-limits. She'd never suspected when she'd started the job that involvement could be a problem. Boyd Chaney? Not if they were the last two people alive on earth. Any of his legitimate children, aides, political cronies, friends or enemies? Uh-uh. Never. No way.

But his illegitimate son… She gave a great sigh. Anytime, anywhere, any way. If only she could. If only it didn't smack of bad judgment, bad taste, a lack of ethics, a conflict of interest or another career-damaging move.

Rising from the bed, she used the bathroom, brushed her teeth and tied her hair back, got a glass of juice and a handful of chocolate chip cookies from the counter, then settled at the dining table, where she'd set up her laptop computer and spread out her notes. She had a file on the laptop named for J.T., and every night before bed, she entered everything that had caught her attention during the day—important or trivial, for the book or merely her own vanity. She'd made a note that J.T. had called her pretty, that he'd claimed to like her hips, that he'd looked at her as if he'd felt the same pull she did. They were silly comments which had no place in the book and certainly wouldn't be repeated to the senator, but she'd recorded them all the same.

Like a lovesick girl scribbling in her diary.

Sitting cross-legged in the chair, she booted up the computer, then opened the file that contained multiple beginnings to Chapter 1. The first two didn't tempt her to do more than correct a couple of typos. By the time she finished reading the third, she was ready to write, picking up where she'd left off, losing herself in the early days of a life story she knew as well as her own.

She worked until a knock at the door pulled her back to the present. A glance at the kitchen clock showed that it was seven-thirty, the sun had risen, and the day was going to be light, bright and hot—again. Carefully she got to her feet, easing kinks out of stiff muscles, then padded barefoot down the hall to the door. A tingle deep in her stomach as she reached for the knob told her who was on the other side, but that didn't make seeing him any less pleasurable.

He wore jeans and a T-shirt and looked considerably more approachable than over the breakfast table the other three mornings. His hair was damp, he smelled of shaving lotion and cologne, and he looked amazing. Like every sexy fantasy she might have in the future.

"Good morning," he said, and she dazedly repeated the greeting.

"Just wanted to let you know that breakfast will be ready in about ten minutes."

"O-okay. I'll be over in a minute."

His gaze moved over her, starting with her hair and working its way down to her toes and back, leaving sweet heat everywhere it touched. "You might try getting dressed first. Not that I have any complaint with what you're wearing, but Jordan is just a kid whose hormones are on full alert all the time."

She glanced down at the night clothes she still wore—a ribbed-knit tank top that clung to her curves and a pair of matching shorts that lived up to their name—and her face heated with a flush. "I—I was just working."

"Too bad you can't wear that to work all the time. But if you did, none of us would ever get anything done, would we? At least…no work."

Suddenly her mouth was so dry that she couldn't swallow, and her nipples were hard and achy. She tried to take a deep breath, but it was hard when the air was so heated and she felt as if she might spontaneously combust right there if he didn't stop looking at her that way. It was just a tank top and shorts. Thin and snug, yes, but perfectly decent. The outfit revealed less than any of her swimsuits—but maybe that was part of the problem. It hinted, not showed. Suggested. Gave ideas. And face it—she could be wearing a high-necked, floor-dragging flannel gown, but one look from his sexy, dark eyes would have the same effect.

She took a breath that seared her lungs and left her starving for air. Another breath—gasp—didn't help, while he looked as cool as a person could be in summer hell.

She tried to bluff, to act as if nothing out of the ordinary was going on. She wasn't sure how successful she was, though, what with the steam rising from her pores and the huskiness that damn near robbed her of her voice. "Do you want to come in? I need just a few minutes to get ready."

For a moment he hesitated, and she thought he might turn her down. Then he grinned wryly, and she realized he wasn't as cool as he appeared to be. "You and me in the same house while you're changing clothes? You think that's wise?"

His response made her feel better. Stepping back, she gestured down the hall. "I'll lock the bedroom door."

"It doesn't have a lock." But he came in, anyway, his boots making clunking sounds on the way to the kitchen.

"Then I guess you'll have to be on your best behavior, won't you?" she teased. "I'd offer you some coffee except I don't drink it. There's juice and tea in the refrigerator, and some cookies on the counter."

He glanced at the package of store-bought cookies and shook his head. "Ask Jordan to make you some of his oatmeal-raisin cookies sometime. Those things taste like cardboard in comparison."

"He cooks *and* bakes. If only he were fifteen years older..."

"He's growing up fast enough as it is. Don't try to speed up the process."

Natalie laughed as she left the room, but by the time she reached her bedroom, her smile had faded. She'd never met a family quite like the Rawlinses appeared to be. Jordan and J.T. were closer than any uncle and nephew she'd ever known—closer than any father and son she'd known. According to J.T., the boy was also very close to Tate, and it was apparent that both males loved Lucinda dearly.

Sometimes she'd envied the people she'd known with families. Her schoolmates had complained about their pesky brothers and sisters, and co-workers had offered plenty of gripes about in-laws, troublesome relatives and kids. She would have loved to have had a brother or a sister, no matter how pesky. Grandparents, aunts, uncles, cousins—she'd wanted the whole shebang. What she'd gotten was a father who wouldn't speak to her.

But most families weren't like the Rawlinses. If she'd been given a large family, it probably would have been a curse rather than a blessing. She would have wound up like most of those schoolmates and co-workers, avoiding phone calls from their mothers, making excuses to miss dinner with their in-laws or visiting their grandparents. She would have been envious of people like herself, with no demands on their time.

It seemed she just couldn't be satisfied, she thought with a rueful smile as she checked her appearance in the dresser mirror. Her dress was a green sheath, cool and comfortable enough to make her forget the triple-digit heat. Not bad. Not Cheerleader Barbie perfect, but not too bad.

When she returned to the kitchen, J.T. was sitting in the chair she'd vacated, his attention on the computer monitor. She'd completely forgotten the files opened on the small screen, and said a silent prayer of thanks that his own file wasn't among them and was password-protected, so that even if he'd found it, he couldn't have accessed it. That was a lesson she'd learned from experience with Boyd, Jr.

Though she'd made little, if any, sound, he was obviously aware of her standing behind him. "I would ask if you'd ever considered writing fiction," he said quietly without turning, "but if this book is Life According to Chaney, it'll be at least partly fiction."

"I'd love to interview your mother so I can present both sides."

"No one who knows her will believe his lies about her."

"But if she doesn't dispute them, everyone who doesn't know her will."

"And that doesn't bother you?"

Reaching past him, she used the mouse to close each file, then shut down the computer. As it whirred into silence, she sat down in the nearest chair. "I'll make it clear that Chaney's version of events may not be completely accurate, but the sad-but-simple truth is that most people are going to believe him no matter what. It'll be the word of a wealthy, powerful, familiar man versus a poor single mother they don't know from Adam. Unfortunately, women do tend to pursue wealthy, powerful men. Also unfortunately, women do deliberately get pregnant in order to get something from the man—marriage, money, whatever.''

Her stomach growled, and she latched on to it as an excuse to break the somber mood. ''I'd like to talk with you in depth this morning, but can we get breakfast first?''

He nodded, and she led the way next door. They were in his kitchen, halfway to the table where Jordan waited, when J.T. finally spoke. ''We can't talk this morning. Jordan and I are going to church.''

She couldn't help it. She stopped dead in the middle of the room and turned an astonished look on him. ''Church?''

''You know, big building, steeple on the roof, singing and preaching and that sort of thing?'' He circled around her and took his seat on Jordan's right. She followed more slowly.

''I think it's probably safe to say that none of your—of the senator's other eight children have *ever* set foot inside a church,'' she remarked as she slid into her seat.

''At least for funerals and weddings,'' Jordan said. ''You've gotta go for them.''

She shook her head. ''All Chaney weddings are held at the senator's house. He has a great, old *Gone with the Wind* type mansion outside Montgomery. As for funerals…except for his parents, they tend to be a long-lived people. No family deaths that I can recall in years.''

''Well, Rawlinses go to church,'' J.T. said. ''At least, on Sunday mornings. Jordan and Mom go most Sunday nights.''

Though she'd commented unkindly on the Chaneys' church habits, the Grants weren't much better. Probably the last service her father had attended that wasn't also newsworthy was her mother's funeral. She remembered only the flowers, the confusion and fear that filled her, and the tears—her tears. Thaddeus didn't cry. He never had. "Can I go with you?"

J.T. and Jordan exchanged looks, then J.T. asked, "Do you have a dress that's six or eight inches longer than the one you're wearing?" When she shook her head, he mimicked the motion. "Nope, sorry, you can't."

The refusal took her by surprise, though she should have expected it. He'd made it clear her first day at the ranch that he didn't want her hanging around town—didn't want his friends and neighbors knowing anything about her. Allowing her to tag along to church would raise a lot of questions that he obviously would rather not answer.

Still, she felt…rebuffed.

She smiled brightly to hide it. "Not a problem. I can use the time to get my questions in order. Do you have other traditions, like dinner after church with friends?"

After another look at his uncle, Jordan answered. "Sometimes we go over to Mike's house, or she and her dad come over here, and sometimes some of my friends come out. Usually Grandma fixes pot roast in the slow-cooker, and she buys fresh bread and a coconut cake from the bakery in town after church because that's everyone's favorite." He speared a couple of sausage patties on his fork before asking, "What did your family do on Sundays?"

Natalie took her own sausage and neatly cut it into quarters. "If my father was home, he watched the news programs on TV. He ate lunch in his office or met his friends at their favorite sports bar. He'd come home in time for *60 Minutes,* and spend the evening getting caught up on reading all his newspapers."

Both Rawlinses gave her disbelieving looks. "Every Sunday?" Jordan asked skeptically.

Her smile felt shaky. "Well, he was usually gone two or three Sundays a month, but, yes, that was his routine when he was home."

"And what did you do?"

She thought for a moment, then another. Finally she

shrugged. "Funny. I can't remember. Whatever six-year-old and nine-year-old and fifteen-year-old girls did while they waited for their fathers."

"Guess there's a price to pay for having a great man for a father." J.T.'s tone was flat, his expression grim. Disapproving. Of her? Or Thaddeus?

"My father had a very important career," she said defensively. "It came with a great many responsibilities."

"His first responsibility was raising his daughter. The rest was just a job."

Just a job. If Thaddeus heard anyone describe his career as *just a job,* he would become apoplectic. His career had been the most important thing in his life. He could have survived losing anything—his wife, his daughter—as long as he had his career.

As she spooned up a helping of scrambled eggs, she shook her head. "My parents had an agreement. He would have the career, earn the paycheck, support the family, and she would make the home and raise the children. If anyone abdicated their responsibilities, it was my mother."

J.T. paused, his fork halfway to his mouth, to stare at her. "For God's sake, Natalie, she *died.* Don't you think that negated the agreement?"

Wishing the conversation had never gone so far, she carelessly waved one hand in the air. "Please, let's not get hostile here. It's no big deal. Kids do great with only one parent. Look at you and your brother. Heavens, look at Jordan. He's just about perfect."

"And some kids do okay with no parents at all," J.T. said softly. "Look at you."

She *was* okay, she admitted to herself as she forced her attention to her breakfast.

Unfortunately, as far as Thaddeus Grant was concerned, okay would never be good enough.

That evening Mother Nature teased them with the promise of change. The temperature dropped fifteen degrees after the sun went down, and the wind picked up, carrying the faint scent of rain. Jagged forks of lightning streaked across the dark sky, and on occasion Tate could feel the rumble of distant thunder vibrate through the deck and his chair into his very bones. But it was nothing more than a tease. He'd gotten online to check the weather map after dinner, and there had been no activity to speak of all the way across Oklahoma and Kansas and into Colorado. The only forecast for the state was more of the same—heat and drought.

"Have you ever considered moving someplace where the climate's more hospitable?"

He glanced in Natalie's direction, though she was little more than a shadow among shadows. When they'd come outside to enjoy the cooler weather, he'd shut off the lights that drew bugs, and the clouds moving in from the west kept the moonlight and starlight to a minimum. "Nope, never have. If you don't have allergies, Oklahoma's just about perfect eleven months out of the year…though I have to admit, I could do without August most years."

"Have you always lived here?"

It was on the tip of his tongue to mention the time he and Lucinda had lived in her own home state, but he caught the slip. "Yep."

"Are your mother's parents from Oklahoma?"

"Yeah. They have a ranch a few hours from here. Outside a little town that makes Hickory Bluff look like a bustling city."

"Have you ever visited Alabama?"

"Never had any reason to."

"It's a part of your heritage."

"No," he said flatly. "It isn't." Any heritage he decided to acknowledge besides the Rawlinses' would come from his good-for-nothing, rodeo-cowboy father from Texas. Alabama meant nothing to him except bad memories from the past…and the possibility of a few good ones for the future.

"It's a beautiful state."

"Hmm."

"You'd be treated like royalty once everyone knew who your father—knew about your connection to the senator."

"Meaning they'd treat me like a nobody otherwise?"

"No, I didn't mean—"

"This may come as a surprise to you, Ms. Alabama, but I have no desire to be treated like royalty, and I have even less desire to have anything to do with people whose treatment of others is determined by their family names. I prefer to be judged on my own merits."

"That doesn't surprise me at all—and please don't call me that."

He chuckled. "You don't like sharing a beauty queen title?"

"I don't approve of beauty pageants," she said primly.

"You don't? Or your father doesn't?"

"Don't criticize my relationship with my father when you've never even been in the same state with your father."

"And whose choice was that?"

"It was his—in the beginning," she admitted. "But he's made an effort to make up for that."

An effort, Tate thought scornfully. The old reprobate's secretary had called Josh twice, and there had been two letters. What kind of *effort* was that? Sure as hell not enough to make up for twenty-nine years of denying his son's existence. "You know, Natalie, a boy needs a father most when he's little, but not so much as he grows up. By the time he's thirty—" Josh had just turned twenty-nine, he reminded himself, so he dropped the *four* he'd been about to say "—there's not a whole lot a father can do for him."

"So once Jordan turns thirty, he'll have no further use for Tate?"

The question stirred an ache in his gut that he rubbed slowly. There had been a time when he'd resented not his son, but the *idea* of him. He'd been a kid himself, and he'd had such plans for his life. Having to give them up to stay in Hickory Bluff and take care of a baby had seemed the biggest injustice in the world…until the first time he'd held his son. He hadn't been around a baby since Josh had been one, and he'd felt clumsy and awkward, but Jordan hadn't minded. Only a few hours old, he'd snuggled close and fallen asleep, and Tate had known then that he'd gotten so much more than Stephani had given up.

"That's different," he disagreed. "Jordan has never known any parent but his father. They have sixteen years of growing up together. They love each other. Do you honestly think Chaney loves anyone besides himself?"

She shifted positions in the chair—he heard the faint creak of wicker and the rub of dress fabric against cushion fabric—then stretched out her long legs to prop her feet on a low wicker table. The clouds overhead chose that moment to part so a shaft of silvered light could gleam off her coppery hair and the creamy expanse of skin. She looked so lovely in the pale light, so exotic, that with a pair of gossamer wings and a band of flowers around her head, she could pass for a fairy or sprite of some sort. When she answered his question, he was half-surprised that the words weren't flavored with a wee bit of an Irish brogue.

"I don't know about love, but I do believe he regrets not knowing you. I think he has a tremendous curiosity about you. He's found a lot to be dissatisfied with in his six wives and the other eight children, as well as his grandchildren, and he wonders about you. You've never asked him for money. You've never required his help to get out of trouble. Your name's never been in the national news. You've never been part of a scandal, or done anything that might bring shame to the family. Without ever meeting you, he already knows you're very different from the rest of his children, and he wants to know more."

"Maybe he should have thought of that twenty-nine years ago."

"So…Rawlinses aren't perfect. You at least suffer from a lack of forgiveness."

"I never claimed to be perfect, Natalie. I'm far from it."

If he were perfect, he wouldn't be sitting here having a serious conversation and wondering if her skin was as soft as it looked...if it was the same shade of pale all over...if he could look at her much longer without touching her...if he could touch her without wanting more. "Besides, the old man hasn't asked for forgiveness. He hasn't apologized. He hasn't said, Maybe I was wrong for denying you, or for calling your mother a gold-digging whore, or for paying her to get out of town."

"You haven't given him a chance to say much of anything, have you?"

He shrugged. Josh hadn't taken either phone call or answered either letter. But he'd read the letters. If Chaney cared about making an *effort,* in writing would be a good way to start. "You think because he's decided that maybe he's ready to be a father, I have to forget the past twenty-nine years and accept him?" Before she could speak, he raised his hand. "Wait, don't answer that. Of course you do, because you're still hoping that someday Thaddeus will decide *he's* ready to be *your* father, and you want to be there, ready and waiting. You want to believe it can happen and everyone can live happily ever after. Well, I *don't* believe it. Sorry."

After a long silence she said, "You know, I've interviewed about sixty-five people for this book, half of them in depth. You are far and away the most obstructive of the bunch."

"I'll take that as a compliment."

"I didn't mean it as one."

"I know." He grinned. "Tell me something, Natalie. Do you ever relax and forget about the job?"

"I forget more often than I should."

"Meaning?"

Her chair creaked as she got to her feet. She crossed the short distance to the railing, turned so it was behind her and leaned against it to face him. "You said the other day that you couldn't always tell whether I was making conversation or conducting an interview. Well, sometimes neither can I.''

''So you make a habit of getting chummy with your subjects.''

''No, I don't. When I was interviewing the other children, I never forgot.'' Then she gave a shake of her head that set her curls aquiver. ''Truthfully, they never would have let me. In their world, a reporter ranks a step or two below a servant and a step or two above the common poor folk. They had to tolerate me because it was what their father wanted, and since he controls the money they all want, they had no choice.''

Tate could easily imagine the type of behavior she described. He'd never known anyone who was truly wealthy, like the Chaneys, but every town had its own family or two who thought they were superior to everyone else. In Hickory Bluff, it was Shelley's family who believed they were so much better, and they never let anyone forget it.

Not that the Chaneys were anything special. Sure, the old man had done a lot, but the rest of them combined weren't worthy of the air they breathed. They certainly had no accomplishments to lord over Natalie or anyone else. For the Chaney kids, particularly, and the grandkids, their claim to superiority was nothing more than an accident of birth.

''But,'' Natalie went on, ''all that aside, *I* never forgot my reasons for being there, for asking all those questions. Here…sometimes…I do.''

After a long silence Tate moved to the railing beside her, but where she faced the house, he looked out across the yard. There was only darkness ahead for the first few miles, until the glow of streetlights and house lights illuminated the bottoms of the heavy clouds that hung low over the town. ''You know, Ms. 'Bama,'' he said softly, ''for someone who has a way with words, you sure are dancing around what you want to say.''

''You think you can say it any better?'' Her tone was

cross, her body language—eyes straight ahead, chin high, arms folded across her chest—unmistakable.

"Yeah, I do." He rested his hands on the rail cap, weathered to a smooth surface and warm as an ember, and curved his fingers over the edges. "You consider yourself as professional as they come—as professional as the eminent Thaddeus Grant would demand. You don't get involved with the subjects of your stories. You've never even been tempted before, certainly not by anyone connected to Chaney. But your interest in me goes far beyond your story. You tell yourself it's unprofessional. We have conflicting interests. You can't afford that kind of mistake. Worst of all, dear old Dad wouldn't approve. But none of that changes the fact you're still attracted to me, and you don't know what to do about it."

Finally she turned her head to look at him. "And you know all this...?"

Tate swallowed over the lump that suddenly blocked his throat. "Because I feel the same way about you."

Somehow the air around them became heavy, pressing against him with unseen force. Breathing was hard, moving toward her harder. Moving away was impossible.

For a long time they looked at each other, though it was too dark to read her thoughts in her eyes, or the emotions on his face. They didn't speak, they barely breathed, and they watched each other. Then abruptly she drew a ragged breath that sounded part hiccup, part sigh. "So what do we do?"

"It *would* be a mistake. I don't even like reporters, especially ones who work for Chaney."

"It's undeniably unprofessional conduct. And I don't work *for* Chaney. He's just cooperating with me. My money's coming from the publisher."

"It could be risky as hell."

"I won't be here long."

"You don't belong here at all." Though she could. If she

gave up her job. Forgot the ambition that had guided her every move. Found the nerve to disappoint her father.

If she wanted.

"So…?"

"So…" A gust of wind rushed through the breezeway that separated the two halves of the house, whipping her hair about her face, trapping a thick, corkscrew strand across her cheek. Though he knew it was foolish to touch her at all, he brushed it behind her ear, drawing his fingertips across her warm silken skin, catching one finger in the fiery silken curl, before reluctantly sliding his hand free. "We remind ourselves that we're responsible adults who make decisions based on reason and logic rather than hormones."

"We do," she echoed, but it was more question than firm agreement.

"You remember that you're here because you have a job to do, and I remember that I let you stay because…well, you gave me no choice. And we act like professionals."

"And we ignore everything else." She smiled faintly. "My father taught me all about ignoring emotions."

Tate's own smile was rueful. "My father taught me all about being ignored. We should be able to handle this just fine."

"Yes," she agreed quietly.

Some part of him regretted that she'd agreed so readily. She could have argued, could have insisted that they were perfectly capable of keeping their business together separated from their personal lives. She probably could have convinced him with very little effort.

That was why, when he should have said good-night, instead he said, "But not without this."

When he should have gone inside and locked the door behind him, he closed the small distance between them.

When he should have been standing alone in the dark inside his house, thinking about what rotten luck he had, he lifted her chin, tilted his head and kissed her.

He'd had his first serious kiss when he was fifteen. It had

been her first real kiss, too, and it was the usual awkward experience—their noses bumping, her glasses slipping, his tongue pinched against her braces. It had also been pretty damn hot. But that kiss had nothing on this one, and not just because they had years of experience between them. This kiss was sweet, full of promise, different and yet familiar, too. It was as if some part of him knew exactly what to expect—how she was going to feel, taste, respond.

And she did respond. Though he would have settled for an innocent kiss, she opened her mouth to him, drawing his tongue inside. He would have been satisfied with no other contact if she hadn't wrapped her arms around his neck and pulled him so close he could feel her breasts against his chest—could feel the soft heat where her hips cradled his. He could have taken one sweet kiss, then walked away, if she hadn't made it one sweet, hungry kiss. Needy. Lusty.

She moved her hands under his T-shirt, stroking his chest with feathery, erotic touches, and he slid his into her hair, trapping his fingers in her curls, and felt the sizzle and spark he'd expected from the instant he'd seen her. If he didn't stop, common sense warned, he was liable to get burned, but instead of stopping, he moved closer. He thrust his tongue deeper into her mouth and ground his erection hard against her belly, and silently, violently, cursed Boyd Chaney, his ego and his damnable book.

He was desperately considering lifting her onto the railing, sliding her dress up and making what could well be the biggest mistake of his life, when the deck lights flashed on, then off again. Reluctantly, he ended the kiss, but he didn't release her right away. Slowly his fingers eased their grip on her, sliding over her scalp, past her shoulders, down her spine to her hips. For one painful moment, he lifted her against him before taking a step away, then another.

She looked dazed. He cupped his hand to her jaw and brushed the tip of his thumb over her full bottom lip. ''Wh-what…?''

''I think Jordan discovered we were having more fun out

here than he was in there. Sometimes having a kid can be a pain, but Mom says it's a kid's job to get in his parent's way.''

"Luckily—" she broke off to clear the hoarseness from her throat "—he's a pain to his father most of the time instead of you.''

Tate bit back his natural instinct to defend his son and instead lightly brushed one hand over her hair. "Wanna do that again?''

She laughed softly, shakily. "I don't think we'd better risk it. Basing decisions on reason and logic sounds really good, but hormones can bring you to your knees.''

"Sounds promising." It was an effort to keep his voice light, when the image of either of them on their knees before the other was enough to make a man weak.

"I-I'd better go inside." She eased away from him and the railing, then took a few backward steps before stopping. "J.T.? This won't happen again, will it?''

She sounded vulnerable, unsure but hopeful. He wanted to lie to her and say of course not, that he'd kissed her only out of curiosity. Now that he'd had his tongue halfway down her throat and his hard-on against her hips, that curiosity was satisfied. But he was lying to her about everything else, and at the moment he couldn't bear to lie to her about that. "Oh, darlin', I think it probably will." Because she was right. Reason and logic didn't have anything on hormones, and no matter how big a mistake he knew it was, he doubted he could say no. He wasn't that strong.

Moving quietly, she went into the house. From where he stood, Tate heard the door close, followed by the click of the lock. Turning back to stare into the darkness, he rubbed both hands over his face, then drew a deep breath that smelled of her. *He* smelled of her—his shirt, his hands, his skin. He could still taste her, could still feel the incredible heat and softness.

Oh, man, he was in trouble.

That sentiment was echoed in Jordan's voice an instant

later. "That might have been the dumbest thing I've ever seen you do." His son joined him at the railing, facing out into the night as if there were answers to be found in the shadows. "Do you think that's wise under the circumstances?"

"No, Jordan, I don't think it's wise," Tate replied testily.

"You can't fall for her, Dad, not when she thinks you're Uncle Josh."

"You think I don't know that?"

"It's bad enough you're lying to her about all the important stuff, but to have sex with her—"

He glared in his son's direction even if the clouds did hide it. "It was just a kiss, Jordan."

"Yeah, right. Anything you say."

"I can't help it if I'm attracted to her."

"But she's a reporter. And she works for Senator Chaney. And she thinks you're his kid."

All good arguments...and they didn't change a thing. He liked her. He wanted her. He couldn't have her. And he shouldn't have kissed her. "I hate this damn charade," he muttered.

"I feel kinda bad about it, too," Jordan admitted. "She's just trying to do her job, and she thinks we're nice people compared to all the others, but at least they were honest with her. All we've done is lie. I understand it's for Grandma and Uncle Josh, and even for me some, but...it still feels wrong."

"It still *is* wrong."

"If she ever finds out..."

"She won't." Tate would see to it that she never met anyone in Oklahoma who might tell her she was spending her time with the wrong Rawlins son. No one in Alabama knew the truth to be able to tell her, and there would be no photographs of J.T. for the book. Much as he hated the deception, he was in way too deep to let the truth come out.

"But if she does..."

"She *won't*." She couldn't.

Unless this thing between them didn't go away. Unless she came back once the book was completed and all the arguments were moot. In spite of the ninety-degree temperature, the thought sent a chill through Tate. How much would she hate them if she discovered the truth? How impossible would she find it to forgive him?

She'd brought the lies on herself, he reminded himself. Josh had refused to cooperate from the start, but she'd refused to accept that. She'd made it clear that he was going to be a part of her book regardless of his own wishes—that she was going to bare his secrets to the world, all in an effort to bring attention to the old man and to make money for herself. If she'd been more reasonable and less aggressive, maybe they could have worked something out. But she hadn't been. She'd left Josh with no choice, and that had left Tate with none. If the truth angered or hurt her, she had no one to blame but herself.

So why did he feel so damn guilty?

"You know," Jordan said conversationally, "I'm sorry you didn't get to play college ball and get a shot at the pros, but…having a father who's famous seems like more trouble than it's worth."

"I'm not sorry," Tate replied. "Truth is, I probably wouldn't have made it into the pros. Most college kids don't. Besides, I like raising cattle and living here and being your dad."

Jordan grinned. "Do you like it enough that you'd talk Natalie into letting me drive her car Friday night?"

"What's Friday night?"

"I have a date with Shelley, and she sure does like convertibles."

"Uh, *no,*" Tate replied with an exaggerated scowl. "But I'll let you take the pickup."

"Gee, thanks. Maybe *you* oughta go out on a date. Find someone to make you forget Ms. Alabama."

"It doesn't work like that, son. Women aren't interchangeable."

"They are to Senator Chaney."

Jordan's dry comment brought a laugh from both of them, then Tate slid his arm around his son's shoulders and started for the door. "Fortunately, old man Chaney's not our role model around here."

At the door Jordan pulled away and looked at him. Thin light through the blinds showed his expression, deep and serious. "Are you sure about that? Lies, deception, pretending to be people we're not—" he shrugged as he went inside "—sounds like a politician to me."

Chapter Six

After supper Monday evening, Natalie kicked off her shoes, sat cross-legged on J.T.'s—rather, Tate's—sofa and patted the cushion beside her. "Move over here."

The look J.T. gave her was steady and wary. It was echoed in Jordan's eyes as he pulled his attention from *The Simpsons* on TV. "I'm comfortable where I am," J.T. replied evenly.

"I want to show you some pictures." From the box she'd put on the floor in front of her, she pulled out a photo album, then patted the cushion again. "You can come, too, Jordan, if you'd like."

The two males exchanged looks and tiny, identical shrugs, then came to sit, one on either side of her. She balanced the album in her lap and opened it to a glossy eight-by-ten of Jefferson Oaks. "This is Senator Chaney's home, though he's never lived there full-time. He spent most of the past fifty years in Washington or traveling on government business. Even now that he's retired, he still keeps an apartment in Montgomery and has a place at the beach at Gulf Shores.''

Jordan gave a low whistle upon seeing the Greek revival mansion. Natalie would have done the same the first time she'd seen it, if she'd been able to whistle. It was a fabulous house—eight thousand square feet of opulence and luxury, of pricey antiques and priceless history. She'd walked up the mile-long drive, counted the huge columns, stood on the second-floor gallery and looked over acres of formal gardens, and tried to imagine living in such a place. Welcome to my home, the senator had greeted her, and she'd thought how wonderfully flexible the English language was, that the same word could describe her cramped apartment as well as his magnificent showplace.

But neither of them held a candle to *this* home. Lucinda Rawlins had found a place for her sons that was everything home was supposed to be—warm, welcoming, comfortable, loving.

She stole a sidelong glance at J.T., who looked neither warm nor welcoming at the moment. His expression was stony and showed no interest.

Flipping the page, she touched the clear vinyl over the photo on the left. "This is Boyd, Jr., your— Will you jump down my throat if I refer to them as your brothers and sisters?"

"You can refer to them any way you want, but they're not my family," he said stiffly.

She thought she hid her impatience fairly well. "Boyd, Jr., is the oldest of the Chaney children. Like his father, he's been married and divorced several times and has three children, each with a different mother. Unlike his father, he's never worked a day in his life. His interests are gambling— he has a particular fondness for the horses—and partying. He also has a fondness for rubbing elbows with Hollywood celebrities.

"This—" she tapped the photo opposite Junior "—is Kathleen, the only child of the senator's second marriage.

She's never married and has no children, but she's made an art of great dramatic affairs that always end badly and publicly. She has dedicated her life to looking fabulous and is a walking testament to the benefits of cosmetic surgery. The only discipline she's ever shown in her life is for her workout program. She's a firm believer that enough hours of aerobics, Pilates, yoga and tai chi can undo any damage her eat-drink-and-be-merry lifestyle might do.''

Natalie couldn't detect even the slightest shift in J.T.'s expression as she turned to the next page. ''Thomas and Monty are actually full brothers, a rarity in the Chaney family. Their mother is Sandra, the senator's third wife. She was the one who persuaded him to buy the mansion—it had once been in her family—and she supervised its restoration. After four years' work and millions of dollars, the house was even better than new, and the Chaneys threw a party to show it off to all their friends and enemies. That was where he met Ginny Louise, wife number four. It says a lot about Thomas and Monty that the most interesting thing about them is their mother. Like Junior and Kathleen, they like to party, gamble and look good. Other than that, they're fairly forgettable.''

When she reached out to turn the page, finally J.T. reacted. He laid his hand over Monty's face and held the page down. ''Why are you doing this?''

''These people are as closely related to you as your brother, Tate, is. I can't believe you truly aren't the least bit curious about them.''

''I can't help what you believe, but it's wrong. They're strangers. They mean nothing to me.''

''Your half brother Gavin raises horses. Two of your half brothers have children about Jordan's age. Your sister Jennifer has her pilot's license, and your youngest sister Paula dates eligible young European princes and very well might end up as a member of some royal family. None of that interests you?''

J.T. remained stubbornly detached, but Jordan's eyes had widened. "Let me see the one that's gonna be a princess."

Natalie flipped through the album until she came to the picture of Paula Chaney. Once again, the boy whistled in admiration. It was easy to see why. That she was beautiful went without saying. Slender and willowy, tall, expertly bleached blond, with a perfect white smile, perfect pert breasts and perfect hips and thighs—perfect everything, in fact. Like the other Chaney women, the best money could buy.

That she was also spoiled, self-centered and vain was also a given. After all, she *was* a Chaney. On top of all that, she was dimmer than a thirty-watt bulb and as mean as a hungry 'gator. By the end of her first day with Paula, Natalie had wanted nothing so much as to turn the young woman over her lap and give her all the spankings she'd never gotten. By the end of the week, she'd known she could sum up everything a person could want to know about Paula in one word: bitch. If pressed for more? Vicious bitch.

"How old is she?" Jordan asked.

"Twenty-three."

"Sheesh, she's gorgeous. Who would've thought, looking at Jo—" Suddenly Jordan broke off and looked at J.T., who was scowling, then flushed.

"Looking at who? What?" Natalie asked.

"N-nothing. I...I was just gonna say...she's awfully pretty, but you'd never guess it to look at the men in the family. But Uncle J.T. is...is one of the men, and..."

Smiling, she nudged Jordan with her elbow. "You know, you're male. It's perfectly acceptable, even preferable, if you find the women more attractive than the men," she gently teased.

His own smile was tinged with relief. "My uncle has a half sister only seven years older than me who's prettier than any *Sports Illustrated* model ever dreamed of being and is going to be a princess someday. I wonder what Shelley would think of that." Sliding away, he got to his feet.

"Guess I'd better get the kitchen cleaned. Mike's coming over after a while to get that part I picked up for her in town this afternoon."

When he left the room, it suddenly seemed smaller, co-zier. Though Natalie and J.T. now had a third again as much room on the sofa, it seemed smaller, too. More intimate. She scooted over a few inches into the space Jordan had vacated, then a few inches more. "Would it do any good—" she cleared her throat "—to show you the rest of the pictures?"

As music filtered in from the kitchen, J.T. shook his head.

"You're a stubborn man. That's a Chaney trait, you know."

"It's also a trait of two-year-olds, ranchers, Oklahomans, Texans and jackasses." He pulled the album from her grip, laid it on the cushion between them and flipped through it. For all the interest he showed, he might as well been scanning blank pages. "Why did you miss breakfast this morning?"

"I…I slept in late."

"Liar," he said softly, politely. "Your lights were on when I left the house."

She felt the slow burn of a blush spreading and tried to bluff it out, giving him a sunny smile. "I was working and lost track of the time."

"And here I thought you were having trouble facing me and/or Jordan after the shameless way you kissed me last night."

"The way I—" Breaking off the protest, she gave him a chastening look. "Mulish and possessor of a highly selective memory. It's a good thing you're vital to this book. Otherwise I might have to write you off and go back to Alabama."

"And why am I vital to the book?"

Natalie could have bitten her tongue. He'd been so opposed to the project that the last thing she could afford was for him to know how easily he could bring it to a screeching halt. The senator had made it very clear—no J.T., no book, no chance to salvage anything that might remain of her once sterling reputation. All her work would be wasted, all her dreams ended and her career lost forever.

"Perhaps 'vital' is a little strong. After all, only a handful of people know you exist. None of the millions of readers out there can miss what they never knew, can they?" She shrugged as if that were a perfectly logical conclusion. "But you and your mother are an important part of the senator's story. An illicit affair and an illegitimate child are so much more interesting than eight legitimate children born of six legitimate marriages. The story's…naughtier. More titillating."

"More sensational," he said sarcastically. "More lurid." He flipped through a few more pages, then looked at her. "What would it take to make you write me off and go back to Alabama?"

"A court order."

"I'm serious."

"So am I. You've made it clear that you don't think highly of my father—interesting, since you've never met him—but he taught me some valuable lessons, some that your mother apparently taught you. One was that you do every job you take to the best of your ability. I accepted a fair amount of money to write this book, and I intend to do it properly. That means no leaving out children."

His dark gaze held hers for a long time. When he finally spoke, it wasn't to change her mind or to argue with her. "For the record, it's not that I don't think highly of your father. Frankly, I don't think anything of him at all, except that the way he's treated you stinks. I think, as a father, he was lousier than my old man. I've never met my father, and like you said, you can't miss what you never knew. But you knew Thad. You tried to be just like him. And he treated you like a nuisance to be dealt with rather than a daughter. Maybe that doesn't bother you, Natalie, but it bothers the hell out of me."

His statement gave rise to conflicting feelings. On the one hand, she wanted to defend her father. He was a great man to be admired, not criticized, and she couldn't sit quietly by while someone did just that. On the other hand, when had anyone ever cared how she was treated? When had anyone taken offense on her behalf?

Not since her mother died. That J.T. did brought warmth to a place deep inside that had been cold for longer than she cared to recall.

Even so, she felt compelled to speak on Thaddeus's behalf. "I appreciate the sentiment, J.T., but...you don't know what it's like to be a single father. I'm sure Jordan's father can relate to some of what my father went through, to some of the choices he made."

"I guarantee you, he can't. Tate never would have put anything ahead of his child's welfare. You know, Mom was willing to raise Jordan. Tate still could have gone to college. He still could have played ball. But he couldn't have been a father to his son, and that was more important than any career in the world could ever be."

"He sounds like a great guy. Jordan's lucky to have him."

"He's the lucky one—to have a kid like Jordan." After a moment he closed the photo album and fixed his gaze on her. "Once again you've gone off on a tangent to get out of answering a question. Were you avoiding me this morning because of what happened last night?"

What happened last night. That made it sound like both more and less than it was. She could tell fifty people about it, and every one of them would wonder why she was making such a big deal of it. It was a kiss, plain and simple. People shared them all the time.

Except there had been nothing plain or simple about it. And she didn't share kisses all the time, certainly not with men like J.T.... Hell, she'd never *known* a man like J.T.

"What happened last night?" she repeated dryly. "We agreed to keep our distance—"

"And the next thing you knew, my tongue was in your mouth. So were you avoiding me today because we agreed to keep our distance? Because I kissed you? Because I stopped kissing you?"

She drew her feet onto the cushion and laced her fingers around her ankles. "Look, my work doesn't leave me much time for a social life. My romantic involvements, for lack of a better phrase, are few and far between, and I don't take them lightly. That kiss..."

"Was one hell of a kiss. It curled your hair." As proof, he gave a strand of her hair a gentle tug, straightening it to its full length, then letting go and watching it curl again. His smile was sweet and sent tendrils of heat spiraling through her, warming her from the inside out. "You weren't prepared for it, were you?"

She shook her head.

"Me, neither, darlin'."

"I don't do things like that. I don't kiss people. I don't get swept away."

"Too bad," he murmured.

Yes, it was, she privately agreed. Maybe if she'd gotten swept away a few more times before coming here, she wouldn't be so susceptible to it now.

Though, truthfully, she doubted previous experiences with any man could have prepared her for J. T. Rawlins.

The mood between them had gotten so quiet, so intimate, that when the doorbell rang, it startled her and made her draw back guiltily, even though half the sofa separated them. She looked toward the door, where a tall shadow showed through the frosted fanlight, then at J.T. "Should I hide in the hallway?"

"Nah." There was a part of him, Tate admitted as he went to the door, that wanted to say yes—to keep her his and Jordan's secret. But Mike had surely already seen the Mustang with its Alabama tag parked under the tree, and presumably, since Jordan was expecting her, he'd already given her a heads-up.

"Hi, Mike," he greeted the girl when he opened the door. She stepped back, and he pushed open the screen door, too. "Come on in."

He noticed as she moved past him that she was only a couple inches shorter than him. She'd been coming over here all her life. It seemed just last week she'd been a squat, stocky, nondescript kid whose pigtails were the only clue that she was a girl. When had she gotten so tall, and developed breasts, and grown those long legs? Had she grown up so fast...or had he just not paid any attention to her in the past few years?

"Is Jordan here?" she asked, though her gaze kept flickering to Natalie. Tate hoped she was merely curious because she knew about their deception, and not because this was the first time in sixteen years she'd come over and found a woman there with him.

"He's cleaning up after dinner. Unless you're in a hurry, have a seat."

She hesitated, then sat on the arm of Jordan's favorite chair.

"Natalie, this is Mike Scott, Jordan's friend. She and her dad live down the road, and she keeps our trucks running when we can't. Mike, Natalie Grant." Though he was fairly certain Jordan had already confided the whole Natalie story to Mike, Tate felt as if he should add something to the introduction, but what? He could describe Natalie as a friend, but she wasn't. As a reporter, but not when they were supposed to keep her presence pretty much a secret. As a prospective lover? Not something he felt the need to acknowledge to anyone—even, at the moment, Natalie. So, in the end, he said nothing.

"It's nice to meet you, Mike," Natalie said. "What is that short for?"

"Michaela."

"What a lovely name. Does anyone ever call you that?"

"Just my granddad. I...I didn't like it when I was little, but..." She shrugged.

"It's the sort of name you grow into—like Natalie. When I was a kid, I wanted to change my name to Catherine so I could go by Cat, but the closest I ever got was being called Nat and Natty for a short time as a child. By the time I was fifteen, I was happy enough with Natalie."

"Yeah. Sometimes I think maybe Michaela's not so bad."

"Hey, Mike!" Jordan shouted from the kitchen. "Come on in. I'm almost done."

She stood up, brushed her hair from her face, then nudged her glasses back into place. "It's nice meeting you, Ms. Grant."

"Nice meeting you, too."

After Mike disappeared into the kitchen, Tate sat down again on the sofa. Natalie was giving him a smug look that made him want to haul her close and—and kiss it away. "What?" he asked, faking a scowl.

She leaned closer so she could lower her voice. "You see that girl on a regular basis, and tonight's the first time you noticed that she's grown-up."

He lowered his voice, too. "Don't be silly. You reporters aren't the only ones with good powers of observation. Of course I'd noticed."

"Yeah, about five minutes ago. I saw you look at her chest and her legs with that sort of stunned look men get when they realize the kids they know aren't kids anymore."

From the kitchen Jordan called, "Uncle J.T., we'll be outside," a mere second before the back door slammed.

Tate stretched out his legs, resting both feet on the coffee table, then shook his head in dismay. "I swear, last week she was a foot shorter, twenty pounds heavier, and the only curves she had were baby fat. I don't know what happened."

Natalie treated him once more to that smug smile. "The physical development of teenage girls is God's revenge on teenage boys. It's punishment for all their misdeeds."

"And torture for their fathers. I bet Mike's dad is having fits."

"You said she lives with him. What about her mother?"

Even though the kids had gone outside, he lowered his voice. "She cleared out when Mike was about six—moved to Tulsa to be an exotic dancer. She got into a bit of trouble at the club where she performed—got into a lot of trouble with the men at the club. Last I heard, she'd just gotten out of jail and was working as a bartender at the same dive. Nobody talks about her much around here."

Abruptly, he realized what he'd said and looked sharply at Natalie. She gave him a chastening look, but said nothing to defend herself.

"So...who called you Nat and Natty?"

"The kids at one of the numerous schools I attended. My father found out and instructed the teacher to put a stop to it immediately. Those were the only nicknames I ever had. What about you?"

"Just J.T." It felt good to tell her the truth for once.

"Which stands for Joshua Terrell. Are they simply names your mother likes, or do they have significance?"

"They have significance to me," he said dryly. "But if you mean are they family names, no. No Joshuas, no Terrells, no Jeffreys or Tates or Jordans or Thomases in her family."

"Just the three of you J.T.s."

He shrugged, then gestured toward the photo album. "Come on over here. Show me the rest of your pictures."

"You want to see them? Really?"

"No...but I kinda like it when you're sitting that close."

She gave him another of those chiding looks, but slid across to sit beside him, almost close enough to touch but not quite. Close enough to smell the flowery fragrance of her shampoo and her subtle, exotic cologne and, barely there, the cocoa-butter scent of her sunscreen. Close enough that all he'd have to do was turn toward her and lean forward an inch or two, and he could kiss her. Close enough that he could hear the soft rhythm of her breathing, not as steady now as it was five minutes ago.

Close enough to make him a glutton for punishment.

She opened the album to a blank page, where, he presumed, the uncooperative son belonged, then gave him a rundown of the remaining four siblings. Their photos were followed by pictures of the exes, the grandkids and a variety of houses. Only one photo in the entire album interested him. Unlike the others—professional portraits or, in the case of the houses, top-quality photos from Natalie's camera—this one was a snapshot. The color was bad, the image off center, the setting shabby. He stared at it a long time before murmuring, "I remember that."

Natalie gave him a curious look. "How? You weren't born yet."

Startled, he glanced at her, then shrugged and lied. "Mom has a copy of it somewhere. I've seen it before." Truth was, he'd seen it as the photo was being taken. Chaney had come to their apartment for some reason—the first of only two times he'd set foot in their part of town—and Lucinda had coaxed him into posing for a picture together. The teenage girl next door who'd baby-sat Tate while his mother worked and met with Chaney had snapped the picture with utter disinterest before returning to the phone calls that filled most of her baby-sitting hours.

Lucinda was smiling in the photo, but it didn't reach her eyes. She had tried to step in close to Chaney, but he'd held her at arm's length, scowling fiercely as if contact with her might somehow contaminate him.

The photo roused Tate's anger, both with Chaney and with Lucinda. She'd let the man seduce her, use her, discard her and threaten her—had let him turn her into someone, at the moment the shot was taken, to be pitied. *Why?* Why hadn't she had more dignity, more pride?

"Was she in love with him?" Natalie asked softly, looking from him to the picture and back again.

"I don't know." That was the truth. It was a question

he'd never thought to ask Lucinda, an answer he'd never cared about. To his way of thinking, Chaney had been just another mistake, like her fling with Hank Daniels. He'd assumed her excuse for both men was a combination of youth, lust and a desire for something more than the little-better-than-nothing she'd always had.

But love?

"Have you ever been in love?"

Sharply he looked at her, and found her much too close. He wanted to scoot away, but he was already hugging the sofa arm. He could move to the chair where he usually sat, or could close the album and put a stop to the conversation…or he could pull her closer and make her forget she'd ever had a question to ask.

He closed the album and stood it on end between them, his hand spanning the cover, his fingers pressed hard against it. "Who hasn't been in love at least a time or two by the time they're twenty?"

"Me."

"Really?"

"Really."

"Then you need to make up for lost time."

"And you accuse me of avoiding answering. Have you ever been in love?"

He had been crazy for Stephani from the moment he'd met her, but he'd never considered having a future with her until she'd told him she was pregnant. Since her, he hadn't had a lot of time for pursuing relationships, and a lot of women, especially in the first few years of Jordan's life, had drawn the line at getting seriously involved with a single father. They'd been perfectly willing to sleep with him, even to play at a relationship with him, but it was one thing to be nineteen or twenty and dating a man with a two-, three- or four-year-old son. It was another entirely to consider marriage and being a mother to that son. Still, there'd been a few…

"Yeah," he admitted. "I guess I have a time or two."

"Obviously, you didn't marry either of them. What happened?"

"The first one, Robin, was the oldest of five girls, and the younger four were all married and raising families, and she felt it was her turn—*past* her turn. She figured if we loved each other and were going to be together, there was no reason not to get married right away. *I* figured if we loved each other and were going to be together, there was no reason *to* get married right away. Considering Mom's track record with relationships—"

"And Tate's," Natalie interrupted.

Stiffening, he looked at her. He didn't *have* a track record—at least, not anything unusual. "Tate's?"

"Single father? Never been married?" She shrugged as if that said it all. It didn't, not by a long shot, but this wasn't the time to go into it.

"Anyway, I wanted to wait, to be sure. While we were waiting, Robin ran off and married someone else."

"Were you heartbroken?"

"Hurt. Obviously, though, her feelings for me weren't quite what she'd claimed." Before she could ask about the other woman he'd loved, he asked his own question. "Who broke your heart?"

"Who says it's been broken?"

"You're thirty-one and single. It's a natural assumption."

She retreated to the other end of the couch, and Tate wasn't sure whether he was relieved or regretful. On the one hand, she wasn't tantalizingly close anymore. On the other, she wasn't tantalizingly close anymore. But at least he had a better view.

"I've never been in love," she replied airily.

"That was your question, not mine. I asked who broke your heart."

For a long time she sat motionless, barely breathing, a distant expression on her face, as if lost in time. Then she blinked and quietly spoke. "Her name was Candace."

Her? He kept his jaw from visibly tightening, his eyes

from widening and the surprised question from popping out, and instead waited for her to elaborate.

"She was my best friend—the only best friend I ever had. We met when she came to work at the paper in Montgomery about six years ago. She had studied with my father—had been one of his prize students—and we became very close very quickly."

The light and pleasure were gone from her eyes, leaving them shadowed with pain and something uncomfortably close to shame. Tate wanted to tell her to forget the question. Though she was the one who'd sent the conversation off into such delicate territory, he wanted to end it.

But not as much as he wanted to know this intimate detail about her.

"Have you ever noticed how people say that someone is like a brother or sister to them, to demonstrate an unusual degree of closeness? But most people I know aren't nearly as close to their siblings as they are to their best friends. I can't imagine having a sister who could possibly know and understand me as well as Candace did...." Her words trailed off and the wistfulness faded, replaced when she spoke again with an icy chill. "Which made it that much harder when she—" Once more she broke off, took a deep breath that wasn't quite steady, then offered a sickly smile. "Let's just say she betrayed my trust and leave it at that."

Tate didn't want to leave it at that. He wanted to know more—wanted details on exactly what Candace had done and why, how Natalie had reacted to it and how it still affected her—and then he wanted to make it better.

But it wasn't his business. They were supposed to be keeping their distance, remember? Being cool, logical, responsible. But he felt neither cool nor logical, and just for a time, it would feel damn good to not be responsible. All his life he'd been responsible—had done the right thing, put others first, worked hard. And what had it gotten him? He made a decent living, but he worked damn hard for it. He was single, and more likely to see his son married before he found a wife himself. He probably wouldn't have any other kids, any other future, any other life but more of what he'd already had. Being the responsible one. Sleeping alone at night.

Just once he would like to put himself first, and worry about everyone else later.

Then he looked at Natalie, still gazing off into the distance, still looking wounded and vulnerable, and knew that he couldn't just put himself first. That wasn't who he was, wasn't who he wanted to be.

His own smile wasn't much better than her last had been when he deliberately changed the subject. "I told you there'd been a couple of women. I'll warn you, the second one's not a pretty story. It's about a beauty queen, a clown, a flock of emus and a Corvette. You wanna hear it?"

Slowly the wounded look slipped away, and she smiled dryly. "Sounds like my kind of story. Tell away."

"Well, once upon a time…"

On Wednesday morning Natalie turned down a chance to go out and check the herd with J.T. and instead settled at the kitchen table, computer on, her chapters opened on-screen, her cell phone resting beside it. She wasn't typing, though—wasn't looking over her notes or proofing what she'd already written. She'd drawn her feet onto the chair seat, rested her arms on her knees and was staring out the window over the sink at the pale-blue sky, empty but for the contrail some distant jet had streaked behind it.

She would have liked to go out with J.T. this morning, but she was expecting a call back from the senator any minute now. He hadn't shown the least interest in reports on her interviews with his other eight children. In fact, when she'd tried to bring up a few questions that they'd raised, he'd had no interest in hearing them. He didn't much care what his children thought or said, he'd told her. He'd brought them into the world, and he'd supported them all their lives. He figured that was about all he owed them.

But J.T. was different. He was way past curious about and bordering on obsessive over the son he'd never met. He wanted to know everything.

She didn't want to tell him anything beyond the basics.

When the phone rang, she flinched but didn't hesitate to answer. It was the senator's secretary, a dour woman who always looked as if she'd sucked one persimmon too many and her face had frozen in that sour, scrunched-up way. Natalie hadn't liked her from the moment they'd met, and she didn't like her any better all these months later.

A moment passed before Chaney came on the line. "Well? Do you have information for me?"

On every other occasion that they'd spoken, the senator had been overwhelmingly polite and friendly, like a good-ole-boy politician, which was exactly what he was, retired or not. She was thrown off balance by his blunt, all-business question. She cleared her throat as the screen went dark on her laptop and brilliant tropical fish began swimming from one side to the other.

"I've spent the last week in Hickory Bluff," she began. "I'm staying at the Rawlins Ranch."

"Really? How'd you pull that one off?"

No way was she going to admit that it had been one of J.T.'s requirements before he would cooperate with her. "I'm resourceful. That's one of the reasons you picked me, remember?"

"Resourceful, indeed," Chaney said with a booming laugh. "So you've met my son. What is he like?"

She started with a physical description, then went into character.

When she finished, the senator was silent for a moment, then he said, "He sounds like a damn saint. You sure you got the right boy? Lucinda's got two of 'em, you know."

She couldn't blame him for wondering. When he had eight spoiled parasites, it must be a refreshing change to find out that the ninth child was 180 degrees opposite. "He's the right one."

"What about his family?"

"I haven't met Tate, the older son. He's been out of town. Lucinda's gone, too. She and Tate are visiting a family friend. But I've met Tate's son, Jordan. He's a great kid— a hard worker, polite, dependable, much more mature than you'd expect a sixteen-year-old to be."

"Sixteen. Hard to imagine the brat I remember having a kid that old. Of course, he was only four or five back then."

And not a brat at all, Natalie would wager. Even without meeting Lucinda Rawlins, she was convinced the woman knew how to raise kids. J.T. and Jordan were proof.

"What about the rest of the family?"

"That's it. There's just the four of them."

"No stepfather? No mother for Tate's kid?"

"No."

There was a pause while the senator spoke to someone in the background. In all the times they'd talked, she'd never had his undivided attention. There were always papers to sign, calls to take, conferences with the sour-faced secretary or the assistants who passed through his life on a monthly basis. He was a busy man, he'd reminded her more than once. A busy, *important* man, had been his real message.

"Tell me more about Joshua," he said when he returned his attention to her.

"J.T. That's what he goes by. I think I've pretty much covered the basics. He has no children. He's never been married. He's worked on the ranch all of his adult life. He doesn't seem to have any vices—no drinking, no gambling, no running around, not even much swearing that I can recall."

"Are you *sure* he's my son?" Chaney joked again. "If you told any of my other boys they couldn't get drunk, play the ponies, whore around or cuss, they'd have to go stand in a corner somewhere. They wouldn't know what to do."

"Maybe it's the difference in the way the boys were raised," she said, hoping her unintendedly snide tone didn't carry well over the phone. "Lucinda has her boys in church every Sunday. I don't think any of your exes ever considered that.''

"I'm sure they didn't," he agreed. "You have your little portable computer there? And that fancy camera?''

"Yes, sir, I do."

"Send me a picture."

"Of J.T.?"

"No, of the cows. Of course of J.T. Your reason for being there, remember?''

"I...haven't taken many pictures yet." Truth was, she'd shot fewer than a dozen, and not one of them had a human subject. Not that she was averse to taking a picture of J.T. Hell, if she had one of him the way he'd looked that first day—hot and sweaty in tight jeans and boots, no shirt—she would probably put it on the computer as wallpaper and drool every time she booted up.

"I'm not asking for a lot of 'em. Just one. I want to see what the boy looks like. You have my e-mail address?''

"Of course."

"Then send me a picture. Today. Why don't you see if you can get him to smile for his daddy?''

Finding no humor in his sarcasm, Natalie made a face, then politely said, "I'll see what I can do. Anything else?''

"Call me in a few days. Tell me more." Once again came the sound of voices in the background, then Chaney said, "If I'd known retirement was going to be so much work, I might've run for another term. There's no rest for the weary—or is that the wicked?''

Over his coarse laughter, she agreed, "No, sir, I'm sure there isn't. I'll be in touch."

Feeling too restless to sit still and work after she hung up, she wandered into the living room, then down the hall to Lucinda Rawlins's bedroom. The door had been closed the day she arrived, and she hadn't opened it yet. This morning, though, she turned the knob and swung the door inward.

The room was the same width as hers, and maybe five feet longer. It held too much furniture for the space, all of it old, heavy and dark. The walls were covered with a washable paper in a busy floral print—about what Natalie would expect for a practical woman surrounded by men and with little chance to be fussy or frilly. The curtains at the windows were lace, as was the bedskirt, and matching runners covered the tops of the dresser, bureau and night tables. There were a dozen fat pillows on the bed, in contrasting and coordinating fabrics, with bits of lace on this one, ribbons on that one, and the entire room smelled of lavender potpourri.

Natalie felt as if she were trespassing as she finally ventured past the doorway, though there was no reason for it. The room hadn't been placed off-limits to her. J.T. had merely pointed it out as Lucinda's room. But he'd probably been counting on common courtesy to keep her out, when he really shouldn't expect courtesy from a reporter.

But that fact didn't ease her guilt, or excuse her snooping, and that was exactly what she was doing. She didn't expect to find anything regarding Lucinda's affair with Chaney lying around. She just wanted some insight into the woman herself. The odds that a woman who could catch Boyd Chaney's interest could also singlehandedly raise two productive, responsible sons were slim to none. Not one of the exes had even changed a diaper. They'd buffered themselves from their children with nannies and servants, had exerted less influence on their kids than complete strangers had. But not Lucinda. She appeared to be quite a woman.

Lined up along the bureau top in inexpensive frames were a number of photographs. Natalie picked them up one by one, recognizing a young, fresh-faced, pretty Lucinda in several of them. The older couple, she assumed, were her parents, and in each picture they looked at their daughter as if they adored her. Had her affair with the senator changed that? Had they been disappointed when her marriage to Tate's father ended, or disillusioned when she'd taken up with a married man? Had the circumstances of his birth affected J.T.'s relationship with his grandparents? Did they favor the legitimate child over the illegitimate one?

She stopped in front of the last photo. It was a shot of Lucinda, Tate and J.T., taken more than twenty-five years ago. She wore a dress and big hair, and the boys were both shirtless and shoeless in denim overalls, and adorable. Tucked into the corners of the frame were two additional snapshots—one of a handsome, dark-eyed cowboy with a grin so brash and bold a woman would have to be comatose to not respond to it, and the other of a thirty-years-younger Boyd Chaney.

"That's the closest you'll ever come to a Rawlins family portrait."

J.T.'s voice in the doorway startled her, but she didn't jump guiltily. Her fingers tightening on the picture frame and a soft, sudden intake of breath were her only outward responses.

He reached her in three lazy strides, pulled the frame from her grip and returned it to the bureau. "Guess I should have locked the door."

"Or asked me not to come in here. If you'd asked, I would have stayed out." She didn't look at him. "Is that Tate's father?"

"Yes."

"It's easy to see how your mother fell for him. He's gorgeous."

"Gorgeous, charming, friendly, selfish, two-timing bastard."

"Did you ever meet him?"

"Nope." He sounded almost cheerful about it. "He disappeared before I was born."

"Does Tate ever see him?" When he shook his head, she sighed. "So he just walked out of his son's life."

"Some men have a tendency to do that."

"So do some women," she pointed out, thinking of Jordan. Looking back at absentee father number one, she noticed the background—a dusty arena, chutes, cowboys and fans. "He was a rodeo cowboy."

"And a pretty good one. Women came as easy to him as finishing in the money did, and he took advantage of it."

"Women would have come easy to him no matter what he did. Did I mention that he's gorgeous?" She smiled faintly. "Does Tate look like him?"

"Mom always said he did. I'd say…not so much you'd notice." Taking her arm, he steered her back into the hallway, then closed the door behind them. "You know, when you're a guest in someone's house, it's rude to go prying."

"It is, and I apologize. But the pictures were the only thing I touched. I didn't open any drawers, go through the closet or peek under the bed."

"Am I supposed to be impressed?"

She looked up at him, trying to gauge whether he was simply annoyed or truly put out with her. Unable to read anything in his dark eyes, she set the question aside. "I didn't hear you knock."

"You must have been too caught up in your snooping. I rang the doorbell."

"The side doorbell doesn't work. Lightning strike, remember?"

Emotion flickered across his face as, obviously, he did remember. "I knew there was something I was forgetting. I promised Mom I'd fix that while she's gone."

"When will she be back?"

"When will you be gone?"

She gave him a surprised look, then headed for the kitchen. "You're kidding, aren't you? She's not coming back as long as I'm here?"

"She doesn't want to talk to you."

"But we agreed that I wouldn't talk to her."

Stopping beside the table, he moved the mouse and the screen saver disappeared. There on the screen was her address book, and the name highlighted was none other than Senator Chaney. He glanced at it, then picked up the cell phone, pressed the key to bring up the call log and compared the last number she dialed to Chaney's. His mouth tightened in a thin line as he returned the phone to the table.

Her smile was unsteady, her laugh phony. "Hey, you can't expect me to write the definitive biography of the man without talking to him."

"I keep forgetting not to expect anything at all of you."

Stung, she folded her arms across her chest. "That's not fair, J.T. It's not as if I'm lying to you or deceiving you and pretending to have no contact with your father. I called him this morning. I wasn't trying to hide it. It's not a big secret. I just didn't know how to work it into the conversation when you were accusing me of snooping through your mother's room."

Her words, apparently, struck a nerve. She'd hardly started to defend herself when a peculiar look crept across his face. She didn't know whether to take advantage of his remorse and make him forget the phone call, or use it as grounds to suggest they forget the past fifteen minutes and start over.

"I assume you had a reason for coming over," she said at last.

"Uh, yeah. Jordan's gone into town to meet a couple of his buddies before football practice, and I've got to pick up some supplies. You want to go along?"

She couldn't stop the bright smile that stretched across her face. "Really? You're offering to actually set foot off the ranch with me? You wouldn't prefer to lock me in the closet until you return?"

He gave her a grudging look. "I would, but there are laws against that, you know."

"Have I mentioned that you're the only one of Chaney's nine children who has a sense of humor?" Without waiting for an answer, she raised her arms from her sides. "Do I look okay?"

He checked her out, starting with her hair, pinned up in a curly mess, sliding over her barely made-up face, down her throat, across her breasts. His gaze moved slowly all the way to the very short hem of her very snug-fitting dress, then swept down to her feet, and everywhere he looked, heat followed, with a tiny tingle of awareness. Anticipation settled low in her belly, and her nerves rippled as if the contact were physical.

Every woman should experience a man looking at her like that at least once in her life.

"You look fine. You ready?"

"Yes." That was the simple answer, the polite one. The *real* answer was locked inside her, louder, greedier, much more emphatic. *For anything, cowboy.*

Anytime, anyplace, anyhow.

Chapter Seven

Though they were only four and a half miles from Hickory Bluff and nineteen miles from Dixon, when Tate pulled out of the driveway he turned left, away from both towns. He felt Natalie's curious gaze, but she didn't say anything. She probably assumed he was just taking a different way into town, not taking her out of the way to a different town.

With its shocks shot, his pickup wasn't the most comfortable ride on smooth pavement, and very little of the county's road maintenance budget went to dirt roads such as this one. Still, the air conditioner worked, and in Oklahoma in August, that mattered.

Little more than a half mile down the road, they passed the Scott place. Gesturing toward the mailbox, Natalie asked, "Is that where Mike lives?"

He nodded.

"Where *you* live?"

"You've seen—" Abruptly he broke off. She'd seen Tate's house, but he was supposed to be Josh, which meant he was supposed to live in Josh's cabin. "There's a cabin on the property, set back in some trees. You haven't been near it."

"Will you show it to me?"

Tate's fingers tightened around the steering wheel as he tried to remember what had been in Josh's cabin the last time he'd gone there. Some photographs of Josh and various lady friends. Personal papers. Any number of chances for him to trip up. It wasn't a risk he was willing to take. "No."

"Why not?"

He gave her a sidelong glance. "Because it's *my* place and I said no. You forced me to let you come here. You coerced me into talking to you. But you can't make me take you to my home. I don't want you or Chaney or anyone else knowing exactly where I live."

"Oh." She looked as if the vehemence of his answer stunned her before she turned her head away to stare out the side window. "Okay."

The next mile passed in silence, then... "Look, you're getting a lot more than I ever planned to give you."

"Okay."

This time he waited three-quarters of a mile. "I have a right to some privacy—to not be harassed in my own home."

"I *said* okay."

The odometer marked less than a half mile when he scowled at her again. "You can't expect me to trust you with that information."

"I suppose, in all fairness, I can't expect you to trust me at all." Her voice was soft, her tone wistful, as if it mattered...and damn it, it did, apparently to her and more than he wanted to him.

"It's not that I don't trust you—"

"But you don't. I understand."

No, she didn't. Not taking her to Josh's house had zero to do with his trust and everything to do with protecting his lies. He was in too deep to let something as simple as a photograph, a piece of mail or a message on the answering machine ruin this deception. Of course, he couldn't tell her that…but he could tell her *something*.

He brought the truck to a stop in the middle of the road, shifted into Park, then faced her. She stirred uncomfortably, checking the outside mirror, then glancing over her shoulder. "You'd better move. Someone might come along."

"This section of road probably doesn't get even five cars a week." There were easier, quicker ways to get everywhere it went—part of the reason he'd come this way. "You don't understand squat."

That made her meet his gaze. Tension turned her eyes a deeper shade of blue and flattened her mouth in a thin line. "You've made it perfectly clear, J.T."

"Then perhaps you could enlighten me."

For a moment he thought she was going to refuse to answer. Then she proved him wrong. "You despise your father and the way he treated your mother. You dislike reporters in general and me in particular, except you have this perverse desire to have sex with me, even though it would be the biggest mistake either of us could ever make. You're a hostile participant in this project, you feel you've been forced to cooperate against your will and you won't be happy until I'm out of your life. What's not to understand?"

"Sweetheart, you haven't *seen* hostile yet," he warned. Sweeping off his Stetson, he tossed it on the dash, then combed his fingers through his hair. "You're right. I despise the old man and the way he treated Mom. If you can find anything admirable there, how about pointing it out to me, because it's sure as hell escaped me. You're also right that I don't want to be a part of this damn project, but that was easy enough to figure out, since the only response you ever got to your requests for an interview was *no*. And I *was* forced to cooperate—easy enough, too, since you're the one who forced me. But—" He leaned across the bench seat, caught a firm grip on her arm and hauled her to him, sliding his arms around her, holding her tight when she tried to pull free. His voice just naturally lowered and turned husky, his body temperature shot up about twenty degrees and, in the space of a heartbeat, he went from irritated with her to wanting her more than he'd ever wanted anyone.

He saw the instant she became aware of his arousal pressing against her. Her eyes widened, softened, and she became still. "But...what?"

It took him a moment, then another, to remember what he'd been about to say. It wasn't easy when so much of her warm, soft body was pressed against so much of his hot, hard body, but soon enough the words came back. "There's nothing perverse about my wanting you, and though it seems like a really bad idea, I can't help it if it feels really good. And as for my not liking you..." He removed the clip that held her hair in a mass on top of her head and let it fall, then tunneled his fingers into the thick, electrified curls. "Did I ever tell you my biggest weaknesses are red hair, long legs and thick Southern accents?"

As the question faded away in a murmur, he kissed her, taking possession of her mouth. After only one kiss her taste was familiar, full of promise. He felt as if he knew her intimately...and not at all. She was enticing, intriguing, tempting, and he—sweet damnation, he was lost. They could have all the rational, reasonable conversations in the world, but no way was cool logic going to convince him he didn't want this—didn't want her.

She whimpered deep in her throat and wriggled closer, maneuvering until the only way she could get closer still was to sit on his lap—which seemed a fine idea to Tate. He didn't care who was on top, who was on bottom, where or when or how, as long as he got to bury himself inside her, as long as he could touch her, feel her, kiss her—

"No...no...*no.*"

Those soft little pants weren't what he wanted to hear, though it took a moment for their significance to sink into his dazed brain. By the time he understood, Natalie had already twisted free. By the time he got his eyes open, she was plastered to the passenger door, staring at him in shock.

"We can't—"

When she didn't go on, he grinned wryly—or, at least, tried. It wasn't easy, when he was feeling like a starving man who'd been given a taste of the most delectable treats available, only to see them snatched away. He was hungry enough for her that he ached with it. "We shouldn't, darlin'," he corrected. "But we most certainly *can*."

"It would be wrong," she breathed.

It might end badly—almost definitely would, since she was going back to Alabama sooner or later, and he was staying here—but it wouldn't be wrong. Maybe not wise, not practical, not cool and reasonable and logical, but not wrong. Instead of trying to convince her, though, he took a stab at teasing. "Okay, I admit, it's the middle of the day and we're on a public road. But, darlin', if you haven't done it in a pickup or the back seat of a car, you can't pass for a native around here. Every girl I went to school with and most of the guys—myself included—lost their virginity in a vehicle on a deserted country road."

The corners of her mouth twitched with a smile she didn't let form. "You left out that small detail when you told me about your first time."

He shrugged. "I figured it went without saying. Guess you folks down in Alabama do things differently."

Finally she did smile, but it slid away seconds later. "We can't— We shouldn't—"

"You're right. Jordan's gone for at least three hours every afternoon, and at night he sleeps like a rock. No point in working up a sweat out here when we can do it in the comfort of a bed at home."

"J.T...."

The half chiding, half pleading tone of her voice made him relent. "Okay. You want me to drop it, I'll drop it." He faked a petulant look. "You'd probably just break my heart, anyway."

The sobering thing was, that wasn't a joke. If they had an affair, she probably *would* break his heart. He'd never learned how to separate the sex from the emotion. He figured he was constitutionally incapable of living and making love with her without falling in love with her. And then she would go home—she was too ambitious to give up her career as a reporter to relocate to Hickory Bluff, which didn't even have a newspaper. He wouldn't even have the option of following her, because she believed he was Josh and if she found out the truth...

An ache twisted in his gut as he remembered her words earlier that morning. *It's not as if I'm lying to you or deceiving you...* No, he was the one doing all the lying. He was the one betraying her trust. If she found out the truth, she would never forgive him.

He damn well hoped Josh appreciated everything he was doing for him.

He particularly hoped he survived.

After straightening in the seat, he shifted into gear and pulled away. When one mile of silence turned into two and was well on its way to becoming three, he glanced across the cab. "All right, Natalie of a Thousand Questions. We could use a little of your nosiness about now." If she didn't start talking to him, he was going to keep thinking about wanting her. He was even liable to convince himself that he *could* get involved with her without suffering too much when she left, and then he'd prove just what kind of fool he was by seducing her into breaking his heart.

"Okay. Um...where are we going?"

"Burning Bow."

"Are the supplies you need available only there, or are you willing to be seen with me only in a place where people don't know you?"

"You've never lived in a small town. Gossip is the life blood of a place like Hickory Bluff. If only one person in town found out that a beautiful woman from Alabama was staying at the house with Jordan and me while Mom and

Jo—'' for the first time in days, he almost said his brother's name ''—and Tate are out of town, we would be the prime topic of conversation all over town. I don't like being gossiped about.''

"You could just say, 'This is Natalie and she's writing a book about my father. Her visit here is strictly business.'"

He slowed down to steer the truck over an ancient bridge. The steel span was entirely covered with rust, and the board planks that stretched from one side to the other clattered noisily under the truck's weight. "Well, for starters, everyone in town believes my brother and I have the same father. Telling them otherwise would mean a lot of questions and gossip that he and Mom and Jordan don't deserve.''

"And?"

"That little bit of information wouldn't satisfy them at all. And…'' He let his glance slide over her, lingering on each curve. "They wouldn't believe that 'strictly business' line for a second. I have a reputation for having a fine appreciation for beautiful women, and you are certainly beautiful. They would be imagining all kinds of wicked things going on in that house.'' And if his foolish side had its way, their imaginings wouldn't be the half of it.

"So you're the ladies' man in the family, and Tate is the staid, settled family man.''

He resisted the urge to snort disdainfully. She made him sound like a sexless, lifeless sort of guy. Settled? No more than Josh, except he had one major consideration restricting his social life—Jordan—that Josh lacked. Staid? Okay, so maybe he wasn't much for partying, hadn't enjoyed the last night of drinking he'd indulged in, could barely remember his last date and couldn't remember the last time he'd had sex. That didn't make him staid…did it?

"You don't want to acknowledge being a ladies' man?'' Though her tone was light, there was an intensity to her gaze that belied her casual attitude.

Okay, so Tate's social life was virtually nonexistent, and Josh's was in overdrive most of the time. He should stay in character for Natalie the reporter and admit that yes, he liked women—a lot. But he thought it was more important that Natalie the woman know the truth.

"Jordan has a fine appreciation for restored muscle cars. Mom appreciates intricate, hand-pieced quilts. That doesn't mean cars and quilts are the only things in their lives."

"Not bad dancing yourself," she remarked, a reference to his comment a few nights earlier. *For someone who has a way with words, you sure are dancing around what you want to say.*

The dirt road they were following ended at the highway just outside the town limits of Burning Bow. Tate brought the truck to a halt at the stop sign, saw a line of oncoming traffic and turned his attention to her. "You want me to be blunt? Okay. I like women. I think they're wonderful creatures. I like one woman—you, Ms. Alabama—in particular. That said, I don't meet a lot of women these days. I don't drink much. Cigarette smoke gives me a headache, so I don't hang out in bars at all. I do go out on dates, and sometimes I enjoy them and we have sex, and sometimes I hope I never see them again and we don't even kiss goodnight. I know that doesn't begin to measure up to the old man's style, or his kids', and if that disappoints you, I'm sorry. But if I'm allowed to make requests, I'd really rather not see any mention of the fact that I haven't had great sex in a long time anywhere in your book."

For a long time there was nothing but silence between them. Her gaze searched his face, as if looking for confirmation, darted away, then came back. With the tip of her tongue, she moistened her lip right where the cupid's bow curved upward, then huskily asked, "How long?"

"Long."

Nodding, she looked away again, then gestured toward the highway. "It's clear."

Not by a long shot, he thought as he checked in both directions, then turned onto the paved road. There were still plenty of obstacles in their way—his deception the biggest and most impossible of them all. It alone put severe limitations on anything that might develop between them, first and foremost that it couldn't outlast her time here. She could never know the truth, which meant they could never have more than a few-nights' stand.

But he'd learned to settle a long time ago. If he couldn't have what he wanted, then he would accept what he could have. Whatever that was with Natalie, he wanted it. He would surely regret it, at least for a time, but not as much as he would regret having nothing.

At least, that was his hope.

Burning Bow was, quite possibly, the most unusual town Natalie had ever seen. It was, not to put too simple a spin on it, perfect. Perfectly designed, laid out and maintained. Perfectly clean, efficient and lovely. Perfectly...creepy in a *Stepford Wives* sort of way. The sign in the town square announcing that it was a planned community was unnecessary. Only someone who'd lived his entire life in a cave couldn't guess that. Every house, every shop, every patch of grass—emerald green in spite of the unending drought—was designed to support the vision of an affluent, turn-of-the-last-century, never-never-land town, and they succeeded.

J.T. pulled into the first empty parking space they came to downtown, and she slid out of the truck. She half expected the temperature to be perfect, too, but unfortunately, it was 111 according to the thermometer attached to the outside wall of the hardware store. Even planned communities couldn't mandate the weather, though she wouldn't be surprised to find out they'd tried.

Stepping onto the sidewalk—the flawlessly smooth, uncracked, level sidewalk—she turned in a slow circle before facing J.T. "This is incredible. I've never seen anything like it. Even the lake—" she gestured toward the water visible two blocks and a slight decline away "—couldn't be more perfect if they'd…'' Noticing his grin, she trailed off. ''They built the lake, too?''

He nodded. ''There's a real lake about five miles north, but it wasn't picturesque enough, so they designed this one instead.''

''Amazing. Can you imagine living here? They must require you to check your free will and individuality at the town limits.'' When she would have turned toward the hardware store, he caught her elbow and steered her toward the heart of the town.

''I've got a few friends who live here,'' he said as they strolled. ''It's not so bad.''

''Yeah, until the day you decide to paint your house sunshine yellow, or dig up the yard and put in a rock garden instead, or come home from vacation with a tacky pink flamingo to stick in your flower bed. Then I bet they either force you to move out or they brainwash you into conformity.''

Laughing, he traded her elbow for her hand and pulled her across the street and into a Victorian house whose ruffly and flourishy sign identified it as Miss Mirabelle's Tea Room. ''Not hardly. They're just people who like things to be just so.''

''Fussy, nitpicky people.''

''I bet Thaddeus would fit in here just fine.''

Probably so, she admitted as the hostess showed them to a table. He loved a sense of order, except when it came to his work space. For him, clutter in the office translated into creative energy. Clutter elsewhere—his or anyone else's— was intolerable. This place would delight him.

''It's all very pretty and charming,'' she said as she spread a lace-edged linen napkin over her lap, ''but I'd take what little I saw of Hickory Bluff anytime.''

''Me, too.'' J.T. handed her a menu, waited until she opened it and had scanned the first few lines, then asked, ''What happened between you and your father?''

She stilled, then forced herself to continue studying the

menu. She hadn't realized she was hungry until that very minute, so hungry that her stomach threatened to grumble loudly. She wondered if there was some city ordinance against growling stomachs and other rude bodily noises. Probably a person could get a ticket here for hiccuping in public.

After deciding on a walnut chicken-salad sandwich, she closed the menu and folded her hands in her lap. She hadn't discussed her last meeting with her father with anyone in the fifteen months since it had taken place. The only person she'd ever been close enough to, to have such a discussion with was Candace, who'd been a part of Natalie's great scandal. They'd stopped speaking before she and Thaddeus had. But she wanted to tell J.T.—to tell him the whole ugly story in the hopes it would make him understand why she was doing this book, why its success was so important to her and how vital his full cooperation was.

But if he knew, he would be perfectly within his rights to refuse to talk to her any further. Why not? The newspaper hadn't wanted her around anymore. Her journalist friends had pitied her, scorned her and forgotten they ever knew her. Her own father had been too ashamed to maintain contact with her.

Only one person knew the details and didn't care—Senator Chaney. The mistakes she'd made weren't important, he'd said. Whether she'd learned from them was. She had assured him that she'd learned her lessons well, and he'd offered her the job as his biographer. Truthfully, though, she'd never really understood why. Because he'd respected her work that much? She wished. Maybe he'd thought she could deal with J.T. in ways the men he'd interviewed couldn't? Because, as everyone had suggested, maybe for a time he'd been interested in her himself?

"I realize it's not a simple question," J.T. said quietly, "but it shouldn't take so long to come up with an answer."

Her smile was faint and tinged with wistfulness despite

her best efforts to hide it. "Are all parent-child relationships so impossible? You and your father, my father and me..."

"I get along fine with my mother. Jordan and his father have an excellent relationship. Mom and her parents are very close. You and I and our fathers are more the exception than the rule." He paused while they gave their orders to the waitress, then repeated his question. "What happened? Other than thirty-one years spent trying to please a man whose ego is bigger than Texas and whose job was more important to him than his only child?"

"I let him down. I let everyone down. I did something really stupid, and I had to pay for it." She was embarrassed by the quaver in her voice and the tears that welled up in her eyes. When he reached for her hand, she tried to pull away, fearful that any show of sympathy would cause her to burst into tears right there at the table. Instead she tried to unobtrusively wipe her eyes, then forced her brightest, phoniest smile.

"This really stupid thing... You did it deliberately?"

She shook her head.

"So it was an accident, more or less."

This time she shrugged.

"You helped a convicted felon to escape from prison."

"No."

"You bilked a bunch of helpless senior citizens out of their life savings."

"*No.*"

"You caused someone to die."

"Of *course* not."

"Then what did you do that was so awful your own father couldn't forgive you?"

She studied him for a moment, then her smile tightened. "Oh, you're good, J.T. Last time this came up, I told you it was none of your business. So you wait a few days, bring it up again and get that much more out of me without my even realizing it. You're *very* good."

Her words, meant in part as a tease, in part as a way to

change the subject, left him looking annoyed. "I'm not trying to manipulate you, Natalie. That's your game, not mine. I was just asking because I'm interested."

"I'm not playing games," she said stiffly. "This is my career, and I take it very seriously."

"I bet you do."

Her first impulse was to argue with him, but a man who thought so little of journalists in general and those in the good graces of Senator Chaney in particular wasn't easy to sway. Neither was a man as stubborn, ornery and hard-headed as J.T. had proven to be.

Instead, she forced a smile onto her lips and sweet words out her mouth. "What is this problem you have with reporters? Was your mother frightened by a newspaper when she was carrying you?"

Abruptly he grinned, and her own smile immediately became more natural. "Maybe," he drawled. "And I bet your mother wasn't scared of anything, was she?"

When the waitress brought their food, Natalie took advantage of the interruption to look around the dining room. She was no expert on Victorian architecture or interior design, but every last detail, to her untrained eye, looked true to its period. It was all lovely, feminine, civilized. "My mother was delicate, soft-spoken and as malleable as a ball of clay...with a backbone of steel," she remarked when they were alone again. "My father thought he ruled the family, but the truth was she just let him think so. She decided what she wanted, then gently prodded him until he thought he'd reached that point on his own. She was beautiful and fragile and the perfect example of the well-bred Southern belle, but she had this laugh that was way too big for her body. It just bubbled over and was loud and booming and made everyone around look at her. Of course, she was so pretty that everyone looked at her, anyway."

"You take after her."

She risked a quick glance at J.T., then fixed her gaze on separating her sandwich into halves. This being a tea house, she'd expected dainty portions, perhaps with the crusts removed from the bread and a few bites of fancy lettuce on the side. What she got was a sandwich big enough for her and J.T. both. The bread was fresh baked and soft as cotton, and the chicken salad spilled over the edges. Surrounding it were scoops of potato salad, fruit salad and cottage cheese.

Before trying to pick up one sandwich half, she scooped up a forkful of chicken and chewed it slowly, then responded to his comment. "I've seen enough pictures of her to know that I look like her, though her hair was blond. But she was so much more than I'll ever be."

"You appear deceptively delicate. You're stubborn. You prod people until they give you what you want. You're a perfect steel magnolia. And you're beautiful."

She laughed to cover her embarrassment. "I'm flattered...I think." Quickly, then, she redirected the conversation. "After she died, my father never mentioned her name again. When I grew up, there were so many things I wanted to know about her, but he couldn't bear to talk about her. I probably know less about her than you do about your father."

He didn't respond to her calling Chaney his father. "So write a book about her. Research her. Find the answers to all those questions."

Once before he'd suggested that she find her mother's family, but she'd written off the idea without fully considering it. She didn't know where to start. It would infuriate her father. What if they were no more interested in Thaddeus's daughter than they were in him? What if the only other family she had were to reject her just as her father had?

They were solid arguments...but only on the surface. She didn't know where the Stevensons lived? So find out. That was what reporters did. Thaddeus would be angry? He hadn't spoken to her in fifteen months. How much angrier could he get? As for rejecting her... She was alone. She had no friends, no family. If they rejected her, she would still have no friends or family. All she had to lose was hope. All she risked was another broken heart.

Making an attempt at a casual air, she said, "Please don't talk me into something that could prove dangerous. Trouble finds me easily enough on its own. I don't need to go looking for it."

"You consider your own family trouble? Or does Thaddeus?"

"*You* consider the Chaneys trouble."

"At least I know something about them. I'm not blindly following the lead of a mean-spirited, selfish old man." When he went on, he sounded annoyed again. "You know, Natalie, you'd probably fit in here just fine, too. Apparently, you checked your free will a lifetime ago."

She wanted to be offended, but couldn't summon the energy, especially when he was right. It was easier to follow her father's dictates than to risk his wrath and find out about her mother's family for herself. Maybe J.T. had been right the other day, too. Maybe the Stevensons would be happy to meet her.

And maybe she was too big a coward to find out.

"It's time to change the subject," she said brightly, "to something less depressing and/or tougher to argue. Tell me more about Stepford—I mean, Burning Bow. Who knows? I might get assigned to do a Halloween piece someday, or maybe something on the country's ten creepiest places to live, or maybe I'll get the urge to write a horror novel. It could come in handy."

"If you don't quit calling it Stepford, you'll be the first person banned from entering the city in its entire six-year history," he warned, then shrugged. "You're the reporter, remember? Ask your questions. I'll answer what I can."

They were three-quarters of the way home when they met an approaching pickup. Tate recognized it as belonging to Casper Littrell, a distant neighbor, former rancher and nosy retiree, and inwardly groaned when the truck slowed and a thin, bony arm extended out the window.

"Not even five cars a week, huh?"

He gave Natalie a wry look as he brought his own truck to a stop and rolled down the window. The heat rushed in, heavy and draining, and rooster tails of dust that had followed each vehicle slowly drifted away. "How are you doing, Mr. Littrell?" he called, his voice pitched loud enough to compensate for the old man's hearing loss.

"Aw, I shouldn't complain."

But he often did, Tate thought with a suppressed grin. Most days old Casper had a list of complaints a mile long at the ready, covering everything from the weather to HMOs to the high school football team, from politics to the cost of living to the pitiful amount of hellfire and brimstone in the pastor's last sermon.

"How's your granddaddy?"

"He's fine."

"I hear your mama and that shiftless brother of yours went to help out while he's ailin'."

Tate could almost hear Natalie's ears perk up. He shifted in the seat to make her participation in the conversation difficult, if not impossible. "My brother's not shiftless, Mr. Littrell."

"Aw, don't you be foolin' yourself none, Tate. R'member, he used to work for me. You and your mama was always too easy on him."

As pain radiated through Tate's right hand, he realized he had the steering wheel in a death grip. He forced his fingers to relax, then did the same with the muscles in the back of his neck and his jaw. Being called by his proper name in front of Natalie wasn't a big deal, he told himself—at least, not in these circumstances. He could handle it, and she'd never be any the wiser.

"And you were always tough on him," he responded to the old man's remark, making his face crinkle into a mass of wrinkles as he laughed.

Casper leaned forward and narrowed his sly gaze to see past Tate. "Who's that you got with you?"

For an instant Tate froze. Then, with a grin, he offered the first response that came to mind. "Isn't she pretty? She's this week's special at the hardware store over in Burning Bow."

"Huh. And Dunleavy in town only gives out yardsticks. No wonder business is better over there." Casper shifted into gear. "Guess I'd better git along. I cain't sit and talk at ya all afternoon. Give my regards to your granddaddy and your mama."

"I will."

With a nod, the old man drove off. Tate rolled up the window before the dust could find its way inside, then pulled away himself.

"He had you confused with your brother," Natalie remarked, her tone amused.

"He always has." Tate said a silent prayer for forgiveness. Casper might be older than the state of Oklahoma, but his memory was sharper than most people a third his age. "I gave up correcting him about twenty years ago."

"What's wrong with your grandfather?"

"He—" Abruptly he glanced at her. "This isn't for your book."

"I'm not asking for the book."

Searching her face, he found nothing but sincerity—and more than a little irritation—in her expression. "His horse threw him about a week and a half ago and he broke his leg. Gran insisted she could run the ranch herself, but Mom and...Tate thought that wasn't such a great idea."

"So your mother really didn't leave town just to avoid me."

"I told you she didn't."

"Yes, but I didn't believe you. I also can't believe that Tate went and you stayed here, when you could have easily left him here while you disappeared."

The heat of guilt made the neck of Tate's T-shirt feel a

good three inches too small. He slid his finger between the ribbed fabric and skin slick with sweat, tugged the shirt loose, then immediately felt strangled again as soon as he let go. "Would you have been that easy to get rid of?" If she said yes, he swore he would make Josh pay for all the lies, the guilt and the dishonor he and Jordan had been coerced into.

Her laughter was clear and pleasant enough to bring an automatic smile to his lips. "You waste your breath asking. I would have stuck around as long as it took to find out where your grandparents live, and then I would have tracked you down. I consider myself the Royal Mounties of the journalism world—I always get my man…or story."

"Or man," he said quietly. He would like her about a thousand times better if she was looking for a man and not a story. Hell, if she would forget this particular story, he might even fall in love with her.

But that wasn't going to happen. Not the forgetting, and for damn sure not the falling.

"What would you have done if I'd shown up at your granddaddy's ranch?" she asked with a teasing, tantalizing flutter of lashes as he pulled into the driveway.

He parked beside the pickup Jordan normally drove, shut off the engine, then faced her. "I would have had you arrested, and then I would have made you damn sorry you'd ever heard of Boyd Chaney, J. T. Rawlins and the entire damn state of Oklahoma."

Ignoring her startled, hurt look, he swung out of the truck and began unloading the supplies from the back. He heard the passenger door open, then close, but paid no attention. He kept his focus narrowly on the task at hand until Jordan joined him to help transfer everything to the storage shed and the barn. "What're you doing home so early?"

"The air conditioner's out in the weight room. Coach sent us home. Where have you and Natalie been?"

"Burning Bow."

"Long way to go just to buy some barbwire and fence posts. You guys have a fight or something?"

"No."

"You're just not speaking right now." When he got no response after a moment, Jordan went on. "Uncle Josh called while you were gone. He wanted to know how much longer he's gonna have to stay at Granddad's. They're having fights, too. Granddad says Uncle Josh don't know nothin' 'bout nothin', and Uncle Josh says Granddad is a mean old goat who wouldn't admit he's wrong on threat of death. Why don't they get along?"

"Probably because they're too much alike. Leave it to Josh to go off and leave me here to handle *his* problem, then complain about his escape."

Jordan gave him a superior look. "Well, of course he's complaining. When has he ever been in the same room with Granddad for five minutes and not complained? Just be grateful you're here and not there. Grandma and Granny Anna have to listen to 'em both." His sidelong look turned sly. "You want to trade places with Josh, all you have to do is tell Natalie the truth."

Tate wasn't sure he could imagine how angry she would be...or how hurt. At least then neither of them would have to worry about the inappropriateness of any relationship they might have. She would hate him. Period. Never forgive him, never want him, never let him explain. "Telling her the truth isn't an option." Would never be an option.

"But losing her when she's finished with the book is."

Tate's muscles tightened until he felt real pain. "That's not an option, either." It was a simple, cold fact. "Besides, she's not mine to lose. That book is the most important thing in her life. You and me—we're just part of the story."

Jordan murmured an obscenity that would have brought a threat of a mouth washing if his grandmother had heard it. Tate didn't have the energy to warn him to watch his language. "Come on, Dad. I *saw* you kissing her. I saw *her* kissing you back. There was a lot more going on there than just her story."

Because there was a lot more going on—and *not* going on—than Jordan guessed, Tate deliberately spun the conversation off in another direction. "I know what your motive is, son, in trying to push Natalie and me together—you're looking to drive that car. Well, let me tell you, your chances of that are somewhere between slim and none. Even if Natalie said okay, I doubt her insurance covers teenage drivers, and my insurance sure as hell doesn't cover sports cars."

"Aw, Dad, you think I would try to marry you off for a *car?*"

Tate looked at the Mustang, then Jordan. "Yes."

A grin stretched across Jordan's face as he gave the car a longing look. "Oh, well…you can't blame a guy for trying."

Nice line, Tate thought as he headed for the barn. Maybe he'd try it next time he kissed Natalie and she came to her senses long before he was ready to stop. As beautiful as she was, as needy as he was, and as damn much as he wanted her…

You really couldn't blame a guy for trying.

Chapter Eight

On Friday, for the first time since arriving at the ranch, Natalie ate both lunch and supper alone in her paper-littered kitchen. Supper wasn't much—a TV dinner she'd found in Lucinda's freezer, microwaved into something resembling food, and a juicy, red tomato, fresh from the garden and lightly sprinkled with salt. Jordan had come over around six-thirty to see if she was joining him and J.T., but she'd begged off. She'd been working since 6:00 a.m. and wanted to squeeze out every single word that would come while she was on a roll.

It was quite a significant amount, and now she was pooped, both physically and mentally. Rising carefully from her chair, she planted her feet apart, then bent from the waist. Every millimeter her taut muscles and ligaments stretched brought relief, and the audible pops as her spine realigned itself made her grunt aloud. As soon as she straightened again, though, the aches returned. There was a burning between her shoulder blades, a stitch in her ribs, her butt was numb, and her arms... She gave them a surprised look. The muscles in her arms were actually fatigued from so much typing.

And here she'd thought writing a book couldn't possibly be too different from writing newspaper articles.

Picking up her tea, she shuffled across the kitchen, down the hall and outside onto the deck. The sky was a soft, dusky melange of colors—blues, purples, roses. On the western horizon, bands of gold stretched from one end to the other. On the eastern horizon there was nothing but velvety darkness. No city lights, no stars yet, no moon.

There was only the slightest of breezes, and the thermometer hadn't yet noticed that the sun had gone down. Grateful for her shorts and tank top, as well as the elastic band that held her hair off her neck, she crossed the deck and eased into a chair still warm from the day.

Though J.T. might have exaggerated about the five-cars-a-week bit, Rawlins Ranch Road wasn't a busy throughway, by any means. The last car she'd heard had been an hour ago, and had come from right next door. Jordan heading out to spend a Friday night in town with his friends? Or J.T. going off to spend a few hours with *his* friends? Maybe a female friend in particular.

Not that she cared, of course, except where the book was concerned. She had little doubt one of the first questions in every reader's mind would be how much the secret son took after his much-married father. Would anyone believe that a child of Boyd Chaney had had only two serious relationships in his entire life?

Then she laughed out loud. Right, Natalie, she thought scornfully. *Your only interest in J. T. Rawlins's love life— or his sex life—is for the book. Anyone who believes that, step right up for first dibs on a piece of fabulous swamp land.*

"What's so funny?"

The voice came out of the darkness and made Natalie jump. Her feet hit the floor with a thud, and she sloshed cold tea over her leg before placing the voice with a name—Mike Scott. Peering into the shadows, she could just make out the more solid shadow of the girl and the horse she rode standing placidly fifteen feet away.

"You startled me."

"Sorry." Mike nudged the horse closer to the flower beds that edged the deck. "I just assumed you heard us."

"I'm used to listening for cars, not hoofbeats. What are you doing out so late on a horse?"

"I ride a lot at night. There's a trail from here to our house."

Moonlight rides. Sounded romantic…and scary. Though if she had the right companion to make it romantic, then it couldn't possibly be scary. She couldn't imagine the situation in which she could be afraid with J.T. at her side.

"Can you tie him up and sit for a while?" she asked. "I'll get you some tea, and I have some great cookies." They were oatmeal-raisin, baked this morning, and Jordan had delivered them along with the invitation to supper. She couldn't afford the calories of one more of them, but Mike was tall and skinny. They might do her some good.

After a moment Mike dismounted and led the horse into the darkness again. Natalie went into the house, and when she returned with a tall glass of tea and the plate of cookies, the girl had pulled a chair close to her own and was sitting there, looking uneasy.

"Is…is Jordan here?"

"I don't know. Would you like me to find out?"

In the dim light that came from the bulb over the door, Natalie could see the color heating Mike's face. "I…I don't—"

"It's not a problem." Particularly since she wanted to know whether it was Jordan or his uncle who'd left earlier. "Let me check."

She rang the doorbell, waited, then rang it again. She was about to turn away when the lock clicked and the door slowly opened. She couldn't help but smile at the sight of

J.T. in jeans, a black T-shirt and barefoot, as usual after work. His dark hair was tousled, and his eyes wore a sleepy, dazed look. "Did I disturb you?"

He rubbed one hand over his face. "I dozed off on the couch, I guess."

"Sorry. I was just wondering if Jordan's home."

"Isn't he a little young for you?"

She gestured toward Mike, and a sympathetic look crossed his face. When he answered, he lowered his voice to a just-for-her murmur. "He had a date with Barb—Shelley tonight."

Ouch. "Too bad."

"We missed you at dinner."

The words sent a rush of longing through her that threatened to sear her lungs and curl her toes. "You did, huh?"

"Yeah, I did."

Her mouth suddenly dry, she swallowed hard, then wished for her iced tea—not to drink, but to pour over her steaming skin in search of relief. "I—" She cleared the hoarseness, or at least part of it, from her throat. "I had a really good day writing. I figured I should take advantage of it while I could...though my back may never be the same."

"Come over when Mike leaves and I'll give you a massage."

Her gaze dropped automatically to his hands—large, long-fingered, callused, strong. Just the thought of them on her body sent healing heat through achy muscles, made stiff joints relax and damn near melted her bones. In fact, if she ignored the incredible ache that had suddenly appeared deep inside—the emptiness, the hunger, the need—she felt better already. "Thank you for the offer, but...I don't think so."

"Why not?"

She smiled wistfully. "I'm not that strong." To lie down with him beside her, to feel his hands touching her intimately, to be that close, that connected, and not plead for more... Pure and simple, she wasn't capable of it.

His responding smile was sweet. Sinful. "Give me a chance to change your mind."

"Remember, we're supposed to rely on reason and logic, and under the circumstances, you giving me a massage——" just saying it made her bite back a groan "——seems neither reasonable nor logical."

"Reason doesn't keep you warm at night, darlin', and logic doesn't help a bit when you want someone as damn much as I want you."

Her breath caught in her chest. Did he have any idea how erotic it was to be told she was desired in no uncertain terms? Her knees were weak, her brain had turned fuzzy, and her stomach was tied in knots...but her laughter was forced. "You *are* your father's son."

The instant she said the words, she wished she hadn't. They turned his eyes cold and shaped his mouth in a thin, hard line. His touch was gentle, though, when he brushed his fingers across her jaw. "No, Natalie, I'm not, but even if I were, you would never know it."

Leaning forward, he touched his mouth to her forehead in the most innocent of kisses, then stepped back to close the door. "Good night," he said an instant before the door shut her out.

For a long time she stood there, staring at painted wood and curtained glass, and wished she could take back her last words. Accept his offer of a massage and anything that might arise from it. Forget who she was, who he was and why she was here. She wished, for just one night, she could be nothing more than a woman, and he could be no more than a man. Not the key to her future. Not the means of her redemption. Just a man she liked, wanted, needed, dreamed about.

Across the deck Mike cleared her throat, making Natalie wince. As everyone else seemed to do, she'd forgotten the girl completely.

"I guess Jordan's out."

Natalie smiled faintly as she returned to her chair. "Yes, he is."

"On a date with Shelley Hawkins, probably." Slumping back in her seat, Mike propped her feet on the railing and let her chin sink to her chest. Natalie felt like joining her in the down-and-out posture. "She's dumber than dirt...but guys aren't interested in her brains. What does an IQ of fifty matter when you're a size-four blonde with a double-D cup?"

"Kirsten Beecham. That was the Shelley Hawkins of my senior class. Every guy in school forgot I existed when she was around. Beautiful, blond, not a curl on her head. Couldn't put two and two together, but had the best car, the best clothes, the best family, the best guys.... We hated her."

"I keep telling myself that things will balance out. People will realize she's dumb and shallow and selfish. In the end, brains will count for more than beauty." Mike snorted at her own gullibility. "Of course, I know it's not really gonna happen...is it?"

Natalie regretfully shook her head. "As soon as Kirsten finished her reign as Miss Virginia, she married the heir to some French fortune. She now splits her time between homes in New York, London and Paris. She's got three beautiful daughters, she's on a first-name basis with tons of celebrities both here and abroad, and her drop-dead gorgeous husband seems to worship the ground she walks on. My only consolation is that now she's unbearably stupid in *two* languages."

"And guys notice you now. They think *you're* beautiful now."

Not as many as Mike might like to think, Natalie thought...but all it took was one. What was her one doing right now? Had he gone back to sleep on the sofa? Settled in to watch a little television? Headed off to bed? If she'd been smart, she would have accepted his invitation and found out after Mike left.

But would that have been smart or crazy-out-of-her-mind? The best time of her life? Or the worst mistake of said life?

Not knowing the answer and not particularly wanting to figure it out tonight, Natalie forced her attention back to Mike's problem. "You know what? You can make yourself more beautiful, Mike...but Shelley's always going to be dumber than dirt."

Mike plucked at a tear in the knee of her ill-fitting jeans. "I'm never gonna be anyone's idea of beautiful. I'm too tall. I can't see without these stupid glasses. I can't do anything with my hair. I'd make an awful blonde. I'm allergic to perfume and I look like a clown when I wear makeup. I'm a better mechanic and ranch hand than any of the guys around here. Hell—damn—darn, that's what I *am* to them. Just one of the guys."

Surrendering to the temptation, Natalie slid down in the chair and propped her heels on the railing. Immediately the muscles in her back protested, then gradually quieted. "Men like tall women. Glasses can be replaced by contacts, or you could have laser surgery or, hey, how about a pair of *flattering* frames that fit properly? A good cut would take care of your hair—something short, sleek, sassy, that suits your bone structure—and why in the world would you want to be a blonde? Because Jordan likes a particular blonde?"

Pushing her glasses up on her nose, Mike shrugged.

"Blondes are a dime a dozen. Stick with your natural color or—" Natalie grinned wickedly "—add a little red. I know men whose biggest weaknesses are red hair and long legs. Forget the perfume, learn to do your makeup perfectly, add a little jewelry and some clothes that fit, ditch the boy's name for your own.... You'd be amazed at the difference."

Unfortunately, she couldn't say beyond a doubt that *Jordan* would be amazed, because he was so besotted with Shelley. But other boys would. She had no doubt of that.

"You really think...?"

Natalie nodded.

"My dad says I look fine the way I am."

But her dad had never been a teenage girl, and he'd never been judged as heavily on appearance as girls routinely were. And, being male, he probably didn't want to think about his little girl attracting the attention of other males, especially attention that involved lust, hormones and sex.

For a time Mike studied her size nine or ten sneakers before finally nodding once, as if she'd reached a decision. Then she turned toward Natalie. "You have a thing for Jordan's uncle?"

Now it was Natalie's turn to blush. "Um…no…not really…I wouldn't call it…" She sighed heavily. "Yeah."

"But?"

"Pursuing it wouldn't be wise." But, oh, it would be fun!

"Do you have a thing for every man you interview?"

"Of course not."

"So this is special."

"Yeah. It's special."

"I understand not dating every guy you interview, but when it's someone special… It's like ignoring the guy you've been looking for all your life just because you meet him at the wrong time."

"No, it's not. I'm not looking— It's just a—" Blowing out her breath impatiently, Natalie leveled her gaze on the girl. "You know, Mike, I'd—"

"Michaela. That's my name."

Resisting the smile that tugged at her lips, Natalie started over. "You know, Michaela, I'd much rather give advice than take it. After all, I'm almost twice your age, and I do have a little experience with relationships." With bad ones. Deceitful ones. Just plain wrong ones.

But she had no experience at all with finding the guy she'd been looking for all her life because, truthfully, she *hadn't* been looking. She'd always been trying to prove herself deserving of her father's love and respect. She'd wanted to make him proud of her, but instead she'd brought shame on him and herself. She couldn't even think about having a serious relationship with some guy until she'd made things right again with her father and in her career...could she?

"I admit I'm...attracted to J.T.," she began slowly. "But this is a really bad time for me to get involved with anyone, and getting involved with someone who's part of my project is unprofessional and unethical and just plain wrong."

"But you also admit that he's special. And how can there be a really bad time to fall in love with someone? Unless you're married to someone else or dying or something. You're not, are you?"

"No husband, no impending death."

"And what does being professional have to do with being in love?"

Natalie's brow wrinkled as her gaze narrowed. "How old are you? Sixteen going on sixty?"

Mike—no, Michaela now—smiled the first smile Natalie had seen cross her face. It softened her features and drew attention away from the glasses sliding down her nose and the lank hair that wouldn't stay in place, and promised true beauty someday. "My dad was never much good with kids, so he always treated me like a grown-up. Plus my IQ's too high for my own good—that's what my teachers say. Plus I'm just mature for my age."

"No kidding," Natalie said dryly. "Okay, first of all, I'm not in love." Absolutely not. She was just suffering from a case of severe lust and infatuation. "Secondly, this book I'm writing is very important to me and to my career. It can make or break me, and I can't risk it for anyone or anything."

"How can a book be more important than a person?"

"This one book can fulfill every goal I've ever set for my career. How could I risk that for a fling with a handsome stranger?"

"How can you know it would be a fling? How can you be sure he's not the man you're supposed to spend the rest of your life with?"

Now that could be an intriguing idea...if she let it fully

form. She put on the brakes before it could take on a shape or life of its own, and added a bit more insistence to her argument. "I can't. But I *can* be sure that the book's important. It very well might be the most important piece of writing I'll ever do." At the moment the most important writing in her body of work was a series of articles she'd done on life in the inner city and the corruption within the public offices and charitable foundations meant to make that life easier. Unfortunately, it was memorable not for the writing or the acclaim it had received, but for the awards it had won, then lost. The misconceptions, twisted facts and outright fabrications. The lies, the deceit, the betrayal.

If she quit writing now, that would be her legacy. Everything else she'd ever done would be forgotten, and she would be remembered only for her great failure. She deserved better than that, and Thaddeus certainly deserved better. That entire ugly incident should be no more than a footnote on her record. She should be remembered for ably carrying on the Grant family tradition of excellence.

"So the book is important," Michaela said. "It'll be a huge success. *Today* and *Good Morning America* and *People* will be calling. *Time* will want you on their cover. *60 Minutes* will do a feature on you."

Natalie smiled wryly. "My own personal favorite is CBS's Sunday morning show. They do great author segments."

"And they'll say, 'Tell us about your family, Natalie. Is your husband proud of your success?' And you'll say…"

Sitting up, Natalie primly crossed her legs, smiled a practiced smile and said in a sugary Southern drawl, "Why, I don't have a husband, Ms. Scott."

"'Oh. Well, what about the man in your life?' And you'll say…"

The smile slipped. "I don't have one of those, either."

"'Oh. No children? No extended family? No lover? No occasional boyfriend? No one who cares at all for you? Tell me, Natalie, when you found out your book had shot to the top of the bestseller lists and that you are now officially making more money than God, who did you share the fabulous news with?''

Second after second ticked by. Natalie tried to come up with a legitimate answer—someone in her life at the moment who would be happy for her if such success came along. She couldn't think of a single person, other than the publisher waiting for the first hundred pages of the manuscript, the agent who'd negotiated the contract and the senator, all of whom stood to benefit financially from her success.

She scowled at Michaela as she slumped back in her chair once more. ''You're too smart for *my* own good.''

The girl shrugged. ''My grandpa says success doesn't matter much if you don't have someone to share it with.''

But if Natalie achieved the sort of success they were talking about, she *would* have someone to share it with—her father. He wouldn't apologize, but if the book was terrifically good, he wouldn't make her apologize, either. He would act as if the entire Candace-inspired humiliation had never happened…and she would let him, because she would be so pathetically grateful to be forgiven for being fallible.

''No offense to your grandpa, but I say no man is worth giving up every dream you ever had unless you have guarantees that he's worth it.'' *That he'll stick around. That he'll be there for you. That he'll give you unconditional love and acceptance.* But life didn't offer guarantees. It was far more likely a relationship would wind up being a short-term fling than a forever-and-ever sort of love.

Long after Michaela had said good-night and headed home, Natalie remained where she was, gazing up at the night sky. The stars were out now, and her gaze fixed on one in particular that looked as if it dangled by an unseen thread from the tip of the crescent moon. She'd never been the sort to wish on stars—her father believed each person was responsible for his own destiny—but if she were a wish maker, that was the star she would wish on.

And what would she wish for? The healing of her relationship with her father? The success, rave reviews and fat royalty checks all authors wanted?

Or someone who cared about her? Who shared her triumphs and helped her make the best of her failures. Who loved her because...well, just because. Who didn't need reasons to love her and wouldn't look for reasons to withhold his love.

She sighed deeply. There was nothing quite like a sixteen-year-old girl who could get under your skin and make you really think. Someday, when Michaela came into her own, some guy was going to have to work really hard to win her for himself, but she would be well worth the effort.

What if the romantic in Michaela had been right—if this thing between Natalie and J.T. really was special? What if he was the guy she was supposed to spend the rest of her life with, and she passed him by because a relationship would be unprofessional as long as the senator's biography stood between them? What if she blindly ignored what was between them and the book was a huge success and her father deigned to forgive her? Not apologize, not make amends, but forgive her for being human enough to make a mistake. Until the next mistake came along. Until she failed once again to maintain the standards *he'd* set for her.

For a week and a half, she'd watched J.T. with his nephew—had seen the obvious love and respect they felt for each other. Surely he extended the same sort of acceptance to others he loved—his feelings for his mother and half brother were fiercely protective. She couldn't imagine his own child having to earn his love or living in fear of losing it.

She couldn't imagine what it would be like to be on the receiving end of such love, such security. But what if Michaela wasn't just a starry-eyed teenager and there really was the possibility of such a commitment between her and J.T.? And what if she gave it up for the certainty of the book—for the future, for her father?

Just how sorry would she be?

* * *

Tate was standing at the corral fence Saturday morning, watching Jordan work with his newest horse, when Natalie called his name. He swung around and realized she was looking at him through the viewfinder of a camera just in time to duck his head. His Stetson was pulled so low that he had no doubt it obscured his face entirely when he ducked, but still he scowled at her when she joined him.

Turning back to rest his arms on the top rail of the board fence, he muttered, "No more pictures."

"Aw, come on, J.T. Women everywhere would be ever so grateful." She grinned wickedly. "Take your shirt off and get Jordan to do the same, and I can snap off enough shots to fill a cowboy-hunk-of-the-month calendar in no time."

"You think I want women everywhere drooling over my sixteen-year-old…nephew?"

"But it would be okay if they drooled over you?"

Finally he let the scowl slip and smiled crookedly. "I'm used to it."

She made a tsking sound. "I bet you are. The only surprise is that some pretty little cowgirl hasn't yet roped and branded you."

"I'm not looking for a cowgirl."

"I bet you're not looking for anyone at all, or you probably would have found her by now."

"You'd be wrong…on both counts."

His words—or maybe it was the way he was looking at her—brought a flush to her cheeks and made her turn her attention to Jordan as if he were the safer of the two. Tate shifted his gaze that way, too. He shouldn't have made the remark. The hard, cold truth was there was no future for them. No matter how strong the attraction, or that the mere thought of her could make him ache, they couldn't have anything more than a short-term affair. Unless she was the most forgiving person in the world, whatever was between them would end the day her visit did. When she left the ranch to return to Alabama or wherever the book might take her next, that was it for them, too.

Knowing that, they'd have to be fools to let things go any further. But he would. If she turned to him right now and said, "Make love to me," he would do it. Knowing that nothing could come of it. That she believed he was his brother. That she would despise him if she ever learned the truth. He would do it…and pay for it later.

But at least he'd have the memories to get him through.

Letting the small camera dangle from her finger by its strap, she rested her arms on the rail and her chin on her arms. "The senator asked me to send him a picture of you. He wants to see what you look like."

Tate's head jerked around, and he glared at her. "No pictures."

"Just one that shows your face. I can take it right now, download it and e-mail it to him." Though she didn't look his way, she smiled uneasily. "You can even stick out your tongue or make an obscene gesture or something."

"*No* pictures."

"I'll need some for the book." When he didn't respond, she gave a big, put-upon sigh. "Don't make me resort to high school yearbook pictures, J.T. They can't possibly be as flattering as something more current." When he still said nothing, her mouth thinned. "You are stubborn."

He snorted. "If that isn't the pot calling the kettle black. You could give lessons in stubbornness, sweetheart. Something you picked up from old Thad?"

She raised the camera and focused on Jordan, but before she could snap the shot, Tate pulled it from her hand. He held the camera in his right hand, her hand in his left, and she didn't even protest. "I've got a lot at stake with this project. I've got to be stubborn."

"Yeah, fame, fortune, a bit of celebrity for yourself." He didn't try to hide the sarcasm he felt. As far as he was concerned, they were damn poor excuses for screwing around with people's lives. But then, when it was his mother and brother involved, he would find *all* excuses lacking. No one had the right to mess with his family, no matter what the reason. End of discussion.

"I don't care about fame or fortune." Presumably she saw his skepticism when she glanced at him, because she continued. "I really don't. Oh, I admit, when I was invited to Jefferson Oaks to interview with the senator, it crossed my mind that a book on such a prominent figure could sell quite well. But that's not why I wanted the job. Financially I've always been comfortable. My father made good money, and I've done all right. I'd never get rich writing for a newspaper, but I can support myself, and that's all I need. As for the fame…I've lived my entire life as Thaddeus Grant's daughter. That's fame enough for me."

"So why did you want the job? What's at stake if it isn't fame and fortune?"

For a long time she watched Jordan and the horse as if she'd never seen either creature before and found them equally curious. Tate knew horses as well as he knew himself, but sometimes he found himself looking at Jordan that way. Sometimes he was amazed and astounded that this big, strong, good-looking kid was the same colicky baby who'd kept him awake nights—that he and Stephani, two selfish, immature kids themselves, together could create a living, breathing person who embodied the best either of them had to offer.

Had Thaddeus ever been amazed and astounded by his daughter? Had he looked at her when she was a baby and wondered about the people she would be at various stages of her life—the toddler, the teen, the career woman, the wife, the mother? Had he dreamed dreams for her? Had he ever thanked God for having her?

If any of the answers were yes, Tate would be surprised. The man had quit speaking to his only child more than a year ago. No matter what the reason, as far as he was concerned, that said a hell of a lot about the hotshot journalist.

Tate truly couldn't imagine the circumstance that could make him cut off all contact with his child, and he couldn't understand any father who could—his own and the senator included.

After so long that he'd accepted she wasn't going to answer, Natalie finally spoke. Her voice was soft, her tone distant. "I told you the other day that I let my father down. I disappointed him, and as a result, we haven't seen each other since."

Tate nodded grimly.

"This is my first chance to make it up to him. To make things right. To make him proud of me again."

"He's not worth it." He spoke more bluntly than he'd intended, and he felt her surprise in the sharp look that burned into him. "Any father whose affection and pride come with a price tag isn't worth it."

Though she didn't move, emotionally she drew back. "I don't expect you to understand."

"Good. I don't want to understand someone that shallow and cold and worthless, and I don't want to understand what he did to brainwash you into thinking this is normal. He's your *father,* and fathers are supposed to love their children."

"The way your father loves you?" she asked, her voice soft with sarcasm.

"No, my father doesn't love me. But the difference is, Natalie, I don't care. I don't live my life for him. I figure I'm better off without him, while he's missed out on knowing someone who could have made his life richer in some way. I *don't* let him dictate my choices in the pathetic hope that if I live exactly the way he wants someday he'll favor me with a bit of his attention."

One second ticked into another as they stared at each other. Sometime in the last moment her face had gone pale, turning her hair redder in comparison. The blue of her eyes was no more substantial than the cloudless sky overhead, bleached of intensity by the scorching sun, and her lips were parted as if she might heap curses on his head any second now…or burst into tears. He knew as he watched her that of all the things he'd said, she had locked in one single word—one truthful but bad choice of a word that she was going to make him pay for. Because of that, truthful as it was, he'd take it back in a heartbeat if only he could.

When she spoke, she proved him right. "'Pathetic.'"

Though his face flushed hot, he didn't say anything in his defense. Hell, what could he say?

"You think I'm pathetic."

"Natalie—" He tightened his fingers around the hand he still held, but she managed to twist free and back away a few feet. "Aw, hell."

The fence shuddered as Jordan vaulted over it, then landed lightly between them. "Why don't you take care of the horse, Uncle J.T.?" his son suggested. "Natalie and me are gonna run into town and get something for lunch. Okay?" He gave her the same grin that had gotten him his way with everyone in his life, from Tate and Lucinda to Mike and Shelley to the teachers at school. "I've been wanting a ride in that car of yours ever since you showed up, and you don't want the battery going dead from not driving it, do you?"

Her gaze didn't waver from Tate's face as she icily answered, "No, I don't." Probably the only thing she wanted to go dead was *him,* and he couldn't even say he blamed her.

Jordan held out his hand, and Tate slapped a twenty—all he had in his pocket—in his palm, then handed over the camera before climbing into the corral. He approached the mare cautiously while watching them walk away. Jordan gave him an annoyed look over his shoulder.

Natalie ignored him.

They walked to the house together, where Jordan went inside to wash up. She went next door, then met him at the Mustang with her purse and keys. Though Tate watched until they were out of sight, not once did she so much as glance in his direction.

"Hell, I know it was a stupid thing to say," he muttered aloud, though only the mare was there to hear. "But that damned hero worship for her father drives me nuts. The bastard's treated her like she's *nothing,* but she still lives her life for him. Everything she does, every choice she makes... How is any man ever supposed to compete with that?"

Of course he didn't expect an answer, but his gelding would have at least rubbed his head against Tate's shoulder in commiseration, or butted him for attention. The mare... He turned to where she was supposed to be and found only dirt. With another look, he located her, standing in the shade of the barn, totally uninterested in him or anything he might have to say.

Damned female didn't want any more to do with him than Natalie did at the moment. Well, that suited him just fine. He had a dozen better things to do than mess with Jordan's horse.

Like finding a way to apologize.

To make things right.

Without making them *too* right.

Removing his hat, he wiped the sweat from his face, then muttered a curse. He'd been right the day Josh had come up with this stupid plan. It wasn't going to work. He'd already lived to regret it. And he was definitely going to burn in hell.

Chapter Nine

It was a busy morning in Hickory Bluff, according to Jordan, though Natalie wouldn't have guessed it. She'd never lived anyplace where twenty cars constituted a traffic jam. But she had to admit as she drove the length of Main Street that the small town had its own charm...well, provided your standards weren't set too high. Most of the buildings downtown were as old as the town itself, with the notable exception of the yellow brick post office, and most of them offered at least two services—insurance and accounting, clothing and gifts, feed store and lumber yard. The laundromat shared space with a dry cleaner, alterations shop and secondhand store, and the variety store was part five-and-dime, part flea market and part antique store.

Opening his arms wide to embrace the buildings on both sides of the street, Jordan said, "Welcome to Hickory Bluff. If you want, after lunch I'll give you the nickel tour, which, according to my grandmother, definitely gives you your two cents' worth. Speaking of lunch, we have our choice of

Norma Sue's Café or Dairy Delight. They're owned by the same people. Norma Sue runs the café, and her husband Norman runs the drive-in.''

"Norman and Norma Sue?''

He raised his right hand. "I'm not making it up. That's really their names. The food's the same either place. About the only difference is the café's got indoor seating and air-conditioning, and the drive-in's got great music.''

"Do you define great music as coming out of Nashville and involving fiddles and steel guitars?'' she asked dryly.

"Hell—heck, no. That's my dad's music. This is good stuff.''

"Then by all means, let's go to the drive-in.''

Dairy Delight was located at the end of town, with a vacant lot on one side and a gas station on the other. At some point in history, it had been an actual drive-in, Jordan informed her as she parked under a corrugated tin awning, with carhops and everything, but not in his lifetime. Now a person had to place his order at the window on the near side, wait for his number to be called—or, more likely, his name—then pick it up on the other side.

The menu still read like something from ancient history, Natalie thought, offering grape soda, root beer floats and honest-to-God malts. She ordered a hamburger and—after reading the sign that said, Yes, They're Real—onion rings, along with a vanilla Coke. The food was delivered to the pick-up window steaming hot, the onion rings dipped in a light batter and fried to golden perfection. Just looking at them made her mouth water.

"Hi, Jordan,'' the girl who brought the food said with a flutter of lashes.

"Hi, Keri.'' Bending to look inside, he called, "Hi, Terri, Mary, Gerri.'' He grinned at Natalie. "They work together, go to school together and are best friends—mostly because the names confuse everybody.''

A chorus of feminine hellos drifted out.

"Who's your friend?'' Keri asked.

"This is my cousin Nadine. She's visiting from Atlanta."

Natalie said hello, then waited until they were back in the car to comment. "Nadine?" she echoed. "You couldn't have come up with anything better?"

He smiled angelically. "I could have told the truth, but I don't think my dad would have approved."

"To say nothing of your uncle."

His expression went blank for a moment, then he nodded. "Yeah, him, too." After another moment, he asked, "You still mad at him?"

"I'm not supposed to get mad at him. He's part of my job. An interview subject."

"Yeah, well, you're also not supposed to be kissing him, I bet."

Too true. She certainly shouldn't be thinking along those lines after he'd called her pathetic. *Pathetic!* And the hell of it was…he was right. Every major decision she'd ever made had been done with her father in mind. Where to go to college? His alma mater, of course. What to major in? His career field. Where to work, what to write, how to write—all decided for or with him. When she'd researched and written the infamous corruption series, the thought that this would make him proud had always been there in the back of her mind. When she'd accepted its awards, she'd given him credit for it all, and he'd been her primary reason for accepting this job with Chaney.

She was thirty-one years old. Old enough to have replaced Daddy as the most important man in her life. More than old enough to have figured out how to live her life for herself.

"You're right," she said briskly. "I shouldn't be losing my temper with him, and I certainly shouldn't be kissing him. I'll try to see that neither happens again in the future."

"That's not what I meant. I was thinking maybe you should lighten up a bit on the rules. He likes you a lot, and you obviously like him. Why not make the most of it?"

She gave him a steady look as she dipped an onion ring in ketchup. "Have you been talking to Michaela?"

"Michae—you mean, Mike. Uh-uh. Why?"

"Never mind. And by the way, she's decided to go by Michaela."

"Why?"

"Because it's her name. Because Mike is a boy's name and she's a girl." At his blank look, Natalie rolled her eyes. Michaela might have enjoyed being Jordan's best buddy for sixteen years, but she was going to face an uphill battle now, getting him to accept her as a girl or maybe even a prospective girlfriend.

Jordan gave a shake of his head as if clearing away all distractions, and, that easily, Michaela was gone. "Anyway, about you and Uncle J.T.... Why can't you, like, be his girlfriend? You just have to agree that he won't interfere with your book and you'll mind your own business."

"News flash, Jordan—I have a contract at home that gives me a substantial sum of money for writing this book, along with the potential for even more substantial future earnings. Since your uncle is part of the book, everything about him *is* my business."

He considered that while he finished his first hamburger and folded back the wrapper on the second, then shook his head. "I don't think so. I don't think someone can just decide that you've got the right to go nosing around someone else's private life."

"Maybe it shouldn't be that way, but it is," she said gently. "Your uncle's father is a public figure. That puts J.T. in the spotlight whether he wants to be there or not."

"It's not fair."

"No, it isn't, but..."

"Life isn't fair," they said in unison.

After a moment Jordan went on. "He doesn't act this way about a lot of women. I mean, he could. There are a lot of women who'd like to go out with him or even get married or whatever. But he stays pretty busy taking care of the ranch and the family and me. I mean, just in case you're thinking he kisses every woman who comes around. 'Cause he doesn't. I can't even remember the last time.''

"You're very fond of him, aren't you?"

"Of course. He's my...my uncle, and I love him like...a father.''

Natalie's respect for Lucinda Rawlins and all she'd given her children took a giant leap. How many teenage boys could admit to loving an uncle—heavens, to loving *anyone*, with the possible exception of their mothers—without embarrassment? Her father was sixty-one years old, and she couldn't remember a time when words of love had come easily to him.

Of course, that wasn't necessarily reticence. It was quite possible that he just didn't have any love to offer.

Not wanting to consider that, she turned as far toward Jordan as the seat and the steering wheel would allow. "How was last night's date with Shelley?"

A grin spread across his face, making him look young, innocent and so much like J.T. "It was okay."

"That's a whole lot more than an 'okay' grin."

"We had a good time."

"When are you going out again?"

He gathered their wrappers and stuffed them into a bag, climbed out without opening the door and tossed it into the trash can, then came back, climbing in the same way. "I don't know. She's seeing this guy named Kevin who used to live here before his family moved to Tulsa, and they keep a boat on the lake over by Burning Bow, so whenever they come down, she's always hanging out with him. And she goes out with my friend Steve sometimes, and this guy in Dixon her older sister introduced her to."

Even if Natalie hadn't instinctively disliked Shelley on sight, that bit of news would have swayed her to the dark side. It had been her experience as an awkward teenage girl that at a time when dating was vitally important, there weren't enough boys of datable quality to go around—a situation that she doubted had changed in the past fifteen years. Where did Shelley get off claiming four of them—probably the best four—for herself while deserving girls like Michaela sat home alone?

"Does it bother you that she sees these other guys?"

"Well, sure, I'd like to be the only one, but…it's not like I'm looking to get married or anything. There's a lot I want to do before I settle down in ten or twelve or twenty years. I don't want to be like my dad—still a kid and stuck here and raising my own kid. I mean, I'm real grateful he did it, but I'm gonna be grown myself before I have any kids. However…"

He grinned again, the innocence replaced by a sly quality, and still he reminded her of his uncle. "J.T., on the other hand, is a one-woman man. If he's going out with some woman, then she's the only one he sees until it's over. He's not big at all on playing the field."

She couldn't help but chuckle. "How does J.T. feel, knowing that you're approaching single women on his behalf?"

"He doesn't know. Actually, you're the first one I've approached. I mean, he's gotta show some interest first, and you're the only woman he's shown any interest in in a long time. I'd be willing to bet he's the only man you've shown any interest in, too. I mean, besides the senator and all his kids and everything."

"Repeat after me," she said as she started the engine. "Conflict of interest. Inappropriate conduct. Long distance. Your uncle's life is here. Mine is in Alabama."

"You have a computer, a modem, a phone. Seems to me you can write anywhere."

She was about to point out to him that there was more to a life than work, but the truth made her keep her silence. Other people's lives maybe, but not hers. Her life had always had a fairly narrow focus. In school she'd always been the new kid, not particularly pretty or outgoing, never quite fitting in, always working hard at keeping up her grades in spite of their frequent moves. In college and later in the real world, she'd been ambitious and driven. She'd wanted the best assignments, the hardest-hitting stories, the ones that drew attention and won awards along with acclaim. The ones that would make Thaddeus proud. Until Candace, her friendships had been superficial. So had her romances.

After Candace, she'd had neither friendships nor romances.

This book would make up for that…eventually. Never having written a book before, her best guess at a time frame was simply that, but she figured she had another six to twelve months of research, interviews and writing to do, followed by revisions, then the wait until publication. Two years, maybe more, maybe less.

Two years to continue living as she had for the past fifteen months and, to some extent, her entire life. Alone.

That was a depressing thought. To chase it from her mind, she backed out of the parking space, then commanded of Jordan, "Give me that nickel tour you bragged about."

A short while later, as they headed back to the ranch, Natalie acknowledged that there had been more to see than she'd expected. He'd shown her the football and baseball fields where he was a local hero, like his father before him, along with the church they attended, the bars J.T. and Tate had gotten thrown out of a time or two and the jail they'd gotten thrown into some of those times. She'd also seen his schools, the small lake where all the local kids learned to swim and the imposing house looking down on the town that Shelley called home.

They had run into several of his male friends, who had eyed the Mustang enviously, and several female friends, who'd eyed *him* enviously, along with adults who were clearly fond of him. All things considered, Jordan's life and his town were damn near perfect. This was the sort of growing-up experience she would want for her child…if she ever had one. But that wasn't likely to happen if she didn't learn to put the job aside long enough to meet some suitable guy.

But she'd already met a suitable guy, a voice in her head whispered. Handsome, sexy, faithful, a family man, and he liked her. He *wanted* her, too.

Enough to wait a year or more until the book was completed?

Enough to stand by her when the book—and the truth about his parentage—came out? She couldn't imagine it, and as a writer she was blessed with a fertile imagination. But then, she'd never had any experience with men who stuck around through the tough times. J.T. seemed different from every man she'd ever met. Maybe he really was.

There was no sign of him when they got back to the ranch. She wondered if he was off working somewhere on the property—the pickup was gone from its usual space between the house and the barn—or if he'd needed a break…from her. She asked Jordan where she might find him, and his response was a shrug, accompanied by a sweeping gesture that took in the entire countryside. With a thanks for his company and for lunch, she left him on his own stoop and climbed the steps to the breezeway that separated their quarters.

The first thing she noticed as she unlocked the door was that the doorbell had been replaced. The second was the scents that hung faintly in the air when she stepped inside the utility room—sunshine, sweat, leather, grease. The third, as she walked into the kitchen, was the desk. The dining table had been pushed into the corner, and a desk stood where it had been. It wasn't as massive as the oak desk in J.T.'s office, but it was solid, had plenty of room for her papers and, more important, was the right height for working. So was the padded secretary's chair parked in front of it.

Her laptop sat in the center of the work surface, along with an adjustable lamp and a coffee mug to corral the ink pens she'd left lying around. The boxes containing the bulk of her research were neatly stacked under the table, and the files she'd left out had been gathered in a plastic file box.

The last addition was a bulletin board, as wide as the desk and tilted against the wall. Multicolored push pins were lined up along the bottom of the wooden frame, awaiting something to hold.

Wearing a tremulous smile, she pulled out the chair and slid into it. It was well used, worn to a comfortable state, and was going to be so much better for her back than the wooden kitchen chair she'd been using.

It was a simple thing, really—and quite possibly the most thoughtful thing anyone had ever done for her.

Spying her camera on the table where she'd left it, she turned on the computer, then downloaded the single picture she'd taken that morning before J.T. had removed the camera from her. After a bit of tinkering, she set it up as the background for the computer screen, then slouched back in the chair, looked at it and sighed wistfully. Longingly.

He wore dusty, nicely faded jeans that hugged his lean hips and muscular thighs, a white T-shirt that fitted snugly and a straw cowboy hat the color of cream. Just a hint of damp, dark hair curled under the hat in back, and the brim cast a shadow that blocked his face from view except for a bit of beard-stubbled, stubborn jaw. How easily she could envision him gracing a postcard touting Oklahoma tourist attractions or a hunk-of-the-month Wonders of the West calendar.

How easily she could envision him gracing her bed.

"Oh…you're back."

Startled by J.T.'s voice, Natalie jumped, then folded the screen toward the keyboard, blocking the photo from sight. Getting to her feet, she rested both hands on the back of the chair—which sounded so much better than saying she gripped it for dear life. "Thanks for all this. You didn't have to go to so much trouble, but…I really appreciate it."

His dark gaze was wary, his manner endearingly awkward. "It wasn't any trouble. I should have thought of it sooner." He looked down at the tools he held as if he'd forgotten why he had them, then gestured. "I need to tighten some screws on the chair. It's pretty sturdy considering it's been in Jordan's room the past year or so, but it needs a little…tightening.''

She backed away, and he set the wrenches down, then easily turned the chair upside down. "Is the desk his, too?"

"Yeah."

"Won't he need it when school starts?"

J.T.'s grin was the first natural gesture he'd made since walking in. "Nah. He just uses it for holding his dirty clothes. He does his homework at the kitchen table or in the living room—always has. He says he learns better with distractions."

"Life is filled with distractions," she murmured, trying not to stare too openly at her own greatest distraction. "Better that he learns to deal with them while he's young."

"Yeah." Finishing with his task, he stood up, righted the chair, then rested his hands on it—gripped it—as she had earlier.

"The, uh, desk looks…heavy." For someone who earned her living with words, she was having trouble thinking of them at the moment. "How did you…get it over here alone?"

"Mike came over to borrow my truck. She helped. She informed me that in the future, I should call her by her given name. You have something to do with that?"

"Not me. I'm as innocent as the day is long."

Slowly he grinned again, and his voice dropped into bone-melting range. "Oh, I doubt that, darlin'. You haven't been innocent since you were nineteen. You have found someone who wasn't in too much of a hurry since then, haven't you? Because around here we're taught to take it slow, make it good and make it last."

She tried to swallow, but her throat was tight, and the heat searing her lungs made breathing difficult. "You…" To her own ears, she sounded choked, strangled and… embarrassed? Or was that aroused? "You are…"

"Yes?"

Finally forcing a breath into her chest, she exhaled loudly. "You are a tease."

"Yes, ma'am. We're taught that, too."

"So is that an Oklahoma thing, a cowboy thing or a Rawlins thing?"

"Maybe all three of the above. My brother can talk a woman out of her clothes in nothing flat, and my grandmother says my granddaddy could charm the feathers off a bird in the dead of winter."

"And what do they say about you?"

"That I'm a good son," he replied with a look that almost pulled off being angelic. "A hard worker, in church most Sundays, reliable, dependable and a good neighbor. That any woman would be lucky to have me, even for a week or two."

A chill swept through Natalie, making her knees unsteady and erasing the smile from her face. She went to the kitchen, intending to fix herself a Diet Coke so she would have something to occupy her hands. Instead of opening the refrigerator, though, she took a pan from the cabinet, measured water and sugar into it and set it on the stove, then counted out tea bags while she waited for the water to boil.

Finally, her gaze on the corral out back where Michaela's horse shared space with Jordan's new mare, she quietly asked, "Is that all there could be between us—a week or two?"

He moved so quietly that she didn't realize it until he spoke from a few feet behind her. "Or however long you stay. Sooner or later, though, you have to leave. Mom can't stay at her folks' place forever."

And Lucinda didn't want to set foot in her home while Natalie was there. On a professional level, she completely understood the woman's position. On a personal level, it stung.

"When..." She moistened her lips, tried to see him in her peripheral gaze without moving her head, then settled again for the view outside. "When the book is finished and turned in to my editor...I could come back..."

"No. You couldn't."

He said it with such finality, leaving no room for argument, offering no unspoken plea to be persuaded. He was willing to sleep with her now, to make the most of this attraction between them, but when her work here ended, so would their affair. Once the manuscript was completed, once it became a mere matter of time until everyone with the price of a book or access to a library could discover the secrets of his and his mother's past, he wanted nothing more to do with her.

That said an awful lot about the depth of his feelings, didn't it?

"I'm sorry, Natalie."

He laid his hand on her shoulder, but she jerkily moved away, leaving it to fall to his side. "Don't be. Better to know now than to let myself think there might be something..." Her voice did *not* quaver on the last word. She swallowed, took a breath and forced a smile to make sure of it.

"It's just—"

Just that some things were unforgivable. That whatever attracted him to her wasn't so very strong or unusual, after all. That he liked women and being single. It was just one of a hundred possible answers. Or maybe it was no answer at all.

It was just the way things were.

"My mother was raised in Georgia. Did I mention that?" she asked as she removed a pretty crystal pitcher from the cabinet. "Even though her family moved away when she graduated from high school, she never lost her accent, or her fondness for all things Southern. Every day she made a pitcher of tea, boiling sugar and water into syrup, then steeping the tea bags in it. I remember watching her run hot water into the pitcher, so the hot tea wouldn't make it shatter. Then she added cold water, then filled a glass with ice and then with tea, and after giving the glass a swirl, she took the first drink. She always smiled after that first sip—*always,* as if she'd just recalled a wonderful memory."

She filled her own glass with ice and tea, gave it a swirl, then watched the ice start to melt. This tea wouldn't taste the same as her mother's had. Her mother had always added one mint tea bag to her pot, but Natalie was fresh out of mint. But its taste would be familiar—sweet enough, strong enough, to taste like home.

J.T. looked as if he didn't know what to say. She might have taken pity on him if he hadn't just taken some of the hope from her future. Since he had, she remained silent.

"I, uh…guess I'd better get back to work."

He got as far as the hall, then turned back. Whatever he'd been about to say, though, he apparently thought better of it. With a regretful shake of his head, he walked out.

Natalie added more ice to her tea, then returned to the desk. After plugging the laptop's modem into the phone line, she signed onto the Internet, opened the mailbox and attached the photograph of J.T. to an e-mail.

"Dear Senator," she typed. "It's obviously not a great picture, but, unlike you and the rest of the clan, J.T. is camera shy. I'll get his face in the next one. Promise."

Wednesday marked the start of Natalie's third week in Oklahoma and the first day of school for Jordan. Tate hated to see classes start again, and not just because he lost his best helper. More accurately, he hated giving up his buffer. Without Jordan to place between them, how were he and Natalie going to get along?

Not that they'd had much problem since Saturday. On the rare occasions they'd been alone, either they'd talked about her damn book or not at all. Like most people, he enjoyed talking about himself—the interest was flattering. But in this instance…if even one of the thousand and one questions she'd asked him had been remotely colored with personal interest, he still would have been flattered. But the questions had been routine, and the subject—him—unimportant. For all the curiosity she showed, he could have been any one of Josh's worthless half siblings.

He was on his way out of the house after lunch when the phone rang. The temptation to let the machine pick up was great, but Natalie spent too much time in the house. If he or Jordan accidentally played the message while she was within earshot, and it happened to be Josh or their mother or one of a few thousand people who knew he was Tate and not his kid brother...

"Hello."

"There's nothing quite like hearing the cranky grumble of my firstborn's voice to brighten the middle of my day."

He smiled in spite of his mood. "How are things going, Mom? Grandpop and Josh still on speaking terms?"

"*Shouting* is more like it. You know them."

He certainly did. They were frustrating, entertaining, annoying, patience wearing...and amazingly alike. AnnaMae's theory was that they saw themselves in each other—not only the good, but also the bad—but Tate thought it went deeper. His personal theory was that Grandpop was tough on Josh because he figured someday Josh would need to be tough himself. Someday the truth about Chaney would come out, and he'd wanted Josh to be able to deal with it.

Well, someday was almost here...but Tate wasn't sure how well Josh was going to deal with anything. His solution so far—persuading Tate to masquerade as him while he ran off to Grandpop's to hide—was far from ideal. Tate couldn't pretend for him once the book came out. He couldn't handle all the questions and curiosity, couldn't live the changes that were sure to come...though he would if he could.

"Hellooo? Sweetheart?"

Blinking, Tate refocused his attention on the phone. "Sorry, Mom. I was thinking... Did I miss something?"

"I asked when that woman's leaving. I'd dearly love to come home while I'm still young enough to remember the way."

"I don't... We haven't discussed..."

After a moment's silence, Lucinda spoke, a cautious tone to her voice. "What do you think of this Natalie Grant? Is she a fire-breathing dragon? Does she have horns and a pitchfork and belch the fires of hell?"

"She has red hair curling practically to her waist, blue eyes and a Southern drawl, and she could make most men forget their names by doing nothing more than walking into a room."

"Has she made you forget the name you're borrowing?"

"No. Of course not."

Another thoughtful silence, then, "Don't blame me for asking. I just thought you sounded a bit smitten."

"What would it matter if I were? I'm lying to her. I'm pretending to be someone I'm not. Those aren't things that are easily forgiven."

"Oh, Tate, you've gone and fallen for Ms. Alabama. Of all the bad luck."

His smile was bleak and thin. "Runs in the family, doesn't it? Lucky at life, unlucky at—" He didn't finish, didn't want to even think the word *love* in connection with himself or Natalie.

"How serious?"

Absently he rubbed one hand over the muscles knotted in his stomach. "It's no big deal. I'll survive." One miserable day at a time. One lonely day at a time. "I'll find out how much longer she'll be here, then let you know."

Lucinda sighed regretfully. "It's a mess, isn't it? And it's all Boyd's fault. I would wish I'd never met him, except then I wouldn't have Josh. I just wish—"

"What?" he prompted when she didn't go on.

Seconds ticked past, marked by the hum on the line, before she replied. "I wish things had turned out differently. I wish I'd made better decisions. I wish you boys hadn't suffered for my bad judgment."

"We haven't suffered," he said dryly. "Our lives have

been pretty good, considering. As for this thing with Natalie…I'll get over it.''

"You shouldn't *have* to get over it. I've waited thirty-four years for you to get smitten with some lovely young woman and give me more grandbabies, and now that you've met her, my mistakes are forcing you apart.''

"Which mistake? Me or Josh?''

"You hush! You know, I *will* be back home before long, and I can still swat you just like I did when you were a boy. I was referring to my decision to keep Josh's connection to Boyd a secret.''

"You had that right,'' Tate pointed out. "No one but Josh has a right to that information. If you want to blame someone, blame Chaney for needing more time in the limelight. *He's* the one who chose to expose us. *He's* the one who made it necessary for us to lie.'' He paused, opened his mouth, then closed it, then opened it again. "Were you in love with him?''

Again there was nothing but a hum for a long moment. It was broken by a sigh that sounded part regretful and part wistful. "He was the most charming man I'd ever known—handsome, wealthy, powerful—and he adored me. He used to come into the restaurant where I worked, and he flirted with me like all the men did, but there was something different with him. He…*meant* it…at least, for a time.'' Her tone switched, became more harsh. "Yes, I loved him. I know that's not the answer you want to hear, but it's true. Even though he turned his back on me and denied his son, even though he cared far more for his political career than for me, I loved him dearly.''

That sounded almost as if there should be a tag at the end—*and I still do*. Tate didn't want to ask if she did, if that was why her feelings for the men she'd dated in the past twenty-five years had never gone past friendship.

He didn't want to know.

After a time Lucinda spoke again. "Well, I'd better let you get to work. Let me know when I can come back home—and be warned, your granny's threatening to come with me, to get a break from the Battling Rawlins Boys. Give my love to Jordan.''

"I will.''

"And know I love you, too.''

"I do. Love you.''

After hanging up, he left the house by the back door— and came to a sudden stop halfway down the steps.

Natalie knelt beside a flower bed ten feet away, dead-heading Lucinda's marigolds. She wore a sleeveless dress with a full skirt that ended well past her knees, sandals and a floppy straw hat with an electric-blue ribbon around the brim, and she looked incredible. If only the grass were thick and green instead of parched August yellow, she would look the picture of Southern belle perfection.

Even with the straw-colored grass, she looked pretty damn perfect.

He took the remaining steps one at a time, then approached her. "I figured Jordan was taking care of Mom's flowers. I didn't know it was you. She'll appreciate it.''

"I can't have flowers at home. I live in an apartment.''

"Don't you have a balcony or a porch?''

"Yes, but flowers need attention. I've spent too much time away in the past year.''

"That's what friends are for—to pick up your mail, water your plants.''

"I don't have that kind of friends.'' She pinched off the last dead flower, dusted her hands and got easily to her feet. When she eased a few steps closer to her half of the house, he knew he should let her go without another word. When she hesitated, he knew that wasn't going to happen.

"If you're not busy, why don't you grab your camera and go for a ride with me?''

Wariness shadowed her eyes. "A ride…in the truck?''

"Yes, in the truck.'' Not that he wouldn't like to get her on a horse—particularly *his* horse, where she would have to sit close.

"Where?"

"Out there." He waved toward the pasture and beyond.

She looked in that direction, as if she could see more than the barn and a bit of scrubby pasture, as if whatever she couldn't see might make the decision for her. Finally, she nodded. "Should I change?"

"Only if you'd be more comfortable." He hoped not. He liked her looking so delicate and feminine. Of course, he liked her in jeans, too, and shorts and those snug little dresses that barely reached midthigh. In fact, he hadn't yet seen her in anything that he *didn't* like...though he hadn't yet had the chance to see her in nothing at all.

"I'll be right back."

He watched the slow, easy way she walked until she was out of sight, then wiped his forehead on his sleeve. It was too damn hot today to be thinking of anything that raised his internal temperature. He could already use a cold shower. A few hours in the truck with her, and the shower would go from beneficial to vital.

With long strides, he walked to the truck parked in front of the barn. By the time he'd driven back to the point where the driveway passed closest to the house, Natalie had returned with her bag—and she hadn't changed clothes.

Once she settled in, he circled the barn and followed the well-worn road across the pasture to the south timber. When Lucinda had bought the ranch, more than half the acreage had been timber. He'd made it a priority to clear a section every year, though he knew he'd never get rid of it all, or even want to. But every acre that was bulldozed free of timber was another acre that could be planted in grass. Besides, probably 90 percent of the trees was scrub oak or cedar—trash trees, in his estimation. Hell, probably 90 percent of the state was scrub oak and cedar. Nobody would miss the ones he dozed and burned.

"When you have children of your own—" Natalie broke off as the truck bounced across exposed sandstone that was a creek bottom when the rains came. She braced herself, stretching out one leg and gripping the door handle tightly with her right hand. "What are you going to tell them about Senator Chaney?"

"No questions for your book."

"But—"

"If there's something *you* want to know, ask, but no questions for the book." He didn't want to spend the afternoon lying to her, or to continue the deception any more than necessary, just for the next few hours.

She fell silent and remained that way so long that finally he turned on the radio. Just today he'd thought her questions had been routine, tinged with a lack of interest in the subject. Now, in not thinking of a single thing she as a woman wanted to know about him, she'd proven him right when he would much rather be wrong.

Dolly Parton was halfway through an old hit when Natalie leaned forward to shut off the radio. "You call that music?"

"The best. What do you listen to?"

"Classic rock from the sixties and seventies. Nothing more recent than 1980 is allowed to assault my tender ears."

"What—were you frightened by some pop group in your childhood?"

His dry comment, a takeoff on her earlier question about disliking reporters, made her smile smugly. "Just blessed with extraordinary taste."

He'd missed that smile—had missed seeing pleasure in her blue eyes. Seeing it now eased the tension in the muscles in his neck and made his fingers loosen their grip on the steering wheel. "We'll see how extraordinary your taste is. What's your favorite type of movie?"

"Action thrillers. I want to watch people kick butt. Yours?"

"Mysteries and scary movies from the fifties. Books?"

"Nonfiction. What about you?"

"Mysteries and early science fiction."

"Let's talk food. Do you like chicken or beef?"

He gave her a chiding look before gesturing to the Braeford cattle grazing in the distance. "You don't see any chicken coops around here, do you?"

"Wine or beer?"

"Beer, if those are my only choices."

"Seafood or fried catfish?"

"Catfish, of course. No fair when I'm the only one answering."

"I like beef. If wine and beer are my only choices, I'll go thirsty until I can have more choices. I love shrimp and scallops and oysters and crab legs, but nothing beats a done-to-perfection catfish fillet. Now here's the important one—barbecue. Beef or pork?"

He could tell by her expression that she expected him to remain loyal to his profession. With his own grin matching hers for smugness, he replied, "Pork."

"Good answer. There's a saying in parts of the South—if it ain't pork, it ain't barbecue. One more—the sauce. Tomato-, mustard- or vinegar-based?"

"Tomato."

She made an obnoxious noise that sounded remarkably like a buzzer. "And you came so close. Tomato's okay, vinegar's better and mustard is the best. If I were going to be here longer, I'd have some delivered and fix the best ribs you've ever had. But..."

She *wasn't* going to be around long. He'd reminded her Saturday that she would have to leave soon and had told his mother he would remind her again. But not now. It could wait.

He stopped the truck where a fence crossed the road. "You want to get out and open the gate, or slide over here and drive through while I get it?"

"What gate?" she asked blankly.

He chuckled. The gate consisted of a weathered pole, five strands of barbwire and a rusted wire loop that attached the pole to the fence post. In all fairness, with the weeds grown up taller than the post, he could see how easily she might mistake the contraption for just another section of fence.

After he pointed out everything to her, she opened the door and slid to the ground. "Watch out for copperheads in the weeds," he called before she could close the door, and she immediately climbed back in.

"I'll drive," she said sternly. "*You* get snakebit."

He opened the rickety gate, waited for her to pass, then secured it again. When he slid back into the driver's seat, she asked, "Where are we going, anyway?"

"In search of an old American tradition. We're going buffalo hunting."

Chapter Ten

Natalie was entranced when they found the small herd nearly an hour later, grazing between a stand of trees that provided shade and a small pond that offered water. There was one bull, six cows and three calves, and even the smallest baby was massive.

J.T. parked about twenty yards away, and she climbed out, camera clutched in one hand. When she started to move forward, he caught a handful of her dress and pulled her back. "Buffalo aren't the most even-tempered creatures on earth, and in spite of their size, they can move damn fast. The bull is especially aggressive with the calves around." He pulled her to the back of the truck, gave her a boost, then joined her in the truck bed.

"They're magnificent," she murmured as she used the long lens on her camera to get a closer look. "Aren't they beautiful?"

"Yeah, they are." Then he shook his head. "Actually, no, they aren't. I respect them and admire their resiliency after being hunted almost to extinction, but they're big, ugly, moth-eaten and dangerous. *Not* beautiful.''

No sooner had he finished insulting the creatures than the bull looked up. His gaze seemed to narrow as he took a few steps their way.

Natalie laughed. ''I think you owe him an apology. I don't believe he cared for that moth-eaten remark.''

''Well, sometimes the truth hurts, doesn't it, fella?''

It certainly did, she silently agreed. J.T.'s truth—that all he wanted from her was sex, and even that only on a short-term basis—had hurt, and still did.

She concentrated on snapping photos of the herd, focusing her lens repeatedly on the babies. They were incredible, and made her feel insignificant in comparison. ''Is there a market for buffalo?''

''The meat is getting more and more popular. It's lower in fat than most cuts of beef and pretty flavorful. Vern—he owns these guys—just keeps them for sentimental reasons.''

''I don't blame him. I would, too, if I could.''

''You can't even leave flowers at home,'' he reminded her. ''What would you do with a cute, cuddly, two-hundred-pound baby buffalo?''

If she had some land, she could fence in a pasture with three-inch pipe and just keep him there to look at, she thought whimsically. She would name him Bartholomew— or how about Bartholo*muse?*—and he could be her inspiration to write every day, since without writing, there'd be no money for food, and a buffalo without food most likely was neither a pretty nor a happy sight.

''Maybe,'' she said in response to his question, ''I'd buy him a place of his own.'' The profits from the Chaney book ought to make *someone* happy. ''Then I'd have a home where the buffalo roam.''

He winced at her humor. ''Maybe you should start with a dog or cat. If you can handle that, then you could move up to a pony or a llama, and gradually work your way up to the big boys.''

"You have no sense of adventure, J.T."

"I'm a rancher, darlin'. My year can be ruined by rain, hot weather, cold weather, sickness, fluctuations in the market, too much government interference, not enough government intervention. I think I'm pretty damn adventurous. I'm still in business. I'm still standing."

She took a few more pictures, then lowered the camera. "Did you always want to be a rancher?"

He leaned against the cab as if the surface wasn't so hot the thick rubber soles of her sandals felt squishy when she shifted her weight. "Nah. When I was a kid, I wanted to be an astronaut, a race car driver and a cop. When I found out that cops actually had to have a reason for putting someone in jail, I marked it off the list."

She wondered if there had been someone in particular he'd wanted locked up...such as his father.

"When I got older, I wanted to play ball, join the Army, learn to fly. Or go to college and sample a little bit of every major until I found the career I wanted. Or become a vet." He shrugged self-consciously. "I was a kid with every possible option available to me. I figured I didn't really have to choose until I was twenty, maybe twenty-five."

"But you chose to stay here and do none of those things. I understand why Tate stayed—he was stuck. He had no choice. But you had all the choices."

His dark gaze narrowed under the brim of his hat. "Tate wasn't stuck. He had options, too. He just chose the one that was best for both him and Jordan."

He was protective of his brother, a trait she found endearing. How much better would her life have been if she'd had a brother or sister to look out for her? To share the burden of her father's expectations, to make up for his absences and the emotional distance he always kept from her? How much less lonely would her life have been?

"Did you go to college?" she asked to distract herself from a melancholy she didn't want to feel.

"Nope. Never went anywhere or did anything."

"Do you regret it?"

"Not for an instant." His voice vibrated with intensity and unshakable certainty. "Maybe, because family has always come first with Mom, it's become that way with the rest of us. We may not be exactly traditional, what with Tate, Jordan and me all being illegitimate, but we stick together. We look out for each other. Maybe I didn't go around saying 'When I grow up, I want to be a rancher,' but I can't imagine doing anything else or living anywhere else. I can't imagine not having my brother nearby, or my mother or Jordan. These weeks you've been here is the longest Jordan and I have ever been apart from them."

For a long time she simply looked at him—so long, in fact, that he shifted uncomfortably before sullenly asking, "I sound like a sap, don't I?"

"Not at all. You sound like a man who truly appreciates the meaning of family. That's rare in this world. But…it makes me wonder how you can be that *connected* to the family you know, and not have the least bit of interest in the one you've never met."

"Maybe I'm just not a curious man. But you know what, Ms. Alabama? I wonder how family can be so important to *you,* and yet you're afraid to track down your mother's family. Why is that?"

"I told you they didn't like my father. There was a lot of bitterness between them. If he found out I was looking for them, he would never speak to me again."

"But he hasn't spoken to you in more than a year, anyway. He didn't send you a birthday card. Didn't call you and say, 'Congratulations on landing the Chaney biography.' Didn't invite you to spend last Christmas with him. Your mother's family probably would have been thrilled to hear from you at any time in that year. Your grandparents, aunts, uncles and cousins would have welcomed you for every holiday…if you weren't too big a coward to find them."

Was she a coward? Or merely cautious? After all, her

relationship with her father was difficult enough without adding direct disobedience into the mix.

What relationship? J.T. would ask. You couldn't claim a relationship when you didn't speak, see each other or have any contact at all.

From nowhere came a lazy breeze that rustled through the trees and carried with it the faint scent of rain. Natalie closed her eyes and breathed deeply and imagined the temperature cooled a few degrees. Through the loose weave of her hat, she felt the relief on her face when a cloud drifted over the sun, and she smiled wistfully. "Clouds, wind and the smell of rain. Is there a chance? Or is nature being unbearably cruel today?"

She opened her eyes in time to see J.T. scan the sky, and she did the same. To the east and the south, the sky looked exactly as it had every day she'd been in the state—no clouds, pale blue, a wash of color that the relentless heat shimmering in the air rendered thin and stark. To the north and west, though, clouds gathered low on the horizon. They, too, were leached of their stronger colors by sun and distance, making them appear soft gray, lavender, pale blue.

"The forecast didn't call for rain, but we could get some, if that squall line can hold together long enough to get here."

She would wager she wanted the rain as much as he did. She felt parched and in dire need of cool liquid relief. If it came, she would dance in it, or at least stand outside and welcome it.

"We'd better get going." J.T. jumped to the ground, then reached up to lift her down. His hands were big and warm at her waist. She felt their strength, their calluses, their power, through the thin cotton of her dress, all the way through her soul. She wanted him to never let go, but sadly he did...for a moment. His gaze searched her face so intensely she could actually feel it, then he raised his hand. Seconds ticked past as his fingertips hovered a mere inch away, making the air between them tingle and simmer.

When finally he touched her, callused fingers against her cheek, she felt the pleasure and the heat and the shock of it through her entire body. Her eyes just naturally drifted shut in response, and she leaned into the contact, craving more.

The pad of his thumb slid along her jaw, then swept up to brush her lower lip. Her breath caught, and she murmured, "Are you going to kiss me?"

"Do you want me to?" His voice was hoarse, thick, and it wrapped around her, drawing a response from her that required no thought, no reason or logic.

"Yes."

He swept the big-brimmed hat from her head, then cupped her face in his palms, tilted her face up and brushed his mouth across hers, side to side with the lightest of pressure. It was innocent, barely a start, and tempted her with more. Promised her so much more.

He took his sweet time, deepening the pressure, sliding his tongue along her lips, gliding it between and coaxing her teeth apart. His tongue stroked hers, explored, teased, tasted, all with a lazy sense that he had all the time in the world. No reason to rush, no reason to kick up the intensity into full gear. No reason…except she wanted more. She wanted blistering passion, wanted to make the very air steam. She wanted to grab hold and kiss him as if she would die without him.

She raised her hands to his wrists, and her camera bumped against her as it dangled from its strap. Blindly she made her way along his arms to his shoulders, then wrapped her arms around his neck and pulled him closer. For a moment he resisted, but she needed the contact, needed to feel his body against hers.

The instant she pressed her hips against his arousal, he seemed to forget all about taking it slow and easy. He slid his hands the length of her body until they cupped her bottom hard against him, and he took possession of her mouth. There was nothing sweet about *this* kiss. It was wild and hungry and reckless and hot, and it seared through her, leaving raw, jagged need in its wake. It lasted forever…and was over in an instant. He freed her bit by bit, until they each took a step back, then stared at each other.

Natalie wanted to throw herself back into his arms. To climb into the truck as if nothing had happened. To rush off someplace quiet and dark, curl up in a ball and weep. To beg, plead, bargain, for one more kiss.

What she did was look at him. She suspected her face mirrored the emotions clearly visible on his. Desire. Arousal. Surprise. Regret. He looked as if he wanted to say something but didn't have a clue what. She felt the same.

She didn't know how long they'd stood there when a cloud passing overhead reminded her of the heat, the sun and her hat, lying forgotten on the ground where it had tumbled. She picked it up, gave it a shake, then clamped it on her head. Feeling somewhat protected under its brim, she gave a laugh that came out part sigh. "Well…you definitely get the prize for best kiss."

He didn't look amused. "Natalie…"

She waited. If he said he couldn't kiss her again, she was going to smack him. If he reminded her that she could have so much more but only until this trip ended, she would smack him hard.

But after a moment's silence, he shook his head and gestured toward the truck. "We'd better head back."

With a nod she walked the short distance to the pickup. She settled in the seat and put her camera away, then gave the buffalo one last look as they drove away.

They really were beautiful. She intended to frame pictures of them when she got back to Montgomery, and every time she looked at them she would remember this day, and that kiss.

She would probably be the only woman in the world who cried at the sight of buffalo.

For more years than Tate could recall, the first Friday night of the new school year was set aside for the first pep rally, held at the football field. The team and cheerleaders were introduced, grilled burgers and hand-cranked ice cream were served, and the entire town turned out. He and Lucinda had been going for years, though Josh had missed a few since his own graduation.

But this year it was less than an hour until the rally was scheduled to start, and Tate was debating whether to go.

Jordan came into the kitchen, dressed in jeans and his green-and-gold Wildcats jersey. His hair was damp from his shower, his cheeks pink where he'd shaved off the millimeter of stubble that had grown through the day. "You know, it's okay if you don't want to go, Dad," he said, picking up the conversation they'd started before his shower.

"I do want to. I just—" Didn't want to tell Natalie they were headed off to have fun, but she wasn't welcome to go along. He didn't want her getting that look—the damn-I-know-it-shouldn't-hurt-but-it-does one—and he didn't want to try to enjoy the evening when he knew she was at home feeling left out.

"You could take her."

"Which would probably make us the center of attention. She's not exactly the wallflower sort. People look at her."

"People would look at any woman you showed up with. So let 'em look. Let 'em whisper."

"And let 'em come up and say, 'How about an introduction, Tate?'" He shook his head. "I convinced her old Mr. Littrell was mistaken when he called me by my name. What are the odds I can convince her that everyone who knows me has me confused with my brother?"

"So just tell her you've got something to do. We haven't talked about the rally. She won't have a clue."

Tate dragged his fingers through his hair. Not another lie…though, technically it wouldn't *be* a lie. And technically that rationale didn't fly. Not telling the truth was no less dishonest than telling a lie.

"Well, whatever you decide's okay with me," Jordan

said. "I've gotta get going. Coach wants us all there early. What time do I have to be home?"

"Midnight."

"Aw, Dad, nobody's got a curfew that early."

"They should. Besides, Michaela does. And Steve."

"It's a weekend. How about one? Twelve forty-five? Twelve thirty?"

"Keep whining, son, and we'll try eleven."

"Okay. See you."

Tate watched him go, then turned to gaze down the hall to the side door. As he walked out the door and crossed the deck to ring Lucinda's new doorbell, he wished he could take Natalie to the pep rally. It seemed the sort of thing she would get a kick out of—small-town living at its best. But the risks were too great. Someone would surely call him by his name, and someone else would call him Jordan's dad. In fact, a few of Jordan's girl friends usually greeted him with, "Hi, Jordan's dad."

When Natalie opened the door, Tate realized he'd interrupted her at work. Her red hair was piled on top of her head and somehow secured, and a pair of green-framed glasses rested halfway down her nose. The effect should have been spinsterish, but no spinster had ever had skin so creamy and silken, or lips so full and kissable, or incredible blue eyes that shimmered with delight and turned dusky with desire.

And no spinster would wear a ribbed tank top that hugged her every curve, or denim cutoffs that exposed virtually every inch of her mile-long legs. Certainly no spinster should have fire-engine-red toenails on slender, narrow feet that looked impossibly delicate.

Missing one pep rally in twenty years wasn't a big deal. Jordan had probably meant it when he'd said it was okay—more or less. He would understand. Besides, he was one of the honored guests. He would be too busy to notice that his old man wasn't around.

"Hey," Natalie greeted him, when he didn't say anything. "Come on in."

She led the way to the dining room, where she sat cross-legged in the desk chair and waited for him to speak.

The computer was on, with lines of words stretching across its screen, but he made no effort to read them. Instead he swept his gaze over the desk, which was so neatly organized it was frightening. When she'd first seen the disaster area that passed as his office, she'd made a comment about the Thaddeus Grant style of record keeping. He'd asked if that was her style, too, and she'd laughed. Now he knew why. Every bit of data on her desk was annotated, cross-referenced and color-coded within an inch of its life.

"I figured you were already gone," she remarked.

"Gone?"

"To town. To the pep rally/cookout/bonfire." His blank look seemed to amuse her. "It was in yesterday's newspaper."

He frowned. Of course they subscribed to the *Dixon Daily News,* the closest thing they had to a local paper and one that hadn't been a daily in ten years or more. He tossed them in a basket in the living room after he read them and hadn't once thought he should hide them from her. "When did you find time to read the newspaper?"

She laughed. "It *is* only eight pages, counting the ads. I read it while you were on the phone last night."

They'd been in the middle of their nightly game of ten thousand questions last evening when Jordan's coach had called. The conversation hadn't lasted five minutes, but apparently it had been long enough.

"So...are you going?"

"I don't..."

"Aw, come on. The paper said the football team and their families are all going to be there. Since Jordan's father and grandmother can't be there, you have to go."

"You don't mind?" At her nod, Tate had to admit to more than a little relief. Though he could have talked himself out of going, he would hate for Jordan to be the only kid on the team without any family there. "I wish I could ask you to go."

There was the briefest flash of wistfulness in her eyes. "It sounds like fun...but it would lead to too many questions, and it isn't part of our deal. Go on. Have a good time. I'll be working on the final questions I have for you. I've got to get all this information organized and see what subjects we haven't covered yet."

That sounded as if it were one of the final tasks before she packed up and headed home, and that was an idea he really couldn't face at the moment. "I should be home by nine."

"Stop by and tell me how it went."

With a nod he left, locking the door behind him. He drove into town, found a parking space at the middle school and walked the two blocks to the football field.

The rest of the county might have turned yellow and brown from the drought, but the field was so green that a person might mistake it for artificial turf. The parking lots around it were crowded, both with people and cars, and before he'd gone more than fifteen feet, at least five people called him by name.

Jordan sought him out soon after he arrived, handing him a can of pop, then looking around. "Damn. I was hoping you'd figure out a way to bring Natalie."

"Sorry."

"What did you tell her?"

"She already knew. It was in this week's paper."

"Good thing you didn't go in and lie to her, isn't it? Hey, you'd better watch out. Coach's wife's sister is visiting from Chicago, and Mrs. H. was asking if you're seeing anyone. I told her I didn't know, and she said she'd find out for herself."

Tate grimaced. Maxine Halloran fancied herself something of a matchmaker. True, many of those she targeted did wind up married, but he was convinced it was primarily so Maxie would leave them alone. "I'll watch out for her," he told Jordan before moving on.

For the next two and a half hours, he talked with old friends, caught up on all the news, ate, applauded the team members when they were introduced and narrowly avoided Maxie twice. But he really wasn't having much fun. How could he, when all he wanted was to go home and spend what was left of the evening with Natalie?

By the time the rally broke up, the sky was dark except for occasional flashes of lightning that speared across the sky. As Tate walked to his truck, he imagined he heard the rumble of distant thunder. A louder grumble that shook the ground convinced him it wasn't merely wishful thinking. It looked as if their luck was about to change, at least in some small way. What they needed was four or five straight days of a gentle soaker rain. What they were likely to get was a deluge that would dampen everything before running off and doing little, if any, good.

He drove home as he'd done hundreds of times after church or school functions…alone. But this time someone other than family was waiting for him. It was a good feeling, one that could easily be habit forming. Too bad it could never become habit.

The only lights on at the ranch were the ones *he'd* left burning—the pole-mounted light near the bar, another halfway between it and the house and a lamp in the living room. Had Natalie forgotten her invitation and gone on to bed?

He didn't think so.

He parked beside the Mustang, went into the house and tossed his keys on the counter. Sensing something out of place, he stood motionless, then realized what it was—music. Coming from the deck. Country music.

At the side door he tilted the blinds so he could see out. Though the lights were off, Natalie was easy enough to spot. The flashes of lightning that came more frequently gleamed on her pale skin and the copper-penny curls that haloed her head. She was standing at the railing, face tilted to the sky, and her arms were open wide as if welcoming the rain to come.

His chest tightened, and a knot formed in his gut. She was so damn beautiful. So exactly what he wanted—needed—in his life, even if only for a while.

But that wasn't his decision to make.

Quietly he stepped outside onto the deck, but even over the music and the quickening wind, she heard him, or maybe felt him. She straightened her head, let her arms lower to her sides and smiled at him. "How was the rally?"

"Peppy."

She rolled her eyes. "Did all the young girls swoon over Jordan?"

"Enough of them."

"And did all the young women swoon over you?"

"I didn't notice any women." That was true. Other than keeping his eye on Maxie so he could keep his distance from her and her single sister, he hadn't paid any attention to the women in attendance. He'd been too busy thinking about one woman who was absent.

"You didn't notice them at all? Their hearts must be aching."

"Their hearts don't concern me. *Yours* does." He stopped directly in front of her and offered his hand. "Dance with me."

After a moment's hesitation she laid her hand in his, and he drew her into his arms.

The music was coming from the boom box Lucinda kept in the laundry room for working with her flowers or relaxing on the deck. Its lights glowed red in the deeper shadows of the breezeway, and its CD player would keep spinning out tunes until they stopped it. With Natalie's body warm against his, her curls silky against his cheek, Tate wasn't sure he wanted it to ever stop.

"I hate to break this to you, darlin'," he murmured, his breath stirring her hair, "but that's not classic rock, and it's much more recent than 1980."

"But it's all your mother has." She stroked her fingers through his hair, teasing the too-long strands that curled at his neck. "Besides, I was in the mood to try something new. It's not bad."

No, he silently agreed, though perhaps with different meaning. It wasn't bad at all.

Their dancing, when they started, was normal—slow, easy, real steps that anyone could follow. By the third song, or maybe it was the fourth, they were barely moving, merely shifting their weight bit by bit, their bodies gliding against each other's, their breathing shallow and ragged. Instead of resting his cheek against her hair, he found himself brushing kisses over the curls, moving on too easily to her forehead, her cheek, her jaw. Instead of toying with his hair, she was rubbing his neck, his shoulders and back with gentle touches that delivered pleasure and, at the same time, sensitized his skin and made his muscles tighten.

When the first raindrops splashed down on them, she smiled dazedly. "It's raining."

"Hmm." He thought about dancing her to the shelter of the breezeway, but it would mean actually moving, and he'd just slid his hands to her bottom to lift her against him, and he truly thought he might reach maximum pressure and explode if he didn't taste her *now*. Besides, what was a little rain? They wouldn't melt. Just maybe sizzle a bit.

When he took her mouth with his, she opened to him immediately, guiding his tongue inside, drawing on it so hard he felt it all the way through his body. He slid his fingers through her hair, glided them along her jaw, down the length of her throat, over the thin cotton of her top. Her breasts were full and heavy in his hands, her nipples straining against his palms for stimulation.

After a light sprinkling of rain, a roll of thunder swept across the land, vibrating through the ground and everything on it, then the downpour started. In seconds they were drenched, clothes plastered to their bodies, hair limp and dripping, rivulets running down their faces. Tate ended the kiss, dragged in a desperately needed breath, then let his gaze slide slowly down her body.

He'd thought she looked damn good in the white tank top earlier, but the sight of her in the *wet* white top forced a groan from him. When, with slow, deliberate movements, she pulled the top over her head and let it fall to the deck, he was a goner. He considered dropping to his knees and giving thanks. Instead he boosted her to sit on the porch railing, ducked his head and took her nipple into his mouth.

The quivery, quavery sensations rocketing through her made Natalie's muscles go weak. She'd never felt such pleasure—their bodies hot and achy, the rain surprisingly cool, the wild wind, the thunder and lightning. As he suckled, strong and hard, at her nipple, she wrapped her legs around his slim hips and threaded her fingers through his hair, pulling his head closer, silently urging him to take more of her.

After endless moments he raised his head to stare at her, his expression closely reflecting the fierce night. "I want you, Natalie," he said, his voice a harsh, guttural imitation of itself. "I want to strip you naked, lay you down and bury myself so deep inside you that I won't know where I stop and you begin. I want to make love to you, have sex with you, play with you, torment you. I want to make you forget every man who's ever touched you, kissed you, been inside you, loved you, and I want to do it so thoroughly that no other man will ever be able to make you forget me. But…"

She felt a great disappointment inside. There was always a *but…*

"I can't offer you anything else. Once you leave here, that'll be it. There can never be anything between us again. It'll be over forever."

If she were a stronger person, she would tell him no, thanks—or would that make her weaker? Michaela had warned her it would be foolish to turn down Mr. Right just because she found him at the wrong time. Wouldn't it be equally foolish to pass up what promised to be the best time of her life just because it wouldn't last the rest of her life?

Still, she wanted to ask him how he could want her like that but know beyond a doubt that he could never forgive her for this damn book. How could he kiss her like that, look at her like that, and insist he wanted nothing from her once she left?

And how could she settle for nothing now just because he intended to give her nothing in the future? Didn't she deserve whatever pleasure and passion she could find? Wouldn't a few sweet memories make a future alone easier to bear?

"Natalie? It's your choice, darlin'. If that's not enough for you, tell me, and I'll walk away. But if you want it, anyway…if you want *me,* anyway, I'll do my best to make it worth the regrets."

He sounded anxious, aroused, already regretful, wistful, cautious, and she felt all the same things, plus one more— confident. No matter what she decided tonight, she was going to leave Hickory Bluff with a broken heart. She'd waited all her life to feel this way about a man, and she had no reason to think such feelings would come around again anytime in the near future. If her heart was going to break, anyway, she wanted something to show for it.

Her smile formed slowly, lightening the weight on her spirit as surely as the lightning brightened the sky. She cupped his face in her palms, leaned forward and brushed her mouth tantalizingly over his. "I want you, J.T."

"Are you sure?"

"I've never been more sure." And it was true. What they were about to do might be ethically questionable. It was definitely a stupid move in terms of self-preservation. But, for her at least, it was right. It was the only choice she could live with.

He straightened, lifting her with him, but when she would have swung her feet to the floor, he held her where she was. His mouth locked on hers, and his tongue stabbed into her mouth as he carried her to his door. The colder air inside his house raised goose bumps on both of them, but the heat created by his tongue and the thrust of his erection against her hips countered the chill as they made their way through the house and down the hall to his bedroom.

After setting her on the floor, he switched on the bedside lamp, then stepped back to look at her. She felt terribly exposed—and why not, when her top was lying in a sodden heap on the deck—and terribly wanton, because she *liked* being exposed to him. She liked feeling the intensity of his gaze on her naked breasts and her hips and her legs. She especially liked knowing that he was looking at her and getting turned on—that he already *was* turned on, proven by the sizable bulge in his tight jeans.

He pulled his T-shirt over his head and dropped it on the braided rug next to the bed. Leaning back against the dresser, he tugged off one boot, then the other, then peeled off his socks. "You want a towel?"

As she shook her head, she slid her fingertips inside the waistband of her shorts, caught her panties, too, and stripped them off. Her sandals came off with them. "I want you inside me. Now."

Her bold words had a visible effect on him—made him swallow hard, made that sizable bulge even more so. They had an effect on her, too—her nipples beaded more tightly, and hot moisture collected between her thighs.

Tight wet denim was hard to remove, but J.T. managed quickly enough. When he stood naked in front of her, she couldn't resist a long, mouthwatering look from his hair, almost black where the rain darkened it, across his handsome face, over his muscular chest and flat belly and impressive arousal to long, lean thighs and calves and bare feet. Oh, my, yes, she wanted him.

He took her at her word and was prodding between her thighs even as he lowered her to the bed. His weight bore her down, pushing him deeper and harder inside her until she'd taken all of him. She gave a soft sigh. "That feels good."

"Hot."

"Full."

"Tight."

"Perfect," they said in unison, then laughed, and then he kissed her and started moving inside her, and she could barely think, much less laugh.

He filled her with long, deep strokes, pulled back, then thrust in again, longer, deeper, harder. At the same time, his tongue was wickedly, suggestively mimicking the action in her mouth, and his hands were working their tantalizing magic on her breasts, making her entire body quiver and breathing impossible. When he released her mouth to turn his attention to her nipple, her breathing turned to strangled gasps. "Please," she whispered—whimpered—then gave a cry as he slid one hand low between their bodies and so easily located the most sensitive place on her body. "Oh, please!"

Relentlessly he fed her arousal, thrusting with a bone-melting rhythm inside her, suckling and biting her nipples, fingering her in exactly the right way to make her nerves scream with the impending climax but deliberately holding it back, building the intensity feverishly higher, hotter, wilder, until she thought she surely might die from such pleasure-pain if he didn't…

He did, and his timing was impeccable. One last thrust, one tingle-inducing kiss, one final caress—and a cry tore through her as her body convulsed. She was only dimly aware that he was peaking, too. She felt his body go rigid, heard his great groan, felt the hot, liquid release as he filled her, felt her own body's responses to each of his.

Moment after moment passed, and still she couldn't open her eyes, slow her breathing, release her grip on him. Once he tried to lift his weight from her, but she wordlessly protested, the muscles in her arms and legs and deep inside her body automatically clenching to keep him where he was.

He brushed a kiss to her cheek, then nuzzled the curve of her ear. "That was incredible," he said huskily.

She smiled and flexed her muscles around him. "Yes, it

was, wasn't it?'' Better than any sex she'd ever had, because she'd never had sex with a man she loved before. Not that loving J.T. mattered—not to him, not to their future.

Later, when she was alone, she would think about how sad it was that falling in love for the first time didn't matter. She would feel sorry for herself and maybe even indulge in a bout of weepiness. But not now, when he was here, still inside her, still connected with her.

Lifting her head, she caught a glimpse of the clock on the nightstand. ''When is Jordan due home?''

''Midnight.''

''We've got time. Want to do it again?''

Grinning, he tightened his hold on her, then rolled over so she was on top. ''Have your way with me, darlin'. I won't complain.''

She rose onto her knees with an extraordinary amount of wriggling that was designed to torment, and it worked. He groaned aloud, and his features took on a stark, strained look that set off butterflies in her stomach. ''You were both right and wrong, you know.''

''About what?''

''You made it good, but you didn't take it slow.''

He reached up to twist her nipple between his fingertips, making her breath catch. ''If I'd taken it any slower, you would have been screaming. You were already begging as it was.''

Knowing it was true and not feeling the least bit embarrassed, she smiled. ''I've never begged anyone before.''

''I hope you never do again.''

Just him, she wanted to say. She wanted to beg him to change his mind, to forgive her, to give her a real chance once the book was done. But it was a big step from begging for sexual release to begging for love. *That* would be embarrassing. *That* would make her pathetic.

She glanced at the clock again, then leaned forward until

the tips of her breasts rubbed sensuously against his chest. "We have ninety minutes before Jordan comes home. Let's see if this time you can make me scream."

In less than an hour, he did.

Chapter Eleven

Headlights flashed across the bedroom, waking Tate from a restless sleep, disorienting him when they kept flashing. After a moment, when he heard the slam of the truck door, he realized Jordan was home and the ongoing light show came from the storm. The system must have stalled in the region, because it showed no sign of playing out, but he didn't mind. He was home, his kid was home, and Natalie was curled up at his side, sleeping soundly. Building up to a good scream was tiring, he thought with a grin. She'd collapsed and hadn't moved more than a muscle since he'd moved from between her legs, and before he'd settled comfortably beside her, she'd fallen asleep.

Between claps of thunder, he followed Jordan's progress as the back door opened, then closed. The refrigerator door was also opened, then closed, then footsteps moved down the hall to the back bedroom. A moment later came sounds from the bathroom, then the bedroom door closed once more.

After relative quiet settled over the house again, Tate turned onto his side, resting his head on his hand, to study Natalie. She looked exhausted, deeply asleep, beautiful. Her hair was drying about her head in a sort of wanton, well-and-truly-satisfied abandon. No doubt about it, she had the sexiest hair he'd ever seen. Hell, sexiest *everything*.

Gingerly, so as not to disturb her, he eased the sheet down to expose her breasts—perfect full mounds with perfect, sweet nipples. They were flat and soft now, but he knew how easily that could change. One light touch, one hungry kiss, and they would swell…aw, hell, the way *he* was starting to swell.

Deliberately he pulled the sheet back into place, wrapped his arms around her and slid in close. He could wait until morning. She needed rest, and they both needed enough control to ensure there would be no screaming, no crying out, no waking the kid down the hall. He could wait a few hours. It was no big deal.

Living the rest of his life without her…that was going to be the hard part.

He dozed off and on, awakened occasionally by the storm and, later, by the quiet when the storm passed. When he awakened shortly before five, he knew he was going to stay awake—and not because it was almost time to get up, anyway. No, the certainty came from the fact that Natalie was still lying naked beside him, and was stroking and coaxing him into a morning erection with her slender, delicate little hand between his legs. For a moment he lay there and simply enjoyed her skilled caresses, then, with a sudden heated surge of desire, he forced her hand away. When she protested, he slid up until the headboard was at his back, then reached for her. "Did I ever tell you that predawn rides are my favorite? Come over here, and I'll show you why."

She sat up, stretched unselfconsciously, then moved into place. "Good morning," she greeted him as she took him deep and snug inside her.

"Morning. Did you sleep well?"

"Hmm. I can't imagine why." She combed her fingers through her hair, then asked, "Why are we whispering?"

"Because Jordan's asleep down the hall. Let's see how good and quiet we can make this."

Her full lower lip eased out in an enticing pout. "No screaming?"

"'Fraid not. You'll have to be subdued this time."

"Actually…" Leaning forward, she dragged her tongue over his nipple, making it swell and sending an electrical current directly to his arousal. "I was thinking about making *you* scream this time."

Oh, hell… His nerve endings were already tingling, and he was growing impossibly harder inside her, and basically all they'd done so far was talk. He was going to be in for a wild ride.

Shivering with the chilly air, she reached behind them for the sheet, wrapping it around her, then she braced her hands on the headboard and started thrusting slowly along the length of him. At first she refused to settle into a rhythm that he could match, a tactic he found both frustrating and exciting as hell. All he had to do to stop that, though, was work his fingers between their bodies. For a moment, she stilled, head back, eyes closed, the ends of her curls brushing the sheet where it covered his legs, and she let him play. Soon, though, she wanted more than he intended to give at that moment, and this time she perfectly matched her rhythm to his own.

Her body tightened, grew hotter, slicker, where it sheltered him. Knowing she was close, he braced his hands on her hips and urged her to take him harder and deeper. "Come on, babe," he murmured as his own climax began building. "You're almost there. Come on—"

Without warning the door swung open and the overhead light was switched on, flooding the room with light. "You can't sleep in on the one day I need to talk—"

Realizing that he'd interrupted something, Jordan came to an abrupt halt and stared. Natalie looked as if she wanted to dive under the covers and never come out again, and Tate thought he just might join her if she did.

"I, uh…I didn't mean… Aw, hell." Backing out, Jordan slammed the door.

Natalie's eyes were rounded—and regrettably free of arousal. His son's interruption had been more effective on her than an icy shower…not that Tate had escaped untouched. His lust hadn't died a sudden death—he doubted the day would ever come when he wouldn't want Natalie— but it had certainly suffered a setback.

She eased off his lap, taking the sheet with her and wrapping it protectively around her. "What's the protocol when teenage nephews walk in on you having sex?"

"Damned if I know. It's never happened to me before." Of course, he hadn't had sex in the house with Jordan home since the kid had needed help getting out of his bed. "I guess I should talk to him."

"I'll wait here." She curled up against their pillows, looking like a small child with the sheet tugged tightly around her. But there was nothing childlike about her. She was an incredible woman…and he was never going to forget it.

Sliding his feet to the floor, he pulled on a pair of cutoffs, buttoned them and left the bedroom in search of Jordan. He found him in the kitchen, starting breakfast. "Good morning."

Jordan snorted. "Yeah, apparently *real* good for some." He arranged a half dozen strips of bacon in the skillet, then faced Tate. "What happened to, 'It was just a kiss'? That sleeping with her wasn't wise when she thinks—" Tate gave him a sharp look, and he lowered his voice to little more than a whisper "—when she thinks you're someone you're not?"

Tate ignored the flush that warmed his cheeks. "Let me worry about what I do. Save your lecturing for when you have a kid of your own."

"Who needs a kid? I've got a father acting like one. At

least you used a condom, didn't you?'' For a moment he stared at Tate, whose face was burning crimson, then he rolled his eyes. ''Holy—sheesh, Dad, you and Uncle Josh have been drumming that into my head since I was old enough to notice that girls were different from boys. And you go off and spend an entire night with Ms. Alabama and it never crosses your mind?''

''I...I didn't—'' Tate combed his fingers through his hair. ''Her sex life is no more active than mine. I feel fairly safe...''

''I doubt disease is a problem. Getting pregnant, on the other hand...'' Jordan shook his head in dismay. ''Maybe by this time next year, we'll have another illegitimate little Rawlins to raise.''

The idea of having a child with Natalie appealed to Tate far more than it should. After all, in spite of all that had happened, he was still playing out Josh's charade. If she got pregnant, he would have to tell her the truth, and she would hate him, and she would never let him within a hundred miles of their child. Maybe she would hate him so much that she wouldn't *have* his child.

No, he couldn't believe that. She had too much of the unloved child left inside her, had too much love and affection to give. She would have no problem at all loving a baby and despising its father.

''This was *not* smart,'' Jordan said flatly. ''I can't believe you went and fell in love with the one woman in the world you absolutely can't have.''

Tate had nothing to say to that. No denial, because it was true. He *had* fallen in love with Natalie. No confirmation, because it wasn't necessary. Jordan was a sharp kid. He saw things clearly enough on his own.

With some measure of relief, Tate changed the subject from his own stupidity. ''When you came into the bedroom, you said you needed to talk to me. What's up?''

''I wanted to show you this.'' The backpack that held Jordan's school books was sitting on a dining chair. He unzipped it, pulled out a manila folder and handed it over. "Mike gave it to me after the pep rally last night. It's copies of stuff she found on the Internet." He glanced toward the bedroom, then lowered his voice even more. "It's about Natalie."

Jordan went back to cooking breakfast while Tate sat down at the table and opened the folder. The copies were articles that had appeared in various Southern newspapers more than a year earlier, and Natalie wasn't the author of any of them. She was the subject.

He read through the pages, and the cold, empty spot in his stomach that appeared with the first kept getting colder and emptier. When he finished with the last story and sat there, staring blankly at the page, Jordan brought him a cup of coffee.

"You know we're screwed," the boy said quietly. "With that in her past, there's no way she's ever going to forgive what we've done."

"But…if she doesn't know…"

"She *has* to know, Dad. Sooner or later, it'll come out, and if she's already published that book— Her reputation will be ruined. We can't do that, Dad. She doesn't deserve it."

No, she didn't—and she never had. He'd known Josh's idea was a bad one from the start, had known it wasn't fair or reasonable or smart, but he'd convinced himself it was no less fair than Natalie insisting on including his brother and mother in her book. He'd persuaded himself that as long as his family was protected, the lies and the deception were acceptable.

But they weren't. They could have found other ways to deal with her. They should have.

But it was too late for that now. Too late for him now.

"What are you going to do?"

Startled, he looked up at Jordan. "I don't know. I need to talk to Josh and Mom. I need to tell them…"

"When?"

"I'll call them after breakfast, and…I'll talk to Natalie this afternoon."

Jordan nodded. "Right now you'd better get her out of your bedroom. Breakfast will be ready in a few minutes."

Tate slid the papers back into the manila folder and anchored it between the backpack and the chair back, then went down the hall to his room. Outside the door he hesitated, took a deep breath, then stepped inside. The instant his gaze reached Natalie, the desire started building again. He felt helpless against it and tried to ignore it, but it wasn't easy when she looked so damn incredible.

"Is everything okay?"

"Sure." He had to clear his throat to get the lie out. "Jordan was just…surprised."

She sat up on the bed, still swathed in the sheet. "I would have gotten dressed, but my shorts are still wet, and I seem to have left my shirt outside."

He grinned as he sat down facing her. "Want to borrow a shirt, or should I go next door and get you some clothes?"

"A shirt would be fine. An extra long one." She smiled sheepishly. "I've never been caught before. I feel like a kid."

"Oh, darlin', you haven't felt like a kid until you've been lectured on birth control by a sixteen-year-old." He watched her reaction closely, looking for surprise, dismay, oh-this-is-the-wrong-time-of-month relief. He couldn't read anything.

"How about that shirt?"

He grasped a handful of sheet and pulled her to him. "I don't know. I kind of like the idea of keeping you in my bed with nothing but a sheet."

"Let me give Jordan the keys to my Mustang and twenty bucks for gas, and we can play captive and master the rest of the morning," she teased.

At least, he hoped she was teasing. Not knowing one way or the other, his body instantly and intensely reacted. It would be so easy to finish what they'd started. She was still naked under the sheet, and all he would have to do was unfasten his cutoffs. Five minutes—ten, tops—was all they needed…and he would have had another shot at getting her pregnant, and added another sin that would be impossible for her to forgive.

"Sweet hell, Natalie," he murmured. "You could kill me, you know?" He kissed her forehead, then set her away. From the closet he grabbed a T-shirt, pulled it over her head, then led her by the hand through the house and to her door. "Get dressed and come back for breakfast."

"Yes, sir."

"And, Natalie?" When she turned back, he laid his hand gently against her cheek. "Thank you. Last night, this morning… Thanks."

Her smile was unsteady, and her eyes glistened. Rising onto her toes, she cupped her hands to his face and gave him a kiss that threatened to curl his toes, then just as quickly she disappeared inside.

As the door closed, he leaned against the wall beside it, eyes closed, jaw clenched. He'd acknowledged from the beginning that he was going to burn in hell for his part in Josh's deception, but one small fact had escaped him at the time—that he was going to have to die first. One dream, one hope, one love at a time.

But without Natalie, he didn't even want to survive.

As a general rule Natalie tried to not be overly optimistic, but that Saturday morning she couldn't help it. Though she hadn't seen J.T. since breakfast, she couldn't shake the feeling that, in spite of his warnings, they had a chance. He loved her. Even if he hadn't said anything to that effect, she was convinced of it. She *knew* people, and the way he looked at her, treated her, made love to her… She believed he loved her, and she knew she loved him, and maybe he thought he could never forgive her for Chaney's book, but she honestly didn't believe he could simply shut her out of his life when she returned home.

Especially when she told him she wanted to move to Oklahoma. As Jordan had pointed out, she could write anywhere, and it wasn't as if there was anything or anyone waiting for her back in Montgomery. And surely once J.T. saw how sensitively and fairly she'd handled his part in the book, he would be in a more forgiving mood.

He was out with Jordan this morning, replacing the section of fence she'd helped him patch when she'd first arrived, and she'd volunteered to deliver lunch—what they called dinner—to them. They'd left her a map and the keys to Jordan's pickup, and she'd fixed ham sandwiches, potato salad and pasta salad, and had packed it all in the cooler along with cans of pop and bottles of water. Napkins, plates and silverware went into a bag with a dish of cookies, plus wet cloths for washing up. The last item she added was a quilt, stored on a shelf in Lucinda's laundry room, ragged and threadbare.

She was making her second trip to the truck when a horn sounded in the driveway. Turning, she watched as Michaela brought her old truck to a stop, then climbed out. Slowly she smiled.

"What do you think?" the girl asked self-consciously.

Natalie gestured for her to turn in a circle so she could admire her new haircut from every angle. "It looks great. It's exactly what you need." The style was sleek and short—much shorter than the Big-Hair Shelley doll would dare—and the color had been brightened with golden highlights. It was stylish, easy to care for and suggested a certain sass that Michaela had probably never possessed...but could learn.

"Did you get it done this morning?"

Michaela nodded, causing her glasses to slip. "My dad's cousin has a shop in town. When I told her to do whatever she wanted, she was excited, and this is what I got."

"I like it. Have you had lunch?" When the girl shook her head, she gestured toward the truck. "Hop in. I'm taking some food out to the guys. Let's see what Jordan says."

Michaela scowled as she climbed into the passenger seat. "Let's see if Jordan even notices," she muttered.

Natalie gave her the map, glad she didn't have to worry about finding her way herself. Michaela studied it a moment, realized where they were headed and put it away.

They chatted about everything and nothing—about eyeglasses versus contact lenses, red highlights opposed to gold, the best colors for clothing and makeup, writing a book, learning to ride a horse. By the time they reached the work site, Natalie was entertaining ideas of watching Jordan and Michaela grow up...and hopefully together.

J.T. and Jordan stopped working when they saw the truck, put their tools down and headed toward them. They both stopped short when Michaela climbed out of the truck. She raised one hand awkwardly to her hair, and her cheeks turned pink.

"What'd you do to your hair?" Jordan asked, reaching out to muss it when he was close enough. His uncle knocked his hand away before he got the chance.

"Just got it cut," the girl replied sullenly.

"It looks great," J.T. said. "Doesn't it, Jordan?"

"Yeah, looks fine. What did you bring us to eat, Natalie? I'm starved."

"The food's in the truck. You carry it over, and I'll serve it." In a voice designed to carry, she went on. "You know the good thing about teenage boys, Michaela? Eventually they grow into men."

Michaela didn't seem particularly amused.

They sat on opposite corners of the quilt with the food in the middle. Michaela merely picked at her food, Natalie ate a healthy portion, and J.T. and Jordan, as usual, astounded her with their capacity for food. Of course they did work hard—and play hard, she added with a secretive smile, recalling J.T.'s strenuous lovemaking the previous night.

After the meal the kids headed off for the pond the next hill over, and Natalie and J.T. stretched out on the quilt. They lay in the dappled shade of a massive blackjack oak.

It was hotter than Hades, and though last night's rain had left the ground rock hard, it had turned the air steamy, reminding Natalie of home. The combination of heat and humidity, as well as a full stomach, made her drowsy and lethargic.

"Wish we didn't have the kids," J.T. murmured as he tickled a blade of Johnson grass along her jaw.

She brushed away the grass without opening her eyes. "And what would we do without them?"

"Oh, I don't know. Maybe neck a little. Maybe see about getting you a tan...all over."

"Maybe finish what we started this morning."

"Hmm."

The grass brushed her mouth, then down her neck to her breast. There she felt the faintest flutter across her nipple, and it beaded tightly before the sensation continued down into her belly and lower.

"Can I ask you something?"

"Anything." She figured the question would have something to do with sex. She was wrong.

"Tell me about Candace."

Her eyes opened slowly, and she stared up at him. "Why do you want to know about her?"

He shrugged as he tickled her chin with the grass. "You said she was your best friend but she broke your heart. Tell me about it."

She took the shallow breath that was all she was capable of at the moment, then another, but they didn't ease the knot in her stomach. They didn't chase away the queasiness or lessen the hurt in her chest, and they did nothing for the fear. Telling him about Candace would mean relating the worst time in her life to him. Her father, when he found out, had disowned her. What would J.T.'s reaction be?

She supposed it was time to find out.

She sat up, brushed a dead leaf from her shirt, redid her ponytail, then shrugged. "I told you we met when she started working at the paper and that she'd been a student of my father's. She was a good reporter, and ambitious. Of course, that was part of Thaddeus's teachings. If you don't want to be the best, he always said, don't even try at all. Candace wanted to be the best...except I was already fairly well established by the time she was hired. If she wanted to be the best, I was the one she had to climb over. She used to joke that she'd settled for being best friend to the best.

"One day she came to me with a story she'd been working on, on her own time. It involved corruption in several government offices, as well as a number of charitable organizations, all of whom were supposed to be providing support, advice and assistance to the poor in Montgomery. She'd already done some of the legwork—had conducted interviews, documented bribes, skimming and payoffs—but she wanted me to take it over. She felt she was too close to be objective—she grew up in one of Atlanta's poorest neighborhoods and made it to college only with scholarships and bank loans. Plus, she said, the story would gain credibility having my name attached. I was flattered, and after reviewing all her work, I agreed she had a great story. I encouraged her to see it through, but she insisted she needed distance. So I wrote the story, which became a series of three articles, got lots of attention and won the Chaffee Award, which was pretty prestigious. I'd hoped to win it at some point, but I hadn't even let myself seriously think about it yet."

She could remember calling her father to tell him about the award as clearly as if it were yesterday. He'd been so proud of her. There was no doubt she was her father's daughter, he had crowed, and he'd sent her flowers and a bottle of expensive champagne.

"Everything was great for a while...until my own paper broke a new story—that my series didn't stand up to scrutiny. Some of the people quoted denied ever making such statements, and some of the documentation was phony." She swallowed hard. "I had taken Candace's research at face value. I hadn't double-checked her facts, her quotes or anything else. I was on a short deadline, and everything looked good, and…my God, she was my *best* friend.''

''And she set you up.''

''Guess who wrote the article exposing my attempts to defraud the newspaper, the readers and the Chaffee Award people?'' she asked dryly. ''I lost my job and the award. My father quit speaking to me. All my friends also worked at the paper, and they suddenly forgot they ever knew me. I was humiliated, while Candace's career got a big boost. Last I heard, my father pulled a few strings to get her a job at an Atlanta paper. He'd never pulled any strings for me in his life.'' After a moment she sighed. ''The hell of it is, it was all my fault. I was a better reporter than that. I *knew* better than to accept someone else's research without verifying it—even someone I trusted as much as I trusted Candace. I got careless, and I got caught.''

''I'm sorry,'' J.T. murmured. But that wasn't all he offered. After a moment, he took her hand and simply held it tightly in his.

Natalie gazed at his hand. The nails were short and blunt, less than clean, and had never been treated to a manicure. The calluses on his palm were rough, and several small scars were visible on his fingers. Unlike the men she'd known, his were hands obviously accustomed to hard work. They were strong, capable, tender.

''Thank you,'' she said.

''For what?''

''Talking about it didn't hurt as much as I thought it would.'' There was still a sense of betrayal, but not the deep hurt she'd been harboring. Maybe it was true that time healed all wounds. More likely, it was easier to leave ruined relationships in the past when you'd replaced them with promising new relationships.

He remained silent for so long, watching her so intently that she was convinced he was going to kiss her. Already she was anticipating it, growing warmer, achier, wondering how much time they'd need. They wouldn't have to undress—well, she would have to remove her shorts, but she could do that in a matter of seconds—and they could take refuge on the far side of the trucks.

But they didn't get the chance to find out. Just as he started to lean toward her, Jordan and Michaela appeared at the crest of the hill, talking loudly in an obvious effort to warn them.

"Damn."

Natalie echoed J.T.'s low curse, then smiled sweetly. "Well, there's always tonight."

He smiled, too, but there was a tinge of regret to it. Because they'd been interrupted now? Or because she expected more from him later? She told herself it was the former and even pretended to believe it.

"I guess we'd better let you get back to work."

"Thanks for the dinner." He stood up, then extended his hand to her. When he pulled her up, she tumbled into his arms—his intent, judging from the sly grin he wore. He held her hard against his body—or was that against his hard body?—and rubbed slightly, suggestively, against her. "You're one hell of a woman, Natalie Grant. You deserve much better than you got from Candace or your old man."

"You're right. I do. And I've got it…for now, at least."

That brought the regret back to his expression, but she didn't have a chance to pursue it. Jordan stripped his T-shirt off as Michaela shook out the quilt. "Let's get back to work, Uncle J.T., I'd like to finish this job sometime today. I've got plans for tonight."

Good, Natalie thought with satisfaction. So did she.

As soon as the picnic supplies were reloaded in the truck, Natalie and Michaela returned to the house. Despite her best efforts to draw out the girl, it was clear she wasn't in the mood to talk. Had Jordan's reaction to her new look disappointed her, or had he thoughtlessly rambled on about Shelley?

When they arrived at the house, Michaela murmured something about work and left. Natalie cleaned up after dinner, then went to her own quarters to get in a few hours' work. When that was done, she took a shower, dressed with care and went next door to start dinner. The chicken casserole was bubbling, the potato-and-cheese dish browning and the salad chilling, when the doorbell rang. For an instant Natalie stood motionless. She wasn't supposed to have contact with J.T.'s friends or neighbors, other than Michaela, but the only way to know who she was avoiding was to open the door.

She opened it.

The man standing on the porch was the largest man she'd ever met. He was at least six foot six, with shoulders as broad as the doorway, and he wore a Wildcats T-shirt and ball cap with green shorts, the knit kind that no one, according to the sports editor at the paper, but a coach would be caught dead in. His thinning brown hair was cut close to his head, and his expression was startled—and curious—to say the least. "Uh…hi. I'm Dan Halloran, the coach at Hickory Bluff. I'm looking for Tate."

"He's not here."

"I guess I am a little early. Do you happen to know where he's working today?"

"He's out of town. He's visiting his grandparents."

"Since when?"

"A couple of weeks ago."

"Nah, not Tate. I just saw him last night at the pep rally."

Natalie was surprised. She supposed it was possible that Tate had driven back to Hickory Bluff to be at the rally for Jordan, then returned to his grandparents' ranch last night. But why hadn't J.T. mentioned it?

Maybe because they'd been distracted by more important things?

"I didn't know he was here," she said with a shrug, "but he's not today. If you'd like to come in and wait, though, J.T. and Jordan will be back soon."

Now it was his turn to look surprised. "J.T.? Who's that?"

"J. T. Rawlins. Jordan's uncle. Tate's brother."

"You mean Josh."

"He told me he prefers J.T."

"Huh. That's kinda odd. Tate used to go by J.T. years ago, but I never knew Josh to. And if Josh was here, why didn't he come last night? He usually comes to everything involving Jordan."

"J.T.—Josh—*did* go." Smiling at his confusion, she gestured for him to follow her to the kitchen, where she lifted two framed photographs from the wall behind the dining table. Both were old, taken in high school, but each boy was recognizable as the man he'd become. "Tate is visiting his grandparents. I haven't met him yet." She handed his photograph to Coach Halloran. "J.T.'s taking care of things here, including going to the pep rally last night since Tate couldn't." As proof, she held out the second photo.

Instead of admitting his mistake, Halloran laughed. "I guess those Rawlins boys are at it again, huh? Stirrin' up trouble and confusing everyone. Well, sweet pea, let me set you straight." His tone became exaggerated, as if she might not understand if he spoke normally, and he displayed the photo he held. "This is Josh Rawlins. He's the younger of the boys, he's a bit irresponsible, and he loves a good time. I bet you next week's game that he's the one behind this whole shebang. And that—" he pointed at J.T.'s picture "—that's Tate Rawlins, Josh's big brother, Jordan's father and—"

With a grin, he looked past her and stabbed the air with an accusing finger. "Hell, there he is. *That* is Tate, and if he's told you otherwise, well, sweet darlin', he was just flat-out lying."

Chapter Twelve

Tate came to such an abrupt stop inside the kitchen door that Jordan ran into him, and he stared at what had just become his worst nightmare. Danny Halloran, who'd never had a clue when to keep his mouth shut, looked amused as all hell. Natalie looked as if she'd just received the biggest shock of her life.

"Hey, Jordan," Halloran said. "Tate, old man, what kind of game are you and that no-good brother of yours up to now? Does this have anything to do with the fact that Maxie's decided you'd make a perfect husband for her kid sister? 'Cause a simple 'no, thanks,' would have sufficed, honest."

With his lungs too constricted to breathe deeply, Tate came a few steps closer. He'd been hotter than hell when he'd walked in the door, but now cold chills were dancing down his spine. Guilt made beads of sweat pop out on his forehead and set his stomach to roiling. "Hey, Danny," he said quietly. "Natalie."

It was impossible to tell what was going through her mind. She looked too stunned to put three words together, and he'd wager the ranch that she hadn't realized the worst of it yet. Right now she was just considering the personal implications, he figured, but before long the professional ones would hit her. Knowing what he now knew about her and Candace, they would hit her hard.

"Dan, this is a really bad time," he said. "Can whatever you wanted wait until later?"

"Uh, yeah, sure, Tate. Not a problem." Halloran held out the frame to Natalie. When she didn't take it, glance at it or even bat an eyelash, he laid it on the table, then walked to the door. There he turned back. "Jeez, Tate, I hope I didn't—I'm sorry, man."

"Yeah," Tate murmured, his gaze on Natalie. She stood frozen, her fingertips gone white from clenching the second picture frame too tightly. He heard the front door close, then saw movement from the corner of his eye as Jordan stepped around him.

"I...uh...I'll go ahead and take a shower and, uh..." With a shrug Jordan turned down the hall and disappeared from sight.

The clock on the wall ticked audibly in the stillness, like a bomb on a countdown to explosion. Tate wanted to throw it, smash it, anything to silence it. Instead, he removed his Stetson, laid it carefully on the table, then combed his fingers through his hair. He was filthy and sweaty, and up until the instant he'd seen Natalie, he'd wanted nothing more than a cool shower to wash away the effects of a sweltering day's work. Now he wanted...he didn't know what.

After a time she took a sudden breath that seemed impossibly loud. "Judging by the look on your face, he was telling the truth, wasn't he? You're Jordan's father. *Not* Senator Chaney's son." Her voice was soft, quavery, and sounded just this side of heartbroken.

He nodded.

"And you've lied to me, you and Jordan, ever since the

day I got here. Everything you said, everything you did…
lies.''

Reluctantly, though it damn near killed him, he nodded
again.

"Oh, God." Numbly she started to sit down in the nearest
chair, but Jordan's backpack was there. She slid it to the
floor, picked up the folder that fell forward onto the seat
and tossed it on the tabletop, then sank down. *"Why?"*

He pulled out the chair across from her and sat down.
"Josh told you he wasn't interested in your book, but you
wouldn't take no for an answer. When you sent the last
letter, threatening to come here and stay until you got what
you wanted, we decided to give it to you—an interview with
J. T. Rawlins. Just…not…the right J.T.''

"And you thought that was fair? Honorable? Reasonable?''

"No. Well…fair, maybe. You had no regard for what was
fair to my brother and my mother so…we weren't too worried about being fair to you.''

"You're saying it was my fault. I got what I deserved.''

"No, Natalie, I'm not saying that at all. It was a bad
situation. No matter what we did, someone was likely to get
hurt.'' He swallowed hard before finishing. "Better you than
my family.''

She flinched at that, but no more than he did. It sounded
so brutal and cold…but, at the time, it had been true. "So
you and Josh came up with this plan for you to impersonate
him. You would lie to me, string me along, feed me a load
of crap, then Josh would… What? Use it to discredit me
when the book came out? Accuse me of manufacturing that
entire aspect of the book? Sue me?''

"No, that's not—''

"And what was in it for you and Jordan? I understand
Michaela would do anything Jordan asked her to, but what
was *his* motivation? And you got laid, but there had to be
more to it than that. Are you just some sort of pervert who
gets a kick out of making a fool of someone else, or did

Josh promise you a share of any money he gets from suing me?''

''It was nothing like that, Natalie! We just wanted to be left alone. Josh had a right to not be part of that damn book, but since you wouldn't accept that, we decided to control what you could write by controlling what you found out.'' He dragged his hand through his hair again and saw that his fingers were trembling. His entire future was on the line here. If he could magically come up with the right words, he might have one. If not… ''Josh would never sue you. We would never try to discredit you or make a fool of you.''

''That's exactly what you've done!'' she snapped. ''I've got to go back to Montgomery and tell Senator Chaney that I've spent the last two and a half weeks getting screwed, both literally and figuratively, by the Rawlins family! I've got to tell him that I was taken in by your lies—that everything I've told him about his son isn't about his son at all but a stranger he couldn't care less about! I've got to tell him I made the same mistake with you that I made with—''

She broke off, and a look of such sorrow spread across her features. He followed her gaze to find the reason, and the knot in his gut tightened painfully. When she'd tossed the manila folder onto the table, the pages inside had shifted so they extended an inch or two beyond the edge of the folder. In that small space, one word in the headline of the top article was clearly visible—Chaffee.

Her hand shook as she removed the papers from the folder. She looked at each headline, scanned each article, and tears slid silently down her cheeks. He wanted more than anything to go around the table and hold her, to gather her into his arms and let those damned silent tears soak into his shirt and promise her, swear to her on his life, that everything would be all right…but hadn't he already lied to her enough? Nothing was going to be all right, not today, not ever.

When she finished, she neatly stacked the pages together, put them inside the folder once more and closed it.

"Natalie, I can explain—"

"What's to explain? You found out about that, and you decided to use it to your advantage. All's fair in love and war, right? Well, congratulations. You've won this war. My career as a reporter is over. One failure to check my research could, with a lot of luck, be survivable. But two... That's fatal. No editor wants a writer he can't trust, and no one trusts a writer who can't get her facts straight. You don't have to worry about me writing anything about your precious family, J.T.—Tate, or whoever the hell you are—because I'm out of a job."

He stood up when she did and moved to block her way. "We didn't know about that when this started, I swear. Michaela came across it on the Internet and gave it to Jordan last night. I saw it for the first time this morning. Damn it, Natalie, we never would have done any of this if we'd known what happened with Candace. I never meant to hurt you. I just wanted to protect my family."

"You've succeeded. And all you had to do was betray my trust, ruin my career and destroy the only chance I had of getting my father to speak to me again. But the Rawlins boys got what they wanted, and that's what counts, right?"

She sidestepped him and was halfway to the side door when he spoke. "I want *you,* Natalie. If you don't believe anything else, believe that. I know it's bad timing, a bad situation, bad luck, but...I love you."

She stopped, slowly turned. "If you told me the sun was shining, I would have to feel its rays burning my skin before I believed it. So many lies... Enjoy this time I'm gone, J.T., because as soon as the senator gets rid of me, he's going to choose someone else, and they won't be as desperate as I was, or as pathetic, or as easily seduced. They'll be looking for a big seller that will earn big bucks, and they'll know the best way to get it. They'll make you wish for someone as harmless as me again."

"Natalie, please—"

"Go to hell," she said flatly, sadly. Then she walked out.

Tate closed his eyes and breathed as deeply as the sickness that tightened his chest would allow. Part of him wanted to go after her, to grab her and force her to listen while he explained, pleaded, begged. Part of him wanted to feel his hands around Josh's throat and Chaney's, as well, and part of him knew it wasn't fair to blame anyone but himself. No one had forced him to play along. No one had supplied him with all the lies he'd given voice to. Certainly no one had encouraged him to make love with her or fall in love with her or to tell her in such a juvenile way. *He* was responsible for what had happened here. *He* had broken her heart, and his own in the process.

"Dad?"

Tate took a breath. "Yeah?"

"Is she leaving?"

"Yeah."

"Will she ever come back?"

Because he couldn't bring himself to say the word, he shook his head.

"Did you tell her that we were gonna tell her the truth ourselves after supper?"

"I don't think she would have believed me, son."

"So what are you gonna do?"

Finally Tate turned to face him. The apprehension in Jordan's eyes made his big, strapping son look closer to six than sixteen. "I'm going to take a shower," he said, touching Jordan's shoulder as he passed.

Jordan pivoted around and followed. "I mean about Natalie. You can't let her go."

"I can't make her stay."

"Did you tell her you love her?"

"She didn't believe me. Can you blame her, when I'd just admitted I'd lied about everything else?"

"But, Dad—"

Tate went into the bathroom, then blocked his way when he would have followed. "Jordan, I'm sorry. I am so damn sorry…but not as sorry as she is that she ever met me. Just leave it alone right now, okay?''

"But—"

He closed the door in his son's face, leaned against it and closed his eyes tight again. Damn it, he'd known better than to agree to Josh's plan. He'd known practically from the moment he'd laid eyes on her that someone was going to get hurt, had known almost as long that it was likely to be him. He just hadn't had a clue how bad it could hurt…or how long he could live like this…or if he even wanted to.

It had taken Natalie several days to settle into Lucinda Rawlins's quarters, but it took less than an hour to pack everything up again. She worked automatically, allowing herself no time to think, remember, feel. She knew that the moment she began examining her emotions she was going to fall apart, and she wanted to delay it as long as possible, because the putting-back-together wasn't going to be easy.

How could she have been such a fool? One simple question—Can I see your driver's license?—would have ended the charade before it started. But for whatever incredibly stupid reason, it had never occurred to her. She had gone to J. T. Rawlins's ranch on Rawlins Ranch Road, had asked for J.T. and gotten a man reluctantly claiming to be Senator Chaney's son. The idea that she could be dealing with an impostor had never crossed her mind. Even now it seemed too fantastic, too outrageous, to be believed.

She stood in Lucinda's kitchen, everything neatly stacked in front of her—suitcases, boxes filled with research, computer, shoulder bag. She was ready to leave. The sooner she put this awful place behind her, the sooner she could find a way to deal with the awful future ahead of her.

But she didn't move—didn't grab her keys or sling a bag over her shoulder. She wanted to—her brain gave the command, but her body was shaking too badly to obey. All she could do was slide to the floor in a boneless heap and give in to the tears that choked her.

She felt so stupid! Hadn't it all been too good to be true, right from the start? The man who'd ignored her phone calls and letters for months suddenly had a change of heart and decided to cooperate with her? And just happened to find himself wildly attracted to her? Just happened to be exactly the sort of man she could care about in return?

How many gorgeous men had ever been wildly attracted to her? Zero. How many men had she fallen in love with so easily, so completely? Zero. Men like him didn't get hot-and-bothered over women like her. She should have known something was wrong the first time he'd looked at her as if he'd wanted to strip her bare and do all sorts of wicked deeds. But no, dumb gullible Natalie had fallen for his act. She'd believed every lie he'd told her and asked for more. She'd lapped it all up, breaking every rule of journalism along the way.

No wonder he'd called her pathetic.

"Natalie?" Jordan spoke her name so softly that she barely heard it over her own sobs.

She sucked in a breath, dried her eyes with her palms, then looked up at him. She was furious with him, too, she reminded herself. He'd been as much a part of the lies as his unc—father—but he looked so distressed that she couldn't bring herself to vent on him. Besides, he was just a kid, following his father's orders.

He gave her luggage a wary look as he circled it, then sat down beside her. "I...I'm sorry."

She hated apologies, for their insincerity and their inability to undo the damage already done. She hated the meaninglessness of the words, and the stupid idea behind them, as if words as insignificant as *I'm sorry* could actually make a difference. But she lifted her shoulder in a shrug. "Yeah. Me, too."

"Please don't go. My dad...my dad's a good man, and he...he needs you."

She dug a packet of tissues from her purse and blew her nose. "Tell him not to worry. There are fools and suckers everywhere. He'll find someone else to use and humiliate in no time.''

''He didn't want to do this. Uncle Josh and Grandma and I talked him into it. He never would've done it if it wasn't for us.''

She knew the words were meant to make her feel better, but they deepened the pain instead. Four people she'd never met had gotten together and decided to help destroy her life. Not just refuse to cooperate with her—that she could have understood. But they'd chosen to go far beyond merely saying no. They'd agreed to an approach that, if successful, would deal a fatal blow to her career, and had broken her heart while they were at it.

She gave him a sidelong look. ''So you're saying the entire Rawlins family gets a kick out of lying to and manipulating people they've decided deserve their derision.''

''No!'' Jordan said hotly. ''It wasn't like that! You're the one who was causing trouble, who pushed in where you didn't belong!''

She couldn't argue that point with him. She most certainly didn't belong here. Trouble was, she didn't belong *anywhere*. ''You're right, Jordan,'' she said, patting his knee. ''It was all my fault, and I promise, once I leave here, none of you will ever have to see me again.''

''But we don't want you to go!''

Her eyes burned and her throat was raw. She wished she'd left her clothes behind—just grabbed the computer and the research files and dashed to the car. Clothes and toiletries could be replaced, and she could have been in Arkansas by now—crying, to be sure, but privately. Alone.

She wiped her eyes again, then got to her feet and picked up her purse, the laptop and the larger suitcase.

''Dad loves you, Natalie, and I think you're in love with him.''

She stared at him for a long, still moment, then sadly shook her head. ''Jordan, I don't even know him. All I know is his lies.'' After a pause she offered a pitiful smile.

"Goodbye. And take care." With that, she left the house. She didn't ask him to help load her luggage. She was perfectly capable of handling it alone.

Though the sun was slipping lower on the horizon, the day was still unbearably hot. It felt good, though, relentless heat against the chill that had spread through her from the inside out. She might never be too warm again as long as she lived.

It took three trips to load her car. On the last one she left the house key on the kitchen counter. She stowed the boxes in the trunk, started the engine and put the top down, then stood beside the car for a moment, gazing toward the house.

J.T. was in there somewhere, probably on the phone with his brother, letting him know their plan had succeeded. They had nothing more to fear from Natalie Grant. She'd proven her father's greatest fear—that she was a bad reporter, careless, amateurish, unable to remember simple rules such as: verify everything, and then do it again; don't trust anyone; get it in writing or, better, on tape; don't get involved. She was an embarrassment to her profession and an even greater embarrassment to him.

Slowly her mouth curved up, and she smiled in spite of the tears that were seeping down her cheeks again. She owed Tate Rawlins and his family for one thing: for the first time in her entire thirty-one years, she didn't give a good damn what the almighty Thaddeus Grant thought.

Tate was standing a few feet back from the bedroom window, a towel wrapped around his middle, when Jordan burst into the room.

"Dad, she's leaving!"

"I see that."

"So stop her! You can do it. All you have to do is…is talk to her. Tell her you're sorry. Tell her you'll make it all up to her. Hell, beg her if that's what it takes."

Tate watched as she settled in the driver's seat, secured her gorgeous red hair underneath a ball cap, then pulled around Jordan's truck and headed down the drive, and he felt as if something had died inside him. "Sorry, son," he murmured over the lump in his throat. As far as Natalie was concerned...

He didn't have what it took.

August eased into September, though it was difficult to tell the difference on the ranch. The temperatures remained in the triple digits, and the rain came too little and too long between. Lucinda and Josh were back from her folks' place, Grandpop's leg was healing nicely, and the Hickory Bluff Wildcats' football season had gotten off to a great start. Life was good.

But Tate damn sure couldn't tell it.

"I thought you could use something cool to drink."

At the sound of his mother's voice, he slid out from under the same beat-up old truck he and Jordan had been working on the day Natalie showed up at the ranch. The damn thing ran a few days, then broke down. He kept threatening to sell it for scrap, but he hadn't done it yet. Other than his routine work, he hadn't done much of anything yet.

He accepted the plastic tumbler filled with ice and tea and remembered the day he'd watched Natalie make tea. He'd just told her that what was between them was temporary, that she couldn't come back once she'd left. He'd thought he was warning her. He hadn't realized he was the one who needed to listen.

He'd rather drink pond water.

"You feeling better?" Lucinda asked.

"Than what?"

"Oh, I don't know. One of Vern's cranky old buffalo with a burr up its butt."

He sat down on the truck's running board and leaned back into the shade the cab provided. "Does Jordan have a date with Cheer—Shelley tonight?"

"Changing the subject, hmm?" Lucinda closed the large metal toolbox and used it as a bench. "Yes, it's Saturday, and he's supposed to go out with Shelley just like he has the last three Saturdays. But I'm not broiling out here under this sun to talk about my only grandchild's love life. I came to talk about yours.''

"Don't have one. Quick conversation, wasn't it?''

"Jordan thinks you should ask Ms. Alabama to come back.''

Tate concentrated on the tea as if it could somehow protect him, but instead he remembered long, slender hands counting out tea bags, measuring water, stirring in sugar, dropping ice cubes into a glass...and pulling off her shirt, touching his face, sliding between his— He took a long drink to clear the lump in his throat and choked on it.

"We have her address. Her phone number, too.''

"Don't, Mom.''

"Ordinarily, son, I'd take you at your word—you say you don't want to talk about Natalie, I wouldn't talk about Natalie. But it's not ordinary for you to be moping about like this. You fell in love with her, things went wrong, she left. It's not the end of the world.''

It was the end of *his* world. He was in Oklahoma. She was in Alabama. He wasn't seeing her, talking to her, touching her, watching her. He was sleeping alone at night, spending most of his days alone. Even when someone else was around, he still felt alone. And it wasn't going to change. He loved her, and he missed her more than he could put into words, but she wasn't ever going to forgive him. He had betrayed her in far worse ways than Candace and her father had, and he was going to pay for it for the rest of his life.

"You know, Alabama's only a good one-day drive from here. Just a few hours by plane.''

He drained the tea, then tossed the ice into the dirt. Within minutes the cubes were melted. Another couple minutes and the soil would be dry. There would be no sign they'd ever been there. Just as there was no sign that Natalie had ever been here.

A one-day drive. He could finish working, eat with the family, get some sleep and still be in Montgomery by suppertime the next night. And what could he say that he hadn't already said? *I'm sorry?* Nope, said that. *I can explain? I want you?* Tried those, too. *I love you?* The lump appeared in his throat again. He'd said it for the first time—for real, 100 percent sure, guaranteed—and she hadn't believed him. How could she, after all the lies?

"I appreciate your concern, Mom, but—"

"When I was your age, Tate, I'd had my heart broken twice, and I decided it wasn't ever going to happen again. I was going to stay right here, take care of you and your brother and keep myself safe, and that's exactly what I've done. But you know what? Being safe isn't as wonderful as it sounds. Sure, no man ever got close enough to break my heart again, but on the down side…no man ever got close enough to break my heart. I miss the connection, the emotion, the possibilities. I miss having a partner, someone to share things with. I miss that little flutter of excitement, that surge of passion a person feels when the one he loves walks into a room."

She smiled broadly. "I miss having someone to cuddle with on cold nights—someone to worry about me when I'm gone or to make me feel better when I'm down. I cut myself off from all that on purpose, and I kept my heart safe, but it wasn't a fair trade-off. I've lost so much more than I've gained. And I don't want to see you make the same mistake."

"Fine. As soon as I get some time free, I'll go into town and start looking for another woman."

Leaning forward, she swatted his leg and raised a puff of dust. "That's not what I mean, and you know it. You need to *make* time and go looking for *your* woman, and you need to persuade her that you love her dearly, then bring her back here so everyone can be happy."

"The only thing I can do to make Natalie happy is stay

out of her life.'' It hurt to say the words, but he got them
out, even if the effort did make a muscle twitch in his jaw.

''I don't believe that.''

''She does, and in the end that's all that matters.''

Moment after moment dragged by while his mother studied him. He fidgeted under her steady look, rubbed the back
of his neck, then scowled. ''What?''

''I can't believe I raised a son who would turn his back
on family.''

Dismay and irritation darkened his gaze as he stared back
at her. ''Turn my back— I wouldn't be in this mess if it
weren't for my family! If Josh were any kind of man, he
would have handled the damn thing himself instead of running off to Grandpop's. Besides, who have I turned my back
on?''

''Natalie, of course.''

''She's not family, Mom.'' Though, God knows, he
wished she were.

''Sure, she is. The only way she could be more so is if
you were married. And there's Jordan, too.''

''How have I neglected Jordan?''

''The boy wants a mother. He needs one.'' She made a
great show of looking at her watch, then said with a careless
air, ''I imagine that's why he's gone off to Alabama to find
one.''

After popping the top on a can of Diet Coke, Natalie sat
cross-legged on the sofa, took a drink, then glanced around.
Though her living room was far from empty, it looked pretty
bare. All the pictures were gone from the walls, all the
books removed from the shelves, all the items of a personal
nature wrapped and packed in the boxes stacked around the
room. It was a little disheartening, seeing how little she'd
accumulated in her life. There were a few pieces of furniture
that had belonged to her mother, tons of books and papers,
kitchenware and not much else, but it was all ready to go.

She just wished she knew where it was going.

The weeks since her return from Oklahoma hadn't been the worst in her life, but she'd certainly had better. The first few days she'd spent in bed, surrounded by tissues and chocolate, and she'd cried a lot—well, okay, incessantly. Then she'd pulled herself together and gone to see Senator Chaney.

It hadn't been pleasant, not that she considered any of her meetings with the man particularly pleasant. She'd told him about Tate and Josh's scheme, and how she had fallen for it, and he'd been alternately amused by his son's deviousness and infuriated with her gullibility. He'd called her incompetent, a fool, stupid and a *woman,* in such a contemptible tone that there was no doubt it was the lowest of insults. Then, after unloading all his anger on her, he'd fired her. She'd expected it—was even relieved by it. The last thing she wanted right now was to spend all her waking hours working on a book about Tate's half brother's family. She didn't think she could survive having the Rawlins bunch on her mind all the time—not yet, at least, when it still hurt to think about them.

So she'd screwed up—again. Been fired—again. Was at a loss as to what to do with her life, with her reputation in tatters—again. Last time she'd tried a new career. This time she was trying a new life. She had some money saved. The movers would arrive Monday to transfer all of her belongings to storage, and she was leaving tomorrow. Sunday seemed a good day for a new beginning.

Too bad she didn't know where she was going. She'd bought a road atlas to help her decide, then had packed it away with everything else. She intended to take a couple of suitcases and her laptop, climb into the car and go wherever the road took her. Maybe Florida, maybe New England or Texas or California. Maybe she would find a mountain in Colorado or a valley in Montana, an island off the coast of Washington or a butte in New Mexico. She would find a job that had nothing to do with writing and make some friends, and maybe someday she would even start looking for her mother's family, and she would be happy.

She swore she would, and she believed it, because if the rest of her life was going to feel as bad as the past few weeks had, she'd just have to put herself out of her misery now.

With a sigh she finished her drink and returned to work on the last of her packing. Her mother's china was stacked on the dining table and the bar that separated the kitchen and dining room, surrounded by stacks of empty boxes and huge rolls of bubble wrap. Since other people would be handling it, she was taking great care with every piece. She didn't have much that belonged to her mother, and she didn't want any harm to come to any of it.

With nothing but the radio for company, she worked methodically and the stacks of sealed boxes grew. Her back started to ache after a time, though, and her stomach was rumbling. She was debating taking a break and getting an early dinner when the doorbell rang.

At first she did nothing but simply stare at the door. She hadn't had visitors, not even a delivery man, in longer than she cared to recall. It was probably someone at the wrong address or, with her luck, thieves looking for an empty apartment to burgle, and here she'd have everything packed up to make it easy for them.

When the bell pealed again, she went to the door and checked the peephole. Her jaw dropped open in shock. After undoing the locks, she jerked the door open. "Jordan!"

"Hey, Natalie." The boy swept her into a fierce hug that made her ache—literally. When he released her, she stumbled back far enough to let him in, then asked, "What are you doing here?"

"Since neither you or Dad are willing to be reasonable about this, I decided I would be the adult in the family and come get you."

"Come get me for what?" she asked blankly.

"To take you home. To Hickory Bluff. To Dad."

Pain stabbed through her and made her fingers tighten recklessly on the fragile dish she still held. She stared at him a moment, then returned to the table, leaving him to follow or stay. "I appreciate your intent," she said as she wrapped the gravy boat with much more care than was necessary. "But Hickory Bluff isn't my home, and I'm not going back there."

"Aw, come on, Natalie. Don't you miss him? 'Cause he sure as hell misses you."

Her hands started shaking so badly that the first piece of tape she tore off to secure the wrapping wound up tangled and stuck to itself. She discarded it and tried again. "I doubt that," she said dryly. If Tate missed her, he would have called or written or come to see her himself. He would have apologized again and again and again until she had no choice but to forgive him. He would have suffered and groveled and made all kinds of life-or-death promises to her, and he would have taken her back himself.

But he'd made no effort to get in touch with her. All those letters she'd sent his brother had her address, phone number and e-mail address on them. He'd had plenty of ways to get hold of her. Just no desire.

Jordan pulled up a chair and sat opposite her. "I'm not kidding, Natalie. He's been real upset since you left. He blames himself, and—"

"Funny. I blame him, too," she murmured. But that wasn't the entire truth. For what it was worth, most of the blame belonged squarely on her shoulders. She'd learned a painful lesson from Candace, then, at the first opportunity, she'd forgotten it. Being 100 percent certain of all her details had been of paramount importance on the Chaney project, not only because of her past mistakes, but also because the subject matter was so important.

The identity of the man she was interviewing—and kissing, sleeping with and falling in love with—was a pretty big detail to let go unchecked.

"Here. Put this in that box." She handed the wrapped dish to Jordan and reached for another.

He obeyed, then looked around as if noticing the boxes and suitcases for the first time. "Where are you going?"

"I don't know."

"What do you mean, you don't know? Are you being thrown out or something? Did you lose your job because of what happened with us?"

"No, I'm not being thrown out. Yes, I lost my job because of your dad. And 'I don't know' means *I don't know*. I'm going someplace I've never been before."

"Where?"

She shrugged. "I don't know. It could be anyplace in the U.S."

"If you don't know where you're going, then how will you know when you get there?"

"I'll just know. I'll *feel* it." She'd tried to visualize the perfect place for her—small town or city, desert, mountains or beach, with neighbors or isolated and alone. But every time she'd closed her eyes and imagined the place where she wanted to spend the rest of her life, where she would belong, all that came to mind was the Rawlins place, so she'd given up on visualization.

Abruptly her gaze narrowed. "How did you get here?"

"I flew…and, boy, are my arms tired."

The joke was older than she was, and hadn't been funny the first time she heard it. It made her gaze narrow even more. "Does your father know you're here?"

He looked at his watch, shuffled his feet, rubbed his jaw, then finally admitted, "He probably does by now."

"How did you— *Why* did you—?"

"Grandma bought me the plane ticket, and Mike took me to the airport this morning. Uncle Josh gave me your address, and I got a cab here from the airport. Easy." He grinned broadly. "First time I've ever been on a plane or in a cab or outside of the state by myself."

"Enjoying it, are you?" she asked dryly. "My cell

phone's over there in my purse. You'd better call and let them know you made it here and that I'm putting you on the first plane headed back that way.''

''Nah, I'll just catch a ride with you.''

''I'm not going back there, Jordan.'' In fact, if she headed that way, she intended to give the entire state of Oklahoma a very wide berth. Even the thought of going back stirred more pain than she was willing to face at the moment.

Jordan watched her wrap several more dishes before breaking his silence. ''Pretty dishes.''

''They belonged to my mother—a wedding gift from my father.''

''I've never met my mother. Dad showed me some pictures of her, but she was just a kid in them, not much older than me. He said she was just too young to be a mother, but Grandma said she was just too selfish.''

''Sweetheart, if she was old enough to be fooling around with your father, then she was old enough to accept the consequences,'' Natalie said gently. ''After all, *he* did, and he couldn't have been much older than her.''

''Yeah, but Dad...that's what he does. Accepts the consequences. Takes care of people. Be the responsible one.'' He picked up a scrap piece of bubble wrap and began popping the bubbles, one at a time. ''That's what he was doing with you—taking care of Uncle Josh and Grandma.''

''Protecting them from the big, bad reporter? From *me?*''

Josh smiled faintly as he reached for wrapping and a dinner plate. ''Sounds funny, doesn't it? But...isn't that what a man's supposed to do? Take care of his family? Stand up for them when there's trouble? Stand by them when people are threatening them?''

Natalie thought of her father, refusing to make any effort to get along with her mother's family, turning his back on them completely after her death, more or less turning his back on her, too. He'd asked only one question about the whole Chaffee Award scandal—*Did you verify the information?* When she'd told him no, that was all he'd wanted to hear. She'd tried to explain Candace's role in the mess—how her best friend had set her up and betrayed her—but all he'd cared was that *she* had allowed Candace to set her up.

Then he'd rewarded Candace for succeeding at destroying his own daughter's career.

"Yes," she murmured, "that's what a man should do." How different her life might have been if her father had understood that and put it into practice. And how different *his* life would have been. He would have had a daughter who loved him, and maybe someday a son-in-law who respected him and grandkids who thought he'd hung the moon. Instead, he had people like Candace.

And she had no one.

Finishing with the last dish, she taped up the boxes, marked them Fragile, then directed Jordan to stack them against one wall. "Are you hungry?" she asked as she stretched her arms wearily over her head.

"I can always eat."

"Come on. Let's go get some pizza." Then, when they got back, she would insist he call his father and find out about getting him back home. She would put him on the plane herself, kiss him goodbye, then start her adventure, her new life.

Only problem was, she didn't *want* a new life.

They went to a pizza place in the neighborhood, where Jordan managed to put away an amazing amount of pizza while talking an amazing amount, too. He filled her in on all the Hickory Bluff news—which, in his estimation, consisted mainly of football games and dates with Shelley—and dropped in subtle comments about his father wherever he could fit them.

They were about to leave the restaurant when Jordan stopped her with his hand on her arm. "You know, if you'd come back and marry my dad, you could be my mom."

She swallowed hard. "I'd love to be your mom, Jordan, but I can't."

"Are you never gonna forgive him?"

"He *lied* to me! He lied about his name, about who he was, about who you were, and his lies cost me everything—my job, my reputation, my trust, my future!" And her heart. He'd broken her heart.

"So that's it? He only gets one chance? Like your dad only gave you one chance?" Grim disappointment darkened his eyes as he shook his head. "Dad said you always wanted to be like your father. I guess you've succeeded." Releasing her arm, he walked out the door and across the parking lot to her car.

She stood there, staring after him. It wasn't the same at all—the way she felt about Tate and the way her father had treated her. A father was *supposed* to love, protect and support his child. As long as the child was a good son or daughter, he had a duty to be a good father. Lucinda's parents could have made her pay the rest of her life for her two illegitimate children, but they hadn't, and she'd continued to love Tate in spite of the fact that he'd made the same mistake. Jordan could do a million dumb things, but Tate would never stop loving him. Forgiveness and second chances—and fifth and twentieth and hundredth—were part of being a parent.

And they were probably the most important part of loving. What relationship could survive without forgiveness, without compromise and apologies and kissing and making up? Look at her. She'd made the same mistake in less than eighteen months. She'd trusted someone who'd lied to her, and she'd paid for it both times. If one chance, one screwup, was all a person was allowed, then she was in trouble. She'd already screwed up twice and knew it was likely to happen again in the future—somehow, some way. And if she wasn't perfect, if she required forgiveness, how could she deny it to anyone else?

As she crossed the parking lot to join Jordan in the car, she admitted she was stumped for an answer.

* * *

Big cities didn't sit well with Tate. He'd seen his share of them—Tulsa, Oklahoma City, Dallas—but Hickory Bluff was more his speed, and he meant that literally as the gum-popping cab driver screeched to a halt in front of Natalie's apartment. The squat, three-story buildings stretched out in every direction, at this angle and that. The siding was beige, the trim white, with tiny porches and balconies. They'd been striving for a homey effect, but there was nothing homey about three hundred units crammed together in a few acres.

Every building was exactly alike except for the numbers on the doors and the personal touches on the balconies. The rectangles of grass surrounding each building were identical, too, as were the flowers and shrubs planted around them.

And she'd had the nerve to be offended by the lack of individuality at Burning Bow.

He paid the cab driver, slid the strap of his duffel over his shoulder, then scanned the parking lot. There was no sign of the Mustang. Maybe she was running errands, or had taken Jordan out to eat. Maybe she was on a date, or out of town and Jordan hadn't even hooked up with her yet. Or maybe...

He took the stairs to her apartment two at a time and rang the doorbell.

He was about to ring a second time when he heard his son's voice down below. His chest tightened when Natalie and Jordan came into sight at the foot of the stairs—with relief because his son was safe, and with the raw ache that had kept him company in the weeks since she'd left. She was so damn beautiful, and he loved her so damn much. He just didn't have a clue how to convince her of that.

They both stopped suddenly, then slowly, hesitantly, continued up the stairs. When they reached the landing, the three of them filled the small space, and for a moment none of them had anything to say. Finally Jordan cleared his throat. "There were some guys shooting hoops over at the basketball court. Is it all right if I go over and hang out for a bit?''

"Yes." Tate couldn't take his gaze off Natalie long enough to warn his son that he was in a world of trouble for sneaking off the way he had. She looked a few pounds thinner, a few shades paler, as if the past weeks had been as difficult for her as for him. That was his fault. Hell, everything was his fault, but he would happily spend the rest of his life making it up to her if she'd just give him a chance.

Jordan was long gone when she finally spoke. "I was going to have him call as soon as we got back from dinner."

He nodded once.

"You've come to take him home."

He wasn't sure whether he actually smiled or was just so nervous that his lips twitched upward like that. "I've been having a hell of a time with my family running off lately. First Mom and Josh, then Jordan and you."

A sad, wistful look dampened her eyes. "I'm not part of your family."

"Sure, you are. The only way you could be more so is if you and I were married." His hand was unsteady when he reached out to touch her cheek. "I'm the sorriest man you've ever laid eyes on, Natalie. I know intentions don't matter much, but I never meant to hurt you or damage your reputation or cause you to lose this job. It just never occurred to me that I might fall in love with a reporter who worked for Boyd Chaney, or that she might fall in love with me, too."

"I never said I love you," she whispered.

"I know. That's one of my biggest regrets. Letting you walk away—that's another one. And waiting so long to see you again... You're so beautiful, Natalie, and I'm so sorry, and I love you—" He broke off to swallow. That wasn't how he'd planned things on the flight from Tulsa to Atlanta, then back to Montgomery. He'd thought they would have a reasonable discussion—rational, logical—and he would apologize and *then* he would tell her one more time that he loved her. And here he was, blurting it out before she'd even had a chance to unlock the door.

Not that she looked as if she minded. "And?" she prompted.

He was puzzled. "And?"

"You want to...oh, I don't know. Maybe marry me and spend the rest of your life making love with me?"

For a long moment he stared at her, stunned. Then he nodded. "Yeah. I want to marry you and spend the rest of my life making love and babies with you."

"All right."

"All right?"

"I want to marry you, too. I want to have babies with you and mend fences with you and be Jordan's mom and make love with you and dance in the rain with you and compromise and fight and forgive and kiss and make up with you. I want to be a part of your family, a part of your life. I want to be a part of *you.*"

He slid his arm around her waist and drew her near. "For real?"

"For real."

"This is no joke?"

She wrapped her arms around his neck and raised onto her toes to brush her mouth over his. "No joke. For real. Forever. Say yes and kiss me, Tate, *please.*"

"Yes," he murmured before his mouth settled over hers. Holding her tightly, he backed her against the waist-high wall that edged the porch, then lifted her up to sit on it so he could move between her thighs.

She was pressing hard against him, so hot that he burned where they touched, and he was rubbing hard against her, so swollen that he throbbed, when catcalls and whistles sounded down below.

"Take it inside, guys," Jordan called, the chastening in his voice underlaid with pleasure. "*Parents.* You can't take 'em anywhere. Dad, we're gonna shoot some pool over at the clubhouse."

Tate waved his free hand in acknowledgment before forcing a few inches of space between him and Natalie. "What do you think, Ms. Alabama? Want to take a lonely cowboy inside and ease his aching…heart?"

"Among other things," she said with a giggle. "I would consider it an honor, sir, to carry out this great—" she wriggled against him "—great duty." Just as she'd done once before, she wrapped her long, long legs around his hips, and he carried her inside the apartment, following her directions past boxes and luggage to the bedroom. "But once we get back to Oklahoma, you're gonna have to quit calling me Ms. Alabama."

Like the rest of the apartment, the bedroom was a mess, but it had a bed with sheets, and that was all that mattered. Tate lowered her to the mattress and followed her down, settling between her thighs, and gave a sigh of relief. Of homecoming. "Once we get back to Oklahoma—" he paused to kiss her cheek "—I'm gonna call you darlin' and baby and light of my life." He kissed her other cheek, then nipped at her full lower lip. "And Mrs. Rawlins."

"Natalie Rawlins," she murmured as they hastily stripped off their clothes. Lying back naked in the center of the bed, she said, "I like the sound of that," then gave a great, satisfied groan as he slid inside her, stretching her, filling her.

"Hmm. *I* like the sound of *that*. Let's see if I can make you do it again."

And he did.

Again and again and again….

Epilogue

The package came in the mail, bearing an Alabama postmark and a neatly typed label. It was addressed to Natalie Rawlins—after eighteen months, she still loved the sound of that—and the return address was the post office box that belonged to Jefferson Oaks. She found it on the dining table when she came in from her shower, left there by her husband, she presumed, and picked it up. Heavy, bulky, solid. A hardcover book. Gee, wonder whose? she thought dryly.

As she pulled the tab that would open the long side of the padded envelope, Tate came down the hall. He wore jeans and was buttoning a white dress shirt. His jaw was freshly shaved, his hair slicked back, and he looked incredible. "Jordan around?"

"At your mom's."

"Josh?"

"There, too."

"J.T.?"

"Him, too. And your grandparents."

"Hmm..." He slid his arms around her from behind and nuzzled her hair from her ear, making her tremble. "It's not often we get the house to ourselves."

"Don't get too caught up in the idea. They're all going to arrive through that door in about five minutes."

"Betcha I can make you 'arrive' before they do."

With a shiver and a laugh, she pulled his hands from her breasts to her waist, then leaned back against him. "Behave yourself, cowboy."

"I'm behaving," he said innocently. "It's you I'm trying to get to misbehave." After another moment of nuzzling her ear, he rested his chin on her head. "Is that what I think it is?"

She fiddled with the envelope she hadn't yet looked inside. "Probably. *The Life and Times of Senator Boyd Chaney.*" Of course, the title was catchier, not that she cared. It had been impossible to miss all the hoopla when the book had come out a month earlier. Its author—a highly respected television journalist—had been on all the networks and in all the major magazines. He'd been full of himself, so smug and arrogant that a reasonable person couldn't help but want to smack him—and that wasn't sour grapes. In fact, the description came from her mother-in-law Lucinda. However, Natalie did happen to agree.

"Are you gonna open it?"

Reaching inside, she pulled out the copy of the book. A piece of cream-colored stationery was stuck between the pages, its top edge extending an inch. It was engraved with Chaney's name and bore a short handwritten note: "#1 on the *New York Times* nonfiction list! All this success could have been yours. Bet you feel foolish now."

"Do you?"

"Feel foolish? For what?"

"He offered you fame and fortune and a chance to get your father back. You settled for me."

She tossed the book on the table, then turned in his arms. "*Settled?* I *settled* for you?" Mock outrage sharpened her voice. "I didn't settle for anything, pal. I won the grand prize. I got you, two wonderful sons, a mother-in-law and a brother-in-law whom I adore. I got friends and family and Oklahoma. I got everything. All that guy got was a few weeks in the limelight and a little cash. It doesn't even begin to compare."

"No regrets?"

"Not a one. I love you, and I'd gladly go through all the heartache again as long as I know when it's over, I'll have you."

"You'll always have me, sweetheart," he murmured, and then he kissed her—slow, sweet, lazy, as if they had all the time in the world.

Of course they didn't. They'd hardly started when the side door opened, then Jordan spoke. "Aw, Grandma, they're doing it again. I thought you were gonna talk to them about that…Grandma?…Grandma?"

"Sorry, kid," Josh said with a laugh. "We lost Grandma and Mr. Scott out on the deck. They're…uh, admiring the sunset. We'd better get moving if we're gonna get decent seats for the graduation."

Tate released Natalie and gave her one of her favorite wicked grins—a silent promise that they would pick up where they'd left off later—then took eight-month-old Jeffrey Tate, Jr., from his uncle Josh. Natalie got her purse and camera, and linked her arm through Jordan's as they left the house and headed for the cars.

It was a lovely evening—warm, but still a little early for Oklahoma's blistering summer heat. The sun would be setting before long, and the dark velvety night would fall, and it would be a perfect setting for an event as momentous as a high school graduation.

"Hey, Mom."

She smiled up at Jordan. "Yes?"

"Remember when I showed up at your apartment in Alabama…I asked you where you were going, and you said you didn't know? And I asked if you don't know where you're going, how will you know when you get there? And you said—''

"'I'll just know. I'll *feel* it.'"

"Did you? When we came back here, me and you and Dad, did you know this was the place?"

She thought back to that day. In the span of a few hours she'd gone from heartache to pure joy, from hopeless to very, very hopeful. "I knew before then," she said quietly. "When I saw your father, and he said he loved me, I knew then exactly where I belonged. I felt it."

"What did it feel like?"

They stopped beside the Mustang, and her gaze went automatically to Tate, buckling J.T. into his infant seat in the back seat of Grandma Lucinda's car. He secured everything, then backed away so his grandmother could sit next to her grandbaby. His gaze met hers over the roof of the car, and a sweet, gentle smile curved his lips. She smiled back, so filled with love and happiness that she wanted to laugh, clap, dance around the yard. Finally, misty-eyed, she answered Jordan's question.

"Home, sweetheart. It felt like home."

* * * * *

▼ SILHOUETTE®
SPECIAL EDITION™

AVAILABLE FROM 16TH MAY 2003

WOMAN OF INNOCENCE Lindsay McKenna

Morgan's Mercenaries

Mercenary Matt Davis was a legend to Jenny Wright—until their assignment forced her to go undercover as his wife and discover the man beneath the armour. Could she teach the proud soldier the power of love?

THE BEST MAN'S PLAN Gina Wilkins

Dating Bryan Falcon was just a decoy for the press—Grace Pennington never expected to have *feelings* for the hard-core businessman. Was the attraction real, or was he playing the doting boyfriend far too well?

BIG SKY COWBOY Jennifer Mikels

Montana

Burning desire shook rugged rancher Colby Holmes whenever he looked at Tessa, the stunning psychic he'd enlisted to solve a murder. But when the town turned against her, would his love be enough to make her stay?

ROYAL PROTOCOL Christine Flynn

Crown and Glory

Admiral Harrison Monteque thought lady-in-waiting Gwendolyn Corbin was an ice maiden. But as they searched together for a missing prince, her warmth began to melt his hard-edged heart...

THE RUNAWAY BRIDE Patricia McLinn

Judi Monroe fled her wedding, only to be rescued by rugged Thomas Vance. She feigned amnesia to prolong her stay—but would he overlook her lie and see that she wanted to be with him...forever?

THE MARRIAGE PRESCRIPTION Debra Webb

Colby Agency

Doctor Beth only wanted one night together to exorcise legal crusader Zach Ashton from her system forever. But she had underestimated her heart—as well as the man of her dreams. Because *he* had an agenda of his own...

world's most
Eligible Bachelors

RICH, GORGEOUS, SEXY AND SINGLE!

An exciting new series featuring the sexiest, most successful, dynamic men in the world!

Millionaire to Marry *by Rachel Lee*	18th April 2003
Detective Dad *by Marie Ferrarella*	16th May 2003
His Business, Her Baby *by Dixie Browning*	16th May 2003
That Mysterious Man *by Maggie Shayne*	20th June 2003

Coming Soon!

FREE!

2 Books
and a surprise gift!

We would like to take this opportunity to thank you for reading this Silhouette® book by offering you the chance to take TWO more specially selected titles from the Special Edition™ series absolutely FREE! We're also making this offer to introduce you to the benefits of the Reader Service™ —

- ★ FREE home delivery
- ★ FREE gifts and competitions
- ★ FREE monthly Newsletter
- ★ Books available before they're in the shops
- ★ Exclusive Reader Service discount

Accepting these FREE books and gift places you under no obligation to buy; you may cancel at any time, even after receiving your free shipment. Simply complete your details below and return the entire page to the address below. *You don't even need a stamp!*

YES! Please send me 2 free Special Edition books and a surprise gift. I understand that unless you hear from me, I will receive 4 superb new titles every month for just £2.90 each, postage and packing free. I am under no obligation to purchase any books and may cancel my subscription at any time. The free books and gift will be mine to keep in any case.

E3ZEB

Ms/Mrs/Miss/Mr ....Initials ....

BLOCK CAPITALS PLEASE

Surname...

Address..

....

....Postcode ....

Send this whole page to:
UK: The Reader Service, FREEPOST CN81, Croydon, CR9 3WZ
EIRE: The Reader Service, PO Box 4546, Kilcock, County Kildare (stamp required)